D1525048

THE HUNTER LEGACY

THOMAS COX

AuthorHouse™
1663 Liberty Drive
Bloomington, IN 47403
www.authorhouse.com
Phone: 1-800-839-8640

www.thomascoxbooks.com

Published by AuthorHouse 6/13/2012

ISBN: 978-1-4772-1350-6 (e)
ISBN: 978-1-4772-1351-3 (sc)

THE HUNTER LEGACY

(1845-1950)

Grace Simson Blaisdell (1845-1928)

Son John (1860-1865) (d. smallpox)

Lon Shirley (1852-1927)

Son Daniel Blaisdell (1869-1940)

Grace married Darwin James Blaisdell (1868)

Daughter Louella (1872-1908) (Tony's mother)

Grandson Tony Hunter (1892-1970) (Louella's son)

Dave Hunter (1867-1905) (Tony's father)

1

It was a Monday morning in April of the year 1905, an unseasonably warm day and a special day for Tony Hunter, a week shy of his thirteenth birthday. It was the day he started his job working for his friend, Lon Shirley, the owner of *The Billiards Emporium,* the town's only pool hall.

Any other twelve or thirteen year old boy working in the poolroom would not have raised eyebrows, but this was Tony Hunter of Blaisdell House.

Tony was both a pride and an enigma to his Grandmother Grace Blaisdell, the sixty year-old matriarch of the family and one of the three or four richest persons in Vinton, in all of Osanamon Country to be precise. She had kept her word to him, and now that he was almost thirteen, allowed him to work at the part-time job he selected despite her desire for him to join the rest of the family in the *Vinton Bank and Trust.*

To Grace Blaisdell the poolroom was one more eyesore

on Main Street, and the men who frequented it were lazy and shiftless. Occasionally she slipped and paid a compliment to the proprietor Lon Shirley, although she hastily followed that with a comment as to how Lon could have considerably bettered himself had he not stayed in Vinton to run such a lowlife establishment.

But to Tony the poolroom signaled his acceptance into a sort of club made up of hard working, hard drinking, hard fighting types that had little reverence for much of anything anyway. Though it should be noted that no liquor was sold or allowed in Lon's establishment. Tony Hunter had been touched intuitively years before, some kind of camaraderie felt in the soul of a child, on that day when Lon Shirley had seen him standing in the open doorway and motioned him inside. His grandmother was across the street at the bank.

Lon had taken him under his arms and set him on the counter with both his hands holding a bottle of pop, and other men had gathered around to jostle and joke with him. In Tony's young imagination it had been a passage into something that he couldn't explain. He was having *fun*. Then his grandmother had appeared in the doorway and gave a slightly pointed and accusatory smile at Lon. Lon laughed aloud, lifted Tony down and walked him to his grandmother. When he tried to tell her how much fun he had been having, she only rolled her eyes.

Most other boys his age now worked at harder jobs in much dirtier surroundings, as apprentices or farm hands during the summer months, a fact he had pushed home to Grandmother Grace. With his thirteenth birthday imminent, he was one of the few boys who had continued his eight and a half-months formal schooling every year. Most of the girls remained in school, but girls were not important yet, while the boys had quit school to work at odd jobs, or whatever bit of employment they could obtain for meager wages.

So, it was a surprise to everyone when Tony proudly announced he would be working for Lon Shirley in the town's only poolroom.

This particular morning Lon Shirley, a big man in his late forties with a craggy smile, square chin, broad shoulders and a twisted left arm, crippled since his youth, chuckled at him. "Tony, that's the third time already you swept the floor. I ain't raising your salary."

"Why not?" Tony said, brightly. "Oh, I don't mind. It's my job."

"Once is enough before you go home."

Tony's work was simple enough: racking the balls on the two pool tables, helping Lon behind the counter if needed, and keeping the place reasonably clean. Lon had made it plain that Tony's workday would end at five o'clock, although Tony gladly would have stayed until Lon closed the poolroom at eleven or eleven-thirty, depending on the number of customers. Some nights were better than others. For his efforts Tony was to receive the princely sum of fifteen cents a day plus a bottle of pop.

One of Lon's regulars, a panhandler named Gary, stepped inside, greeted Lon with a hefty snap of his suspenders, and said to Tony, "Hey, Tony, what's your old man been up to?"

Tony frowned as he tilted his head. "How would I know?"

Lon frowned also.

Gary continued, "You ain't talked to him yet? Oh, sorry. I seen him a few minutes ago, going into your gramma's bank."

"You made a mistake," Lon said.

"Don't think so, Lon. I knowed Dave Hunter since we was kids. It was him all right. I wonder what his reason is for him to come back to Vinton."

After a moment of silence, Lon said to Tony, "You okay?"

Tony shrugged. He hadn't seen his father since he was five years old and barely remembered him. "Sure. Why not?"

Gary spread his hands. "Hey, I'm sorry. Shootin' off my mouth like that. Maybe I did make a mistake after all. It ain't my business. I'll see you later, Lon." He ducked out the front door.

"Think he's really back?" Tony asked. He looked past the open front door toward Main Street. "What for?"

Lon shrugged, following Tony's gaze out toward Main Street. "Gary wouldn't have no reason to lie about it." He looked around at the other single customer in the joint. The man was on "time" for five cents an hour, practicing pool shots on the back table. "Keep everything under control, Tony. Don't let anybody steal from us or get in the cash box. I'm gonna take a stroll over to the bank."

"I'll go with you," Tony said.

"One of us has gotta stay here or we don't have much of a business."

2

Dave Hunter looked at Daniel Blaisdell seated behind the desk in his office at the bank. Daniel had not yet invited him to have a seat, though he had, more likely out of curiosity than anything, brought him into the office. While Dave was slender, actually closer to skinny, with a gaunt face and wearing old clothes and boots, his fingernails showing the dirt beneath them, Daniel was an impeccable contrast.

Daniel wore a single-breasted dark suit, white shirt and string tie, with everything creased and clean as befitting a banker. He was a broad-shouldered, square chinned man, with steady, dark, inquisitive eyes. One would not find dirt beneath his fingernails.

"David, you're out of your mind," Daniel said. "You know Mother will never allow Tony to leave with you."

"I'm his father. How can she stop me?" Dave shrugged his narrow shoulders. "Grace Blaisdell only thinks she owns the town and everybody in it."

Daniel smiled. "Let me put it this way. With her contributions and influence she practically owns the politicians, the judge, and the local law. It's a stacked deck, David. Besides, what do you plan to do with Tony?"

"Hey, he's my kid, so I 'tend to raise him. What does anybody do with a kid?"

"Tony won't remember you," Daniel said. "He was less than six months old when you left." He paused, studying the thin man. "What made you decide to come back for him? And don't give me bullshit about how you suddenly decided to be a daddy."

"I seen other men with their kids, so I just think a man ought'a have his son with him."

Daniel scoffed. "Tell me the truth, or you get no support from me on anything. Is it some of my mother's money you're after?"

"That's low," David said.

"But accurate," Daniel said. "What kind of life would you arrange for Tony? You want it to be his life or yours? No stable home? Is that what you plan?"

"It works for me," Dave said. "We'll travel. He won't be sitting here in this bank, growing old, counting other people's money. Like you."

Daniel made a sucking noise between his teeth. He tilted his head at the other man. "And school?"

"School's overrated. Look what it got you."

Daniel made a vague gesture at his large, clean office. "Yeah, look."

"Okay, you think you're a smart guy, and maybe you are. We took different roads, that's all." Dave smirked. "You sit here every day beneath that portrait of your old man." He pointed generally toward the oil portrait on the wall behind the desk. "Think he's proud of you?"

"I don't know, or care," Daniel said. "The bank's the family business. I'll help my mother every way I can. Now if Tony decides the bank's not for him, and it's his decision, then I'll see what I can do to help him."

With a wry look at the portrait, Dave shook his head. "Daniel, you don't even look like your old man."

"That's a blessing. What do you think Louella's going to do when you announce that you're stealing Tony away? She is his mother, you know."

"She could come with us."

"You're dreaming, Dave. She's not well. She wasn't when you left. If anything, she's getting worse."

Dave looked down and brushed at his clothing. He wore old work pants, work boots, and a plaid shirt with the sleeves rolled to just below the elbows, a contrast to Daniel in his dark business suit that had been imported from Chicago. He said, "I reckon I have to take him, Danny. I am the boy's father."

"Try telling that to Judge Parks. He and my mother—" Daniel paused to cross his middle finger over his index finger. "She'd have every right to send the law after you."

"That won't be nothin' new," Dave said. His eyes drifted to the baseball bat propped in one corner of the office. "You still play ball?"

"When I can," Daniel said. "Lots 'a guys don't want me on a team. I'm too rich. How about you? You used to be a decent pitcher."

Dave laughed. "Better than you are a hitter. Look, I come here today to tell you how it's gonna be. Maybe I had a tiny hope I could count on your backing."

"Nothing I can do," said Daniel. He steepled his fingers and rocked back. He nodded an invitation to a chair across from him. "Hell, I like you, Dave. We always got along, but I won't cross my mother. In fact, I agree with her. Tony should learn this business and be my partner in the bank someday."

Dave grinned but declined the offer to sit. "Town's changed, ain't it, Danny? So much in just a few years. I see automobiles now—couple anyway. Bet you and your mommy's got one?"

"We do," Daniel nodded. "Bought a Packard a few months ago—gas powered. The gasoline is shipped in by rail or river from Elston. Hell, we even got a mechanic here in Vinton who's learning the in's and out's of internal combustible engines. He's opening a gas station so in the future we don't have to ship the petrol in from Elston. And we got another guy who's pretty good on the electric cars."

He tilted his head. "You know, Dave, that might be a good job for you if you ever want to use your head. Of course, we still got the lumber mill by the river and the livery stable. It's hard work but pays fairly well. Then there's the coal mine near Elston. Dirty work, but again it can be profitable."

"What are you driving at?" Dave asked.

"You abdicated your responsibility to the boy." Daniel drew a deep breath, studying the other man. "You need to get some for yourself, and prove that to my mother."

"Well, I ain't got no intentions of being a logger or a

miner, or fucking around with those stinking cars. Where is Tony now?"

Daniel hesitated before replying. "Tony, so far, is not agreeing to become a banker. He talked his grandmother into letting him work for Lon Shirley across the street."

"Good. Lon can teach him some things." Dave twisted his features into a light scowl. "You say Louella's not well? I'm sorry to hear it."

"She's not a strong woman, Dave." Daniel shook his head. "The doctor can't pin down anything. He says she may have a sickly constitution, or it might be a cancer. She's lost weight, and she's in bed most of the time."

"I'm surprised Grace didn't call in specialists."

"She did. They couldn't confirm an actual illness one way or another. One suggested she might be unstable." Daniel tapped his temple. "So Tony is Mother's pride and joy. She wants him to carry on the family tradition. But he persuaded her to allow him to take the job with Lon Shirley on the promise he'll stay in school 'til he graduates. He's a smart boy, David. Before you go dragging him off somewhere to live like you do, from hand to mouth, think about it. What's best for him? How do you see him five or ten years from now?"

"Dan, I quit school and went to work at thirteen."

"Tony's smarter than you."

Dave laughed and shook his head. "Okay. Good for him. In the meantime, with Lon, he'll learn something other than what goes on in Blaisdell House. Bet Grace is having a pissy fit."

Daniel also chuckled. "Yep. But a promise is a promise." He leaned forward in his chair. "Look, Dave, you won't get any help around here. The people you know can't help you if they wanted to. My hands are tied. Louella won't oppose Mother. You left the boy here. Then, for the last eleven years, there's not a word from you. Mother confirmed with Judge Parks that possession is nine-tenth's the law. You don't even know if Tony *wants* to go with you. Kidnap him, and that's not helping him any. Think about it."

"I see you don't have the guts to help me." Dave stood thoughtfully. Then he asked, "How's our other girl?"

Daniel's face clouded momentarily before he shrugged. "Annie's married now."

Now Dave reacted in surprise. "Annie Pyle? Married? To who?"

"Ivan Coaker."

Now a look of utter disbelief settled on Dave's face. "You're shitting me, Danny. Not the Ivan Coaker I knew. Hell, him and his brother lived in a shack in shantytown."

"The same."

"Why in the hell would Annie marry somebody like that?"

"I don't know," Daniel said. "She must have had a good reason."

"Where do they live?"

"The Coakers still live in shantytown. But I understand Annie spends a lot of nights with Amanda Hopper. Amanda was Annie's employer, this was after you left."

Dave couldn't stop shaking his head. "Annie married," he repeated. "That's a real kick in the ass. And to Coaker? Hell, somebody's gotta rescue her."

"Not you."

"Why not?" Dave grinned. "Are you jealous?"

"No, that was over a long time ago."

"Why? Ah, I see the ring on your finger, Danny?"

Daniel nodded. "I married the minister's daughter, Ruth Jones. You don't know her. She and her father weren't here when you left."

"You married a preacher's kid?" Dave laughed aloud. "Did she save your ass or your soul?"

Daniel just shook his head.

"At least tell me she's good looking."

"She is that," Daniel said. "Very pretty, in fact."

"I expected you to marry a rich girl."

"She also is that," Daniel said. "But that's not the reason we got married."

David said, teasing him, "I never heard of a rich preacher's daughter."

"The Reverend Caleb Jones came to town a couple years ago," Daniel said. "Our former minister moved on after the church burned. Reverend Jones put up the money and hired the help to build the new one. Look down the street and you can see it—the tall steeple. Ruth, my wife, came with her father and was the schoolteacher for over a year. When we got married, she had to stop teaching. She still teaches Sunday school for her daddy."

"Damn," Dave said. "I never knew a rich preacher."

"Caleb Jones inherited his money," Daniel told him. "His family had a large farm back in Pennsylvania. So he doesn't have to worry about what he can scrape in from the collection plate."

"Convenient for you," Dave chuckled.

"Let's drop it," Daniel said, curtly. "And I suggest you stay away from Annie Coaker."

"That might be easier promised than done. Annie was, let's see, fifteen years old last time I was with her." Dave smirked at the other man. "But, 'course, she was older when you put your hands on her."

Daniel stared at him without a reply.

Again, Dave shook his head. "Well, it's good to know Annie spends more time at Amanda's whorehouse than with that bum in shantytown."

"You'll get in more trouble, Dave."

"I expect that from you since you're a church-goer now."

Daniel smiled. "I haven't sunk that far yet. I tried it a little while when I was in college. It didn't take."

"Your wife live with you there in Gracie's house?"

"Yep." Daniel half-smiled. "Don't get any ideas, David. She would be immune to your charm."

Dave grinned and nodded. "You never know. One more question about Annie. What's she look like now?"

"Prettier than ever. Not so little girlish as before. She comes into the bank occasionally to put money in her account."

"I definitely will have to pay Annie a visit."

"Ivan might not like that."

"I won't ask him. Dan, I'll be 'round a little while. You might as well get used to it." Dave stopped at the door. "You might tell Louella I'd like to see her."

"I might, but that's as far as it would go. She wants you out of her life, Dave, and you can't blame that on Mother. Louella won't step up for you."

"I ain't so sure it's all hopeless."

Daniel nodded. "Only chance you'll have getting close to Tony is if you straighten out, get a job here in Vinton, or over in Elston, work hard, save money for a change, clean yourself up, and then make your plea to Mother."

"Yeah? Cut up fuckin' logs or dig coal out'a the ground."

"Telephone business is expanding service from Elston. New wires strung every day. There's maintenance, of course. The road is being graded. You have to settle in to work."

Dave chuckled in spite of himself. "Danny, I can't see kissing even Grace Blaisdell's round little ass." He left, leaving the office door open.

Daniel shook his head. "You are headed for a fall," he said to the open doorway.

He swung around in his swivel chair so he could look out the window of his office toward Main Street. He half-smiled again and softly grunted when he recognized one of the five, as of last count, automobiles in Vinton. It was their Packard, putt-putting down the street at the speed limit of five miles an hour in town. The driver was his mother wearing goggles with a bonnet over her gray hair and tied beneath her chin by a scarf. He almost laughed because of the way her chin was firmly set. Obviously she had heard about Dave Hunter coming back.

3

The main transportation in the small town of Vinton had changed from horses to bicycles, though there still were horse drawn conveyances, buggies, wagons, surreys; ice delivery was by horse-drawn wagon to which, during the hotter months, kids flocked to grab handfuls of ice chunks and chipped off pieces; the milk wagon was also horse drawn; the fire department, all volunteer, had a horse drawn tankard; the undertaker had a horse drawn hearse. The local sheriff did rate higher. Because Osanamon County was a huge area, the sheriff had a car at his disposal, a Studebaker wagon. His regular deputies, and special deputies in outlying towns and villages, still relied on bicycles or horses. The other few such vehicles, all of them electric cars, belonged to the other rich people in town.

From where he sat looking out the window, Daniel Blaisdell could see his mother's scowl. She was driving slowly, carefully, because other than a bricked three-block section Main Street was gravel on tar. If you drove too fast it kicked tarred rocks onto the undercarriage and fenders of your car and created a hellacious problem in getting the vehicle clean again. Daniel's mother would have nothing other than the cleanest automobile in town. She had even learned how to crank the engine.

He watched her angle park the car between a horse and buggy and a mule and wagon tied to posts, spooking the horse. It didn't take long for bad news to spread.

"Oh, yeah," Daniel said to himself, reaching for a cigar from the humidor on the desk, biting off the end, and lighting it. The smoke drifted up around the somber features of his late father, Darwin James Blaisdell, in the portrait on the wall, a smaller version of the portrait that hung in the study up at the house.

Indeed, Daniel did not resemble his father in the portrait. The old man was nearly gaunt in physical stature. His suit hung on him like clothing on a scarecrow in the field, and the stiff high collar looked ungainly although the artist had done as much as he could to make it look formfitting. His nose was oddly large for his thin face. Daniel glanced at the portrait and shook his head.

"What part of you did I get?" he asked the empty office.

Outside, before stepping into the street, Dave Hunter stopped and watched Grace Blaisdell get out of the car. He gave her a smirking smile. She stared without expression back at him as she removed her goggles. For a few seconds they held those poses. Then Dave saw Lon Shirley standing one building down on the same side of the street. He nodded and stepped toward Lon.

Lon was looking past him, looking at Grace Blaisdell.

For a sixty-year-old woman she was remarkably strong and attractive with her oval face and clear complexion except for two scars, one on her upper lip and the other a crescent-shaped one beneath her right eye. Her gaze held with Lon's for several seconds. There was even a slight lifting of one eyebrow. The corner of Lon's mouth quirked in a small smile, and he gave a little wave.

Grace's right hand, on the knob of her black, silver tipped walking stick, trembled slightly. She raised one index finger in response to Lon. Anybody seeing her would not have noticed, but it made Lon Shirley smile wider.

Grace didn't need the walking stick because there was nothing infirm about her. She had adopted it as sort of a symbol after old D. J. Blaisdell died and made her a widow, as well as co-president of the *Vinton Bank and Trust.*

Lon Shirley shook hands with Dave Hunter.

"Heard you'd come back," he said. "You want to see Tony? He's across the street at the poolroom. He works for me now."

"So I heard," Dave said. "Not just yet, Lon. I think both of us got to get used to the idea. Right now I need a beer. Seeing Grace Blaisdell leaves a bad taste in my mouth."

"She's a helluva woman," Lon said. "You got money for a beer?"

"I can manage it."

Lon slipped him a dollar. "First couple's on me. Come to the poolroom when you feel like it."

4

Three men in the poolroom halted their game of "Boston" to stare in disbelief when the stranger stepped inside the door.

The man was not a stranger to the town—countless times they had seen him making purchases and transporting them in the basket of the bicycle back to Blaisdell House—but a stranger in this building. It was the first time anyone could remember seeing a Negro, one of the few in Vinton, set foot inside the poolroom.

Everyone became quiet and looked at him.

He was a tall black man, broad of shoulder and narrow of waist, with a rugged face that looked like he'd seen his share of hard times, a man of indeterminate age. But he was not suffering hard times now. He worked for Grace Blaisdell and, with his wife, lived in the huge house on the hill. Grace never referred to him as a servant but rather as her friend and caretaker. He was the carpenter, roofer, gardener, and all around handyman. You could tell from the coarseness of his big hands that work never bothered him. This afternoon he wore dark trousers and a white shirt, the way Grace Blaisdell wanted him to dress when he wasn't doing manual labor. His black shoes were shined.

His name was Carter Foote, but he was known only as Carter. Almost no one in Vinton knew whether it was a first name or last name, or only name, and no one cared. Everyone knew that, for some reason, he was devoted to Grace Blaisdell.

Lon Shirley raised his head from the weekly newspaper he had spread on the counter and looked over his reading specs when one of the customers coughed emphatically. With no expression, Lon took the corncob pipe from his mouth and said, "Good afternoon, Carter."

If Carter noticed the other stares, he gave no indication. He was looking straight at Tony. He acknowledged Lon's greeting with a nod.

"Mr. Shirley, I came to bring Master Tony home. His grandmother wants him to come home now."

Tony came forward. "What is it, Carter? Did something happen?"

Carter gave him a warm half-smile. "You have to come home now."

Tony looked around, embarrassed when he saw that other men were staring at him. "It's not time yet. She knows I work 'til five."

"She asked me to bring you home," Carter said. "Right away. Mr. Shirley will understand."

Tony turned to look at Lon, starting to protest, but Lon merely nodded to the Negro to indicate it was all right for

Tony to go. Tony bit his lower lip, feeling foolish and angry that Grandmother Grace would do this to him in front of others. He said, "The game's almost over on the back table. I got to rack the balls first."

Carter nodded almost imperceptibly. "I'll wait for you in the alley," he said in his soft, well-modulated voice. "You can ride on the handlebars like you used to when I'd bring you into town."

"I'll walk, Carter. I promise. I'll be along."

When Carter turned to leave, without looking at any of the others in the poolroom, one of the customers muttered something about "niggers." Carter went on out and around the front of the building.

The customer continued, mimicking Carter's careful tone: "I'll wait for you in the alley." He went on in his own voice: "Fuck 'im, Lon. You let one nigger in here and pretty soon they overrun the place."

Looking at his newspaper, Lon grunted. "Bertram, there ain't enough niggers in this town to overrun anything."

The other man spat a stream of tobacco juice toward the spittoon and, with the back of his hand, smeared the dripping brown on his chin. "Did you see them pants, and that fine white shirt, and them boots he was wearin'? I ain't never had clothes like that."

"You don't work for the Blaisdell's," another man said. "They got indoor plumbing in that house and two privies. I know because I helped dig that septic tank. I hear they tore down their outhouse and converted their barn into a garage for that fancy automobile."

"That's right," Lon said, not looking up. "And they sold their horses. They modernized."

The second man nodded. "Just like the Gibson's, and the Scheller's, did. If your name ain't Blaisdell, or Gibson, or Scheller, you don't own much around here. Gibson bought up two more farms last month. Scheller owns half the businesses on Main Street, plus the lumber yard, and the Blaisdell's bank holds mortgages on most of the decent homes in Vinton with loans out to everybody else. Like Lon said, it's modernizing."

"I don't care what you call it. That fuckin' nigger looks down his nose at everybody, just as though he was a white man, too," the first man said and spat again, dribbling more juice down his chin. "I agree with President Teddy Roosevelt. They maybe got some rights but they shouldn't be socializing with us. I never figured you'd just let him walk in like that, Lon."

"Well, he's gone now," Lon said, puffing his pipe, looking down at his newspaper. "Tony, you go on now. I'll see you tomorrow."

The first customer, still on the subject of Carter, said, "He acts like he's smarter'n the rest of us."

"He is," Lon said, scanning the paper. "He's an educated man."

"How do you know?"

"I know."

"Well, I'm educated."

Still not looking up from his newspaper, Lon laughed. "Bertram, you couldn't finish fourth grade. The more you open your mouth, the more it's obvious."

"If you insult me, Lon, I might not come back in here."

"That loss worries the shit out of me," Lon said. "Anyway, where else do you got to go in this town?"

The other man scowled and chewed his wad rapidly.

5

Daniel Blaisdell was seated in his soft chair, staring out at Main Street, when the door opened behind him. He did not turn around. He expelled some cigar smoke and said, smiling, "Hello, Mother. What took you?"

"I saw him," Grace Blaisdell said, removing her bonnet and wiping her face with a handkerchief. "He was in here?"

"I hope it didn't spoil your lunch." Daniel turned in the swivel chair. "Oh, yeah. He came back for Tony."

"He can't have him. The gall of that man." She sighed and took the only other soft armchair in the room. "I was afraid this might happen."

"He's the boy's father. You can't deny that."

Grace nodded. She held her black walking stick straight up and down with her hands folded over each other on the silver knob. Her cheeks were slightly flushed. It made the crescent shaped scar high on her right cheekbone redder. "I don't deny it. But Tony he can't have. What's Dave Hunter want? Drag the boy around the country like a bum?"

Daniel shrugged. "I don't think David knows. Someday Tony will go where he wants to. Even you won't be able to stop that, Mother." He drew on his cigar. "Tony pretty much does what he wants now anyway."

"I know. Go ahead and tell me. I spoil him."

Daniel shrugged again, but smiled.

"What do we do?" asked Grace.

"You got something in mind?"

"Dave Hunter cannot be allowed to stay here in Vinton."

"How can you make him leave?" Daniel asked, mildly. "Last time you tried to bargain with him, he took your money and disappeared. Now he's back. Incidentally, he asked about Louella. I'm not sure what was behind that. Maybe he cares for her."

"He's never cared for anyone but himself." Grace scowled vacantly at nothing between herself and Daniel before raising her head. "Perhaps Sheriff Buckner can help us, Daniel."

Daniel tapped ash from his cigar into his ashtray. "Help us what? Buckner's an honest man, Mother. You can't ask him to run Dave off without a reason that makes sense to him. Sure, he owes us favors, but he'll make his own decisions."

"There are some bad men in this town," Grace said.

"I hope you're merely commenting and not serious," Daniel said.

Grace tilted her head as she eyed him. "You like Dave Hunter, don't you?"

"I did, at one time. Now he's an opportunist. That's my

opinion. I expect him to want you to pay him to leave." Daniel was silent for a moment. "You know he'll try to use Louella against you, against us. I don't know how to feel about that. He did give her a bit of a life. Now she can die with a clear conscience."

"She's not dying."

"Don't expect her to live much longer," Daniel said. "The doctors are pretty sure she has cancer."

Grace sighed and punctuated it with a sharp rap on the floor with her walking stick. Daniel wasn't sure if they were on the same track or she was off on a thought of her own. She gave a little shudder. "You're probably right. And you're right that we can't rely on Buckner. Who else is there?"

"Don't think of crossing into those murky waters, Mother."

"I've taken risks all my life," Grace said. "You're enough like your father I know you're not afraid of risks?"

"No," Daniel said. "I'm just saying be cautious and think."

"There's a time for caution and a time for action, Daniel." Grace considered quietly. "What about that deputy sheriff? Orville Parker? He wants to borrow money from us."

"Orville Parker is not particularly smart. That's why he's in debt to everybody. And he's got a temper."

"I'm not asking for Dave Hunter to be harmed," Grace said. "I'll make that clear to Parker. Daniel, I love you, you're my son, but we have different views on how to handle Dave. We know he can't be bought, not by me. Now, if I have to, I'll fight him any way necessary. I've fought more than once in my lifetime. I haven't raised Tony to see him taken away." She tilted her head toward her son. "What did you talk about?"

"Tony, mostly."

"Mostly?"

"Changes around town."

"How about that other woman? The one he was seeing before he got Louella pregnant."

After a second, Daniel barely nodded. "And after. She was mentioned."

Grace said, "It might be Tony's not the reason Dave showed up. You know, it's possible he might give us the very excuse we need to be rid of him. I bet he tries to see her again. Animals don't change their spots. I'd think you'd be in favor of talking with Parker."

"I told Dave she's married."

"How'd he take it?"

"Surprised."

"She married Ivan Coaker, didn't she?"

Daniel nodded.

"Ivan and his brother could be pretty pissed off if Dave starts sniffing around her."

"Mother, you're back on that illegal edge again."

Grace waved it away. "I'm making noises—trying to figure things out. It's only talk, Daniel. It's my way of reaching a conclusion." She drew a breath. "You could drop a hint to Coaker that Dave Hunter's back in town. See where that takes it."

"I don't trust Ivan Coaker, and neither do you."

"You're not keeping something from me, are you, Daniel? You and that Annie girl?"

"I don't see her anymore, so leave it alone," Daniel snapped. "I made a promise to Ruth."

"Ruth came into town this morning, I suppose to see her father. Agatha told me. She spends more time with her daddy than she does with you."

"It comforts her," Daniel said. "We're having a bit of a rough go."

Grace nodded slowly.

Daniel frowned. "Mother, be careful. Especially around people like Ivan Coaker and Orville Parker. Parker's a poor excuse for a deputy sheriff and a man."

Grace Blaisdell rose to leave the office. With each step of her right foot, she touched the metal tip of her walking stick to the floor. Though it was unnecessary to aid her in walking, it had become symbolic to her without her conscious knowledge. At the door she turned. "Help me in this, Daniel."

Daniel took a last draw on his cigar and mashed it before he nodded. He said, "I'm surprised you don't just ask Carter to do something. He's killed for you before."

"That he has," Grace said.

When she had shut the door, Daniel swung his chair around toward the window and threw the cigar stub into the wastebasket beside his desk. *Damn it anyway,* he thought. She didn't have to bring the woman into it. He hoped that wasn't the reason Dave had come back. That issue was past and dead. Still, he had to admit, there had been the slightest touch of jealousy while Dave was in his office.

Yes, he had no doubt that Dave would be trying to see Annie again. The man had no concept of what he might stir up.

6

In the poolroom, catty-cornered across Main Street from the bank and between the two tallest two-story buildings in town, Lon Shirley greeted Dave Hunter once more with a handshake and slap on the shoulder.

"You're skinnier, if that's possible," Lon said. "Hungry now that you had your beer?"

Dave said he was, and Lon went behind the counter to make them both a ham sandwich, and then returned the ham to the ice box below the counter. Lon made a mental note to get more ice before what was now in the container melted. They ate and drank coffee.

Dave said, "Looks like I'm gonna have to steal Tony from the Blaisdells."

"You get in more trouble than you know. Why do you want to take Tony away from here?"

"Why? 'Cause I'm his old man."

"Bullshit, Dave. Give me a real reason."

Dave thought about it a moment. "I run into lots of guys who take their kids with 'em wherever they go. Made me feel like I should do it, too."

Lon shook his head. "What can you offer him?"

"I'll find a job somewhere. Last couple of years I worked on a riverboat, pushing barges." Dave produced a letter of recommendation signed by the ship's captain of the *Bonnie G*. "I'm a regular old salt."

Lon returned the letter and said, "No salt water in the river. What's your plan? You gonna ship out on another boat and leave Tony on shore to wait? That's real smart."

"I didn't mean another job on a boat."

"Gonna let Tony have a say in it?"

Dave finished his coffee and let Lon pour more into his cup. "I'm his daddy."

"At his age you didn't have much truck with your daddy. I didn't know mine. We were both on the road before we were Tony's age. But times are changing, Dave. He needs school, an education, a feeling of accomplishing something."

"Man's gotta have something in his life that makes him a man," Dave snapped. "What have you got, Lon? This claptrap poolroom with two old pool tables? You ain't never got married, you don't have kids. But you think you know things."

"I might've learned a little through the years," Lon said, kindly.

"But not about me and Tony."

Lon shrugged. "Give him a say in his future, Dave. He's smart. Gracie didn't want him working here, but he talked her into it. So I wouldn't even think of trying to force him to do something."

"Like I said, you ain't a daddy."

"Neither are you."

Dave drew himself up and scowled. His expression softened when he saw Lon Shirley's little half-smile.

Lon said, "You're trying to get back at the Blaisdells. You blame them for all the fucking up *you* done. Hell, Dave, you're the one who left."

"Louella should'a come with me."

"And how would you take care of her? She's not as independent as you are. I don't know the reasons, but that's the truth of it. Maybe old man Blaisdell made her that way when he was alive. He was always telling her how sick and weak she was and how she had to take it easy. She never had an adventure 'til you fucked her."

Dave couldn't resist laughing briefly.

Lon said, "I'm saying I wish you hadn't come back. Not for this reason."

"I think Tony belongs with me."

Lon shrugged again. "Just so you're not doing it to get back at Grace Blaisdell, or Louella. You'll lose, Dave."

"I don't know about that."

"Meantime, you'll need a roof," Lon said. "You can stay upstairs with me. I got a beat-up old mattress we can toss on the floor. Also, you can help me down here. It'll keep you busy while you meet Tony again and decide what to do."

Dave stroked his whiskers. "Yeah, I do need a bath and change of clothes. I got a little money saved, so I can pay my way. But sure, why not, I'll work for you again."

7

Tony tapped lightly on the door and waited until he heard his mother's voice before he went into her room.

She sat up in bed, propped against two pillows, her hands folded on the cover drawn up to her lap. Seeing Tony she smiled and nodded him to the chair beside the bed.

As he sat he was aware of the vaguely uncomfortable feeling he always had in his mother's room. The room itself was pleasant enough, spacious and bright with the large windows and tied back lace curtains, one of the newer cast-iron radiators, nicely decorated and should have been cheerful. But cheer it lacked for him. His mother rarely smiled, and when she did it was a sad little smile that never touched her eyes, never expressed an inner joy. She reached out and took his hand in both of hers. Her hands felt clammy to him.

His mother was quite different from his Grandmother Grace. His grandmother was a woman of vitality and decisiveness, even in conversation, but his mother seemed listless and frail, often timid. Constantly under the doctor's care, she confined herself to her room for long periods of time.

To Tony, her condition was worsening. Her shallow and pinched face reflected a haplessness or hopelessness he couldn't understand. He had seen a picture of her as a young girl, with his grandfather D. J. Blaisdell's arm about her shoulders as though supporting her, and she had been pretty though fragile even then.

"Hello, dear," she said, stroking his hand and making him fidget in the chair. "Is it evening already? I lose track of time."

"He came back," Tony said. "My father. He's in town."

His mother's face clouded. "Oh, God."

Tony leaned forward eagerly. "I want you to make Grandmother Grace keep her promise. I want to work with Lon at the poolroom. I'm afraid she won't let me go back. Today she sent Carter to get me."

His mother's hands trembled as she slipped them from his. She eased back against her pillows, staring straight ahead at nothing. "I was afraid he'd come back someday."

"Why do you hate him so much?"

The blinking of her eyes was her only recoil. "Hate? I never hated him. But he's—he's different."

"You married him," Tony said.

"A mistake. I can't talk about it." She looked at him. "Must you work at that awful poolroom? There are better jobs you can get if you insist. Cleaner jobs."

"I know what I want," Tony said. "Grandmother Grace won't want me to go back as long as he's there."

"Will a few days matter?" his mother asked. "You're so impatient—like him. He never stays longer than a few days."

Tony stood, wanting to leave the room but feeling vaguely guilty about it. He had been wrong to expect help from his mother. She couldn't understand. He adjusted the pillows behind her and asked, "Did you eat anything today?"

"I wasn't hungry." She smiled at him. "Don't worry about me. You can tell Agatha I might have a little something this evening if she'll bring it up. Soup, preferably. I don't feel like coming downstairs."

"Are you sick? Do you hurt?"

"Just tired," she said. "I might sleep a bit. Listen. Don't worry, dear. In a day or two he'll be gone again, and everything will be back to normal."

Tony went to the door and looked back at her. Her head was turned to one side, but the dark shadows were visible beneath her eyes. There wasn't anything he could say. He left the room, closing the door softly behind him.

At dinner that evening he spoke to his grandmother. There were the four of them, Grandmother Grace at one head of the table and Uncle Daniel at the other, and across from Tony sat Ruth, Daniel's wife, who rarely looked directly at anyone else even when spoken to. Grandmother Grace had changed into comfortable pants, her preference around the house, and Uncle Dan had put on work pants and a plaid shirt. Aunt Ruth wore a pale, pink chiffon dress.

Agatha, Carter's wife, served the meal.

The atmosphere was one of palpable tension. Tony sensed it although he wouldn't have been able to put it into words.

"You shouldn't've done it, Granny," Tony said. "Sending Carter to fetch me like you did. It made me look stupid."

Agatha looked at Tony as she ladled soup into Daniel's bowl. There was no particular expression on her face.

"I'm sorry if it upset you," Grace said. "I'm trying to do what's best for you."

"Tony, your grandmother means well," Daniel said, tasting his soup and nodding his appreciation to Agatha. He changed the subject. "How's your mom?"

"She's not coming down to eat. She don't feel well." Tony saw the slight shake of his grandmother's head as she stared downward. He continued, "What's really wrong with her, Granny? What's the doctor say?"

Slowly Grace looked up at him, hesitating a moment. "The doctors don't know for sure, Tony. She suffered a lot of childhood illnesses. More than once, we thought she might die. All we can do is hope for her full recovery."

"Did she ever feel really well?"

Grace's lips twitched, but she didn't respond.

Daniel dabbed his lips with his napkin and said, "She might've had a chance one time, Tony. She showed a little gumption."

"Daniel!" Grace warned.

"It didn't last long," Daniel said. "A brief spark of life. Few months before you were born. I think there was a happy moment in there somewhere."

Grace was shaking her head, her eyes downcast. "Louella has never been strong. Maybe it's my fault. She didn't have it easy when she was an infant. D. J. treated her like a fragile doll. As I said, all we can do is hope."

"Well," said Daniel, "Father felt women should be treated that way and taken care of."

"He missed the boat with me," Grace said wryly as she ate a crust of bread with her soup.

Daniel laughed. "He needed you the way you are, Mother."

Tony said, "Just seems like my mom staying in bed most 'a time in a dark room can't be too good for you. What was it made her happy that time, Uncle Dan?"

Grace and Daniel exchanged looks, hers a cautionary one and his with a small half-smile. He said, "I can't remember offhand, Tony." He turned his attention to his wife. "Tell me about your day, Ruth. Did you go in to see your father?"

Tony was aware of the tension increasing. It had been so for a long time now, as though Uncle Daniel and his wife were sparring with each other.

"Yes, I walked into town," she said. "What I saw was interesting."

Grandmother Grace frowned. "Ruth, I wish you'd let Carter, or Agatha at least, accompany you to town when you want to go. There are unsavory characters about."

"The Lord is my shelter," Ruth said. She gave Daniel a long, rather smirking look. "I stopped outside the bank, and you know what I saw?"

Daniel waited. Finally he shrugged. "I can't guess."

"There was my husband with that woman inside. I saw you through the big front window. All smiles at each other."

Daniel blew out his breath loudly and shook his head.

"No denials?" Ruth said. "It's funny. When I brought

my father's collection receipts to the bank, I didn't see you rush out. You jumped right up and practically ran from your office to see her."

Nobody spoke for a long minute.

Grandmother Grace said softly, "Ruth, I don't think this is proper conversation at the dinner table."

"Nothing to it," Daniel added.

"Right," Ruth said. "You *would* say that. And when you take walks at night into town, which is perfectly fine with your mother, you never see her then?" She got no reaction to her sarcasm. "I'm going upstairs." With that, she pushed her plate and bowl away, dropping her napkin into the soup bowl, rose from the table and headed for the stairway. Over her shoulder she said, "I'm going to pray with my father tonight."

8

The rattling of pebbles hitting the bedroom window brought Louella Hunter alert. At first she frowned until she heard it again. Then she got her legs from the bed, her feet under her, and shuffled unsteadily, holding onto furniture, to the large window. She had to move slowly and carefully, bracing herself, because she felt weak after all the time spent off her feet in bed. She parted the curtains and raised the window.

He was directly below, between the garden and the wall of the house, clear in the moonlight and wearing a big grin on his face. Louella gasped as she nearly stumbled.

"Come on," he said. "Get your butt down here and we'll take a walk."

"Go away!" she hissed. "Leave now."

"I guess you wasn't surprised I came back."

"Go away," she said again. Somehow she couldn't make herself shut the window and go back to bed.

"Come on, Lu." It was what Dave Hunter had always

called her. "It's not cold, but you can put on a robe or coat. We need to talk."

"No!"

"Why not?"

"Just because."

"That's not a reason, Lu."

"Stop calling me that," Louella said. "You're not supposed to be here. What if somebody sees you?"

"Like I give a damn," Dave said and laughed. "Hey, come on. I'll give you a kiss."

"Oh, my God!"

"More than that if you want," Dave said. "Or—I won't put my hands on you if you don't want me to. Remember how we used to sneak out? Sure, you do. You liked it. Now, come on. I want to talk about Tony."

Louella sobbed sharply and said, "Go away!"

Below, Dave heard the snicking sound before he turned and saw the silhouette of the man at the corner of the house. The man held a shotgun resting on the crook of his left arm, his right hand inside the trigger guard, a double-barreled shotgun.

Dave drew in a breath and raised his hands. He said, "That gun ain't necessary, Carter."

"Never know," Carter said, softly. "Gotta do something with you now."

"You mean—kill me?"

"Haven't decided," Carter said. "Maybe save a whole lot of trouble for lots of folks if I do."

Dave looked up at the bedroom window. It was shut

now, and the inside curtains were back in place. He looked at Carter. "You got the gun, you tell me."

"Leave, Mr. Hunter. Walk away."

"I'll come back."

"If you try to come back tonight, I'll shoot you first and answer questions later."

"Is it true you killed men, Carter?"

"You don't want to find out," Carter said. "You got a chance now, so go."

Dave sighed. "Everybody wants me to leave. Okay, but tell Grace I'll be seeing her soon."

He trudged down the hill from the house and made his way to Main Street. The two taverns, *Bagget's Saloon* and *Merryman's Tavern,* were open, and so was Lon Shirley's poolroom. He made a decision and went into the poolroom.

Lon was sitting on a bench, smoking his pipe and dreaming. Dave found the broom behind the counter and started at the back sweeping the floor. They were the only two in the place at this moment.

"Nothing to sweep," Lon said without opening his eyes. "'Tween you and your son, I'll have the cleanest floor in town. Tomorrow you can muck out the stable for Old Bill." "Old Bill" was Lon's horse he kept across the alley in a lean-to stable behind the poolroom.

Dave swept the floor anyway, brushing the dirt onto a newspaper and dumping it into the trash box behind the counter. After he had taken the trash box out back into the alley and emptied it, he returned and asked, "How is Tony, Lon? What does he look like now?"

"A little like you around the eyes and mouth," Lon said, "but he'll be a bigger man someday. He's almost as tall as you right now. Don't know where his size comes from."

"Hell, you're a big man, Lon. Ain't nothin' wrong with bein' big. Tell me, is he a good boy?"

"Of course, after being around me."

Dave, standing behind the counter and facing Lon, leaned his elbows on the smooth top. "I saw Daniel at the bank and wanted to ask him if he's still fucking Annie Pyle on the side. He said she got married."

"Leave it alone, Dave," Lon said in his slow voice. He inspected his pipe, blowing out some debris. "Did Dan tell you who Annie married?"

"He said to Ivan Coaker. Hell, the Coakers live in a shack in shantytown. Why would Annie do that?"

Lon ignored the question and said, "Gracie wants Tony to work at the bank, and I don't blame her. But I suspect the boy might decide for himself. By God, I wish I'd had a chance to work in a nice clean bank when I was a kid. Look at me now."

"You always done what you wanted."

Lon grunted and filled his pipe. He lit it carefully. His movements were slow motion.

"How's the arm, Lon?"

"Depends on what I try to do with it. Hurts when the weather changes."

"How is Louella? Really?"

Lon took his time before answering. He tapped the loose ash out into the spittoon, tamped the pipe with his finger and relit it. "I don't know that she ever leaves the house. Can't remember last time I seen 'er downtown. Tony told me she's sick, but I could see he don't want to talk about it."

"She won't see me," Dave said.

"Expect her to?"

"To hell with it!" Dave smacked his palm against the counter top. "Guess I was a damn fool for getting mixed up with that family. If it wasn't for Tony—" He left it unsaid.

Lon tilted his head toward his friend. "Know something? I can't tell if you're really sincere in your paternal feelings or putting on a show. We known each other a long time, but I can't read you. Suppose I'll find out sooner or later. Let me tell you, Dave. If you do something to hurt Tony, you an' me'll have a major falling out."

"Lon, I might not have anybody to even care about me someday. Tony might forget all about me."

"There is that. I won't have anybody to care about me. Sometimes that's how life is."

"Why didn't you ever get married? Oh, I forgot, you don't like women."

Lon gave a scoffing laugh. "Hey, I got nothing against women."

"But you never loved one, huh?"

"There was one I loved," Lon said. "A very special one who taught me a lot. She was the best ever."

"Here in Vinton?" Dave asked.

Lon nodded slightly.

"Don't tell me you were fucking Annie Pyle, too?"

"No, I never laid a hand on Annie. Way too young for me. She was too young for you, but you wasn't bright enough to know it."

"Is this mystery woman still around? I bet she married somebody else."

"Yes to both," Lon said.

"Tell me her name," Dave teased. "I'll go see her. She might need a change."

"No. Now that's enough." Lon grunted. "You're acting like a caged animal. Got any money?"

"Some."

Lon stood and stretched. He reached into his pants pocket and pulled out a small roll of bills.

Dave waved him off. "No, Lon. Forget it. You already bought me a drink, and you're doing enough."

"Then get your ass out'a here for a while. Take another walk, get a beer, do something to get your mind off the Blaisdell's. I'll close up when it's time, and if I'm in bed I'll leave the back door open for you." He saw that Dave looked thoughtful. "I hope you ain't thinking of visiting shantytown to see Annie."

"No," Dave said, but his voice lacked conviction.

"That's good. The Coakers can be mean."

"How long she been married?"

"I don't know, month or more." Lon shrugged. "Maybe she got to feeling desperate. I only hear things, and I don't put much stock in gossip. Supposedly, she lives with Ivan and his brother in shantytown. That's three of 'em in the same little house. Then on the other hand I hear she comes to downtown and spends most 'a her evenings with Amanda Hopper. They're good friends, you know."

Dave grinned wryly. "Heard she went to work for Amanda after I left. You think Annie got herself knocked up? She was a careful girl, Lon. And she wanted a lot more out'a life than sounds like what she's got."

Lon nodded. "Ever hear of any girl getting married in this town without somebody saying she had to? Anyhow, you keep away from her, Dave."

"Yes, Mother," Dave said and went outside. He stopped in the open doorway. "Maybe Daniel banged her more than he lets on."

"I'd leave Daniel out of it," Lon said. "He's got other problems."

"Like what?"

"It's his business. I said I don't put a lot'a stock in gossip."

9

Dave crossed the alley to *Merryman's Tavern*. He stood at the bar and had a glass of beer. Two of the half dozen customers spoke to him while the others looked him over. When he was almost finished with the beer, another man came inside and stood at the end of the bar. He stared at Dave.

Dave glanced at him out of idle curiosity at first, until their eyes held. A silver star was displayed on the left breast pocket of the man's shirt because the man stood with his hands on his hips, sweeping back his open jacket. His gun belt and holster looked old, the leather cracked. He wore a beaten Derby hat that was darkly stained around the brim.

The bartender asked him, "You on duty or off tonight, Orville?"

"What?" the man said, staring at Dave.

"I asked, are you or ain't you drinking something?"

"Naw," the deputy said, looking at Dave. After a few seconds he came closer until he stood beside Dave.

Dave deliberately turned his head away and drank from his glass of beer.

"You're Dave Hunter," the deputy said. "Bet you don't remember me."

Dave drained his beer before looking at him. There was something odd going on. He had first seen the deputy when he left the poolroom, the deputy standing across the street at that time.

"Yes, I remember you," Dave said. "You're Orville Parker." He nodded at the man's silver star. "I see you changed jobs again."

"Outside," Parker said. "Let's walk and talk."

"I was about to have another beer."

"Outside," Parker repeated.

"What will we talk about?"

The bartender leaned over the counter. "Yeah, take it out of here."

Dave collected his change and went out to the sidewalk where the deputy waited.

The deputy pointed. "We can talk in the alley over there."

"No," Dave said. "We can talk here in the light where people can see us."

Parker spat off to one side. "Town's changing, Hunter. More people getting automobiles now, you see? Not too many horses and buggies on Main Street no more. Hell, even the sheriff's got an automobile. I get to ride in it sometimes when I'm on duty."

"Do you get to drive it?"

Parker snorted. "Sheriff's kind'a protective of that thing. I heard you come in off a river boat."

Dave nodded.

"Bad lot on them boats," Parker said. "Drinkers and gamblers, most of 'em. They disturb the decent folks, and I have to keep 'em in line. How long you planning to stick around?"

"Could be a long time. I got a job. You can ask Lon Shirley."

"Yeah, you two are old buddies. There's a boat come in this afternoon. It's docked down by the park. I got to check it out, so come with me."

"Too dark there," Dave said.

"Naw. We got a streetlight now at First and Main. There's plenty of light. 'Sides, kids will be playing in the park. You got nothing to worry about."

Dave shrugged and fell in beside him.

They reached the end of Main, crossing First Street toward *Riverside Park*. There were breaks in the clouds displaying the occasional full moon. Normally, Dave liked walking by the river, but at this particular time every sense was telling him to be careful. He moved around to Parker's gun side.

They went down the embankment on the graveled road to the river's edge. At either side of the park were the boat docks. They stopped by the water, and Dave heard a boat whistle somewhere upriver. The river was dark, and on the far side, the Kentucky side, were the silhouettes of the trees against the night sky. The only light in the park was behind them now, cast by the street lamp at the corner of First and Main.

Parker stooped, picked up a rock and threw it far out into the water. "You like workin' on a boat?"

"It's okay," Dave said.

"Lots 'a times when boats stop here they're looking for men to fill out a crew," Parker said. He threw another rock into the river. "Get on one, Hunter, and don't come back."

"Why?"

"Because I said to."

"Does the sheriff know about this?"

Parker faced him. "Abe Buckner listens to my advice. You should listen, too. You got one day, Hunter. I don't want to find you anywhere in Vinton tomorrow night."

"Tell you what," Dave said. "Take me in to Buckner. If he's got a reason, he can lock me up."

"I ain't talkin' about locking you up," Parker said.

"I want to see Buckner. Let him tell me."

"You are a stubborn son of a bitch," Parker said and grunted a laugh. "You do what I told you. I ain't supposed to hurt you, or I wouldn't be standing here jawing with you."

"Better idea," Dave said. "Let's go see Grace Blaisdell instead. I can tell her not to send any more cheap errand boys."

"Nobody said I gotta take shit from you." Parker squared his shoulders and stepped forward.

Dave made a motion as if to back off but stepped in quickly, his left fist darting into the deputy's face. He struck Parker full in the mouth. The deputy staggered, his hat fell off, and he shook his head to clear it before Dave could follow up.

Parker came at him, cursing, and swung his big right

fist. Dave ducked and danced out of reach, Parker swung again, and again Dave's head moved out of the way. Dave was watching the deputy carefully, watching his feet and the way he carried himself. He knew he was quicker than the bigger man but not as bull strong.

Dave stayed away from him, dodging the hard rushes. He heard Parker's breath wheezing with the effort. When Parker missed again, Dave ducked in close and snapped a quick left and right into the deputy's midsection and ribs. Parker dropped his arms, and Dave smashed him on the jaw.

Parker hit the ground and rolled over, his right hand reaching for his holstered gun. He got his hand kicked hard and cried out. Dave scooped up the gun. His right hand gripped the weapon by barrel and, in the same motion, swung it in a flat arc, striking the butt against the other man's head. Parker fell with a groan.

Dave shifted the gun in his hand and tucked in inside his belt before he bent and examined the deputy as best he could. Parker was moaning but still conscious. Dave touched the side of the man's head above his right ear and felt the stickiness of the blood.

Nothing could be gained by staying here. Dave felt the deputy would be all right in a little while, and the man would certainly come looking for him again.

Dave straightened and walked up the embankment toward Main Street, pulling out his shirttail and letting it hang over the gun in his belt. He did not think of the trouble he knew he was in now. He was thinking of the person responsible.

10

Tony awakened suddenly, not sure whether he had heard something or had dreamed it. Then it came again, and he knew what it was. Someone was pounding on the front door downstairs.

He climbed out of bed and pulled his pants on, aware of the sounds in the next room also. His Uncle Dan was awake, too.

Tony opened his door halfway and looked out onto the darkness of the landing. A light came on below in the kitchen, and he knew that would be Carter coming from the small room he and Agatha shared in the back.

Tony hesitated in his own doorway as the door to his left opened and Uncle Dan came out buckling the belt of his trousers. He wore an undershirt with his pants but was barefooted, and he carried a .22 rifle in one hand. He went downstairs and turned on the light in the foyer. Tony was unable to see him from where he stood at the top of the curving stairs, but he heard him say, "I'll see to it, Carter."

The light in the kitchen went out, but Tony knew Carter would still be there, in the darkness, probably with his shotgun ready.

Uncle Dan opened the front door and said something softly in surprise. Then Tony heard another man's voice, loud and sharp with anger. "I've come to get my son, Daniel."

"Dave—Dave—"

His father's voice interrupted Uncle Dan. "I'm taking him away, Daniel. We can make it easy or hard, any way you want. If Gracie's got any other ideas, she can kiss my ass and pay for the privilege."

Tony was suddenly frightened. He eased down a few steps until he could sit and peer through the banister posts.

He saw Uncle Dan prop the rifle against the wall.

"Stop it, Dave," Uncle Dan said. "Leave before Mother hears you. This won't help. We'll talk about it tomorrow."

Tony jerked his head around as the main bedroom door opened above him. Grandmother Grace came out. She had turned up the light inside and strode purposefully with it silhouetting her from the back, striking the black walking stick down with each step she took. She wore a wrapper belted at the waist and her gray hair was pulled up and tucked beneath a nightcap.

She came down from the top of the stairs, about halfway, passing Tony without stopping or appearing to look at him. Then, stationary, with her left hand resting on the banister, she peered below toward the lighted foyer. "Who's down there?" she demanded. "Daniel! Carter!"

Tony heard his father's voice again. "You made a mistake, Grandma." Then Dave Hunter pushed into the foyer around Daniel Blaisdell. "I'm taking my son."

The harsh laugh from his grandmother sounded sharp as a dog's bark to Tony. "So it's you, Dave Hunter. Go away and leave us alone. Tony is happy here, and here he'll stay. Get out!"

"Not without him. Bring him down and I'll talk to him. Let's see what he says when he finds out what you tried to do tonight. Whatever you paid Orville Parker wasn't enough. Here!"

Tony saw it, the glint of the object seemingly floating upward in the dimly lighted space to hit heavily on the steps in front of Grandmother Grace. She looked at it but did not pick up the revolver. With her walking stick she hooked the trigger guard and flipped the gun back downward. Tony heard it tumble down several steps before it stopped.

"I am not fond of guns," Grandmother Grace said, coolly. "Take it back where you got it."

"You know where I got it," Tony heard his father say. "I don't like being threatened. You must be scared, Grandma. Afraid Tony wants to come with me?"

"He has a future here, David," Grandmother Grace said. "With us—with the bank. What can you offer him?"

"Choices."

"Poolrooms and whorehouses," she said. "Wonderful. Carter!"

"I'm here, ma'am." Tony heard Carter's voice from the direction of the kitchen.

"Get your shotgun, Carter."

"I got it, ma'am," Carter replied. "It's pointed at Mr. Hunter."

"Hear that, David?" she asked. "Carter will shoot you if I tell him. You are a trespasser here. I want you to leave, and I'll forget about tonight."

"What about Orville Parker?" asked Tony's father. "Will he forget? He's pretty pissed at me."

"I'll take care of him," Grandmother Grace said. "I apologize for him. It was a misunderstanding. He saw me on the street and mentioned he'd seen you. I said I wish you'd never come back and would just go away again. Believe it or not, that's the truth. The man's a brute. Will you accept my apology?"

"Right, and I'll take Tony."

Tony heard more sounds above and saw that his mother had come to the railing at the top of the landing. Wavering slightly, she held her nightgown tightly to her throat as she leaned forward to peer downward. Appearing beside her from a different bedroom was Ruth Blaisdell, Uncle Dan's wife. She was fully clothed as she, too, peered downward.

"I—I heard voices," his mother said. "I was dreaming. I dreamt that Dave was in the house."

"Here!" his father called upward. "Louella, come down and tell your old lady I'm taking our son."

"I'll take care of this, Louella," Grandmother Grace said. "You go back to your room now." It was a soft command.

Ruth was the one who responded, turning and going back inside her bedroom as though she had been the one commanded and shut her door.

"Louella," Tony's father called. "Your mother tried to have me run out of town."

Tony saw his mother clutch her gown tighter. She swayed slightly.

"Louella, I'll handle this," Grandmother Grace said. "Go to your room now."

"Don't—let him take Tony," Tony's mother said softly.

Grandmother Grace struck her walking stick so abruptly against the banister that it made Tony jump. "I won't! Please, go to your room, Louella!" she snapped.

Tony saw his mother move slowly backward, turn, and retreat to her room. She shut the door. He had known she would. Still, he couldn't help the feeling of disappointment. For once in his life he would have liked to see his mother stand up to his grandmother, but he felt that would never happen.

"Damn it, David!" Grandmother Grace said to his father. "See what you made me do. I hate losing my temper. We can resolve this. I'm sure you want money. How much?"

"Now you're talking, Gracie," David said. "I want five thousand dollars from you. Tomorrow night I'll be back. Then I want your promise that I can see Tony and talk to him on my terms."

"I knew you'd sell him," Grandmother Grace said. "Okay, done. Right now, tonight, this is your final chance to leave peacefully. Don't underestimate me. Carter! Count to five slowly and if he's not gone by then, shoot him."

Tony saw Uncle Daniel shaking his head. "She means it, Dave," he said to Tony's father. "We'll clear this up later."

"Why do you let her get away with this, Daniel?"

"Because I think she's right about lots of things," Uncle Daniel said. "Get out of here for now."

Tony watched his father standing below, apparently in indecision, slowly making up his mind. At last his father nodded and went out the front door. Uncle Daniel took the revolver that had been propelled down the stairs and tossed it out the door after the other man.

"Dave!" Uncle Daniel called. "You better take that and get it back to Parker. It'll go easier on you." Then he shut the door.

"Carter!" Grandmother Grace called. "Were you counting?"

"Yes, ma'am."

"Well, that was a damned long five." She turned and looked at Tony. "Go back to bed, young man."

"Where'd he get the gun?" Tony asked.

"Seems like he took it away from Deputy Parker." She chuckled. "Never mind the gun." She saw Uncle Dan starting up the stairs. "I'm coming down, Daniel. Let's talk in the study."

"Meet you there," Daniel said.

11

Daniel carried his .22 rifle upstairs to his and Ruth's bedroom, opened the door and propped the gun in the closet where he generally kept it. Ruth, standing in the moonlight by the window, had turned on the lamp in the bedroom. She peered out toward the dark night. Daniel noted that she had put on bloomers for bike riding.

"I take it I'll be sleeping alone again tonight, as usual," Daniel said. "You're dressed for riding."

"What did you expect?" she said, not facing him. "I'm going into town. I need to speak with Daddy."

"For Christ's sake, Ruth, it's late, and we're all tired. What if I promise I won't touch you?"

"Do not use the Lord's name in vain," Ruth said. "Your punishment will be severe. As for a promise like that, it's too easy for you to break it."

"I've been punished enough," Daniel said, wearily, "for something only in your imagination." He sighed. "You saw your father most of the day. Do you have to go into town tonight? We can talk about this afternoon if you want. I'm willing to meet you more than halfway, Ruth."

Ruth shook her head without turning to face him. She said, "I'm so tired of lies and deceit."

"I've never deceived you."

"You and Dave Hunter—arguing. And it's about that woman, that Annie Pyle, isn't it?"

For a second Daniel was speechless. "No, Ruth. You're imagining things again."

She uttered a short, harsh laugh without humor and hugged her arms about herself. "Always that woman," she muttered.

"I told you that's over, long time ago," Daniel said.

She turned and faced him. "If only I could believe you."

"You want me to be lying." Daniel said. "I made a foolish mistake confessing to you. What you don't seem to understand is that it all happened before we met and married."

"Daniel, I don't like betrayal."

In the dim light, Daniel nodded to himself. This argument was so worn that he really didn't care. He said, "Do what you have to. At least I'm glad to see you'll be taking a bicycle and not walking. I'll be downstairs with Mother."

"Of course you will—you and your mother. If it's real late I'll stay over at the church. Don't worry about me. I'm in good hands with the Lord."

"So I suppose I won't see you before breakfast?"

"I don't know yet. A little prayer wouldn't hurt any of us."

"Jesus, Ruth, do me a favor and let Carter accompany

you as far as the church," Daniel said. "I do worry about your safety."

"I asked you not to blaspheme the Lord's name. Some of us trust in God and his justice." Her tone relented. "If it means anything to you, Carter can follow me in. But I don't want him camping outside the church. I don't like being spied upon."

"That makes two of us," Daniel said. "I'll speak to Carter."

"Just—just go to mother, Daniel."

12

In the study, Grace sighed and shook her head. She took off the nightcap and ran her fingers through her tousled gray hair that tumbled to her shoulders. She had seen pictures and ads in magazines of women in the east who were trending toward shorter hair and considered becoming the first decent woman in Vinton who might get a closer cut. She had decided to give it more thought. She propped the walking stick against a chair.

"Daniel," she said, "I can use a brandy."

Daniel grinned, rubbed one bare foot over the other and went to the cupboard to open a liquor cabinet. The liquor cache was directly below the huge oil portrait identical to the one in the bank of his late father, Darwin James Blaisdell. The old man's somber expression dominated the study and might have had a dark effect on most people, except that Grace and Daniel were so accustomed, or immune, to it that they treated it lightly. The family possessed no picture of the man when he was not somber. Daniel couldn't remember his father smiling very often, and, on occasion when he did, it was always at Grace.

Daniel poured shots of brandy into two glasses and brought one to Grace. As was their custom, they toasted the old man first. Grace said, "Give us a big grin, Sweetie," and Daniel laughed. He knew she was not ridiculing his father. She sat in a soft chair, and Daniel took another chair. The fire in the fireplace had practically burned down.

"If you're cold, Mother, I can put more logs on the fire."

"I'm not cold. I'm exhausted. I was thinking how I manage to mess things up," she said, ruefully, and sipped her drink. "Why do I let that man make me so damned mad?"

Daniel knew she was talking of Dave Hunter. "He's not being smart," he said and took a drink of the brandy. "Eventually Tony will do what he wants. You know that, and it's what we both want. Admit it or not, Mother. And there's not much we can do for Louella. If Louella were more like you, she wouldn't be in this house, upstairs in that bed. She'd be following Dave Hunter wherever he went."

"You think?" Grace winced. "I don't know what to do for her."

"Nothing," Daniel said. "Some people want to live, some want to die. My father convinced her she's sicker than she is."

Grace uttered a negative sound that was half a snort. But she still wore a tiny smile. "We can't blame him. She never was a healthy child. D. J. tried, Daniel. He really tried."

"He could've cared for people a little more."

"He never denied us anything. We're rich, thanks to him."

"So we've got money. Don't start running yourself down." Daniel leaned forward in his chair. "Mother, I saw how much you cared for him, regardless of whatever love was between you—or wasn't. I admit I grew up not understanding how the two of you didn't sleep together. You had your reasons, and I've an idea what they were."

"You think you know more than you do, Daniel."

Daniel tilted his head at her. "Don't you think I heard those rumors that Father would travel in his buggy to the whorehouses in Elston, pay for a girl and watch her undress because he couldn't do anything more. Even the facts of Louella and I couldn't stop that gossip."

"Daniel, there are all kinds of love," Grace said, quietly. "He loved all of us, and for that I'm proud and grateful." She sighed. "The real subject I want to discuss is you and Ruth. It's getting worse."

"I know."

"She spends more and more nights in that spare bedroom in her father's church."

"I'm aware of that," Daniel said.

"Do you have sex at all?"

"Are we sticking our nose in?" Daniel smiled, not mockingly.

"She does spend some nights upstairs with you," Grace said.

"There's an invisible barrier between us that might as well be a wall. She's safe from me. Her daddy preaches sin and guilt, and Ruth believes it."

"What's going to happen?"

"That I don't know," Daniel admitted, frowning.

"Do you love her?"

"That's a tough question. I thought I did. I'm sure I did at first. I don't know what love is, Mother. You'll have to explain it to me."

"Wrong person to ask," Grace said. "Is Annie Pyle coming between the two of you?"

"It's Annie Coaker now, Mother. And, no, she's not. I have not touched Annie since I met Ruth. The only times I've spoken with her is when she's come to the bank."

"But you did see her today?"

Daniel nodded. "She has an account with us. She added to it. That's all."

"You had to wait on her yourself?"

"Yeah, I guess I did."

Grace shrugged and sipped brandy. "Old times' sake."

"You have to trust me, Mother."

"I do trust you," Grace said. "You can tell me it's none of my business, Daniel. You say you've had nothing to do with Annie since you and Ruth married, and I believe you."

Scowling, Daniel drank and pursed his lips. "I've talked to her on a few occasions. She spends a lot of evenings with Amanda Hopper instead of her husband. Who could blame her once you get a look at the Coaker brothers? She sits out on the porch of Amanda's rooming house. She used to work for Amanda. They're friends. I've heard, don't know if it's true, that whenever Annie does go to shantytown she takes a jug of whiskey for Ivan and Clifford. Then the boys run off to the river to fish and drink all night."

"You still consider Annie your friend."

"She listens," Daniel said. "She always listened well. Sometimes I want somebody to understand me, to make me feel good."

"You're treading on dangerous ground, Daniel." Grace broke a smile. "You're a romantic, like your father."

Surprised, Daniel glanced around at the portrait. "My father was a romantic?"

Grace swirled her brandy, smiling into it, and drank.

Daniel laughed softly. "When I was growing up, I used to get in fights all the time on his behalf."

"And mine," Grace said.

"Yours, too. I couldn't let them insult you the way people did. Seemed like every time you hired extra help here at the house for the season, or some construction, the gossip started. How the two of you had separate bedrooms. How you married him for his money. How Louella and I might not even be his children." Daniel shrugged his shoulders. "I'm not criticizing you, Mother. I never would. You held things together. Lucky we had you. I remember him saying that a successful man must have at least one son and one daughter. God knows where he got that crazy idea, but it practically obsessed him. I guess he died happy."

Grace said, "I'm glad you're not like him."

Daniel was a bit shocked at the comment. "You said I am."

"Did I? I meant you're a stronger man than D. J. Blaisdell." She stopped as they heard someone in the front hall, and then the door open and close. She peered at Daniel. "Ruth?"

"Yes. My loving spouse insists she has to talk with

her father. Prayer is what she needs tonight," Daniel said, sarcastically.

Grace shook her head sadly. "All because of Annie Pyle."

Daniel said, "I confessed my poor judgment on our wedding day."

Grace nodded somberly. "In the light of things now, that seems a bit unwise."

"Some people cannot forgive and forget."

"I don't see that there's anything to forgive."

"To Ruth, and her father, a person's past dictates his future salvation. The only problem is, you've got to have some way to make things right. She wants me to agree to attend church and let her father counsel me. Eventually, she says, I can be forgiven with enough prayer and effort. Frankly, that scares me. I don't know if I have that much prayer and effort in me. I know I don't have much faith in something unseen."

Grace smiled ever so slightly. "It might scare me, too. Have you discussed any of this with Reverend Jones?"

"A little," Daniel admitted. "But how do you explain to a man that his daughter is an unreasonable shrew?"

"I'm not one to say," Grace said. "It concerns me that Ruth takes long walks at night, away from the house. You never know the kind of person she might encounter. She might have a hard time explaining to some unsavory character that she's a religious woman going to speak with her father, the minister. They might not care. I've suggested she ask Carter to accompany her, but she refuses. So I've asked him to follow discreetly and make sure she gets to her father safely."

Daniel peered over his glass. "I don't want to see her harmed. I don't know what else to do for her. I spoke to Carter, and he's getting a couple of bicycles out for them now. She wouldn't tolerate my following her. She'd believe I'm spying on her. I tell her, trust begets trust."

Grace cocked an eyebrow at him. "I have to ask. Have you considered divorce, or annulment? You might talk with Judge Parks. That's if the marriage was never consummated."

"That would be one more sin on my account," Daniel said with a slight smile. "Her father married us."

"But you don't have normal sex."

Daniel couldn't suppress a chuckle. "Even abnormal."

"Do you still feel love for her?"

"I don't feel much of anything now."

Grace nodded. "Whatever prompted you to tell her about you and Annie Pyle?"

Daniel snorted a harsh laugh. "Mother, I thought confession was good for the soul. It wasn't good for mine."

"You will have decisions to make regarding your wife."

"I'll get to it," Daniel admitted, shrugged, and finished his brandy.

13

Carter appeared in the open study door and knocked on it lightly. He was dressed and had a light coat on. Grace and Daniel looked at him.

Carter said, "Miz Ruth and I are heading to town now. She doesn't want me to wait for her at the church."

"It's all right, Carter," Grace said. "Just see that she gets there safely and come on home. At this hour I suspect Ruth will spend the night in her father's spare room."

Carter went out, leaving the study door open.

Grace shook her head. "I was so stupid today. I'll have to straighten Deputy Parker out."

"You shouldn't have sic'em on Dave."

"I know, I know." She made a dismissive wave with one hand. "I ran into Parker outside the bank this afternoon and just—well—blurted it out that I wish Dave Hunter would get the hell out of Osanamon County and leave us all alone."

"He took it as a request," Daniel said.

Grace blew out a long breath and finished her brandy.

Finally, after several seconds of silence in which she looked up at the portrait, she said, "Daniel, I wasn't really running myself down. Lots of women in this town think I married D. J. for his money. They're sorry they couldn't get him first."

"Understandable jealousy, Mother. You need more brandy." Daniel went to the cabinet and topped her glass. "We're doing okay."

"Fact is, they're right, Daniel. I did marry him for his money and the security it brought. At the time I had neither."

"That makes you smart," Daniel said. "He was happy with you. I could see that. Regardless of whether I, or Louella, pleased him, he was happy with *you*. When I was little, I remember how worried he was when you had that accident. I think he prayed for the only time in his life."

Grace nodded and absently touched the crescent scar beneath her right cheekbone. "Yes, the accident."

"You got hurt pretty bad for falling off a horse."

"The horse stepped on me," she said. "But—I survived." She changed the subject quickly. "Are you happy at the bank?"

Daniel had to think about it. He took his time seating himself again and crossing his ankles. "It's what I do, Mother. It's what I trained for. I don't know if I ever told you, but when I went to college in the east and studied business and banking, I met a real nice girl."

"You wrote about her. But you let her get away."

Daniel nodded. "Not very bright of me."

"Because you were thinking of Annie Pyle."

"Mother, I was one dumb lump of shit."

Grace thoughtfully sipped her brandy. "Daniel, am I doing wrong by Tony?"

"No, you have his welfare in mind. But he's going to be an independent young man, whether you like it or not. You know something else? I don't believe Dave Hunter will influence Tony's decisions. So we just have to ride this out." He lifted his brandy glass in another half-humorous, half-mocking toast at the portrait. "Dave Hunter seems to bring out the worst in all of us. Would you have allowed Carter to shoot Dave tonight?"

"Of course not," she said. "And Carter would not have done it unless your or my life was in danger. He's protected me before."

"Someday you'll have to tell me about that—and I mean every detail. Especially after you got injured, how he took care of you. I watched him. I used to peek around corners because everybody was so worried for you. Even Lon Shirley came up from town to visit you."

Grace laughed again as she touched the crescent shaped scar on her cheek. "You don't want to know every detail of my young life, Daniel. Then you'd know what a wild and crazy girl your mother was. You'd disown me."

"No, that won't happen. We're a lot alike."

"Where are you going?"

Daniel had risen from the chair and started for the study doorway. He turned. "I feel like a walk myself. Unless there's something else you want from me, I'll get my boots and coat and go out. Can I get you anything?"

"Take the car," Grace suggested, "unless you don't want anybody in town to recognize you."

"I'm not going to see Annie," Daniel said. "It's just for a short walk. We've talked of things I have to think about. Walking helps me think. Don't wait up for me."

"I'll sit here awhile yet before I go to bed," Grace told him.

Tony had crept down the stairs and was listening at the study door that was partially open. He ducked back into the dark kitchen as his uncle went up the stairs. Tony waited there until Uncle Dan came down and went out the front door. Then he peeked into the study and saw his grandmother sitting in her chair and staring at the dying fire.

"Little boys shouldn't listen at doors."

The soft voice behind Tony startled him. He swung around to see Agatha striking a match at the kitchen entrance to light a candle. Agatha set the candle on the kitchen table and grinned at Tony, then pulled out a chair.

Tony went into the kitchen, sat down, and they spoke in whispers. "Do you think he'll come back tonight?"

"Your father? I don't think so," Agatha said. "But you ain't seen the last of him. When he goes for good, he'll want to take you along. How do you feel about that?"

"I don't know," Tony said, truthfully. "Would Carter have shot him?"

"I don't believe my husband would shoot a man like that. But we've both knowed others that needed shooting. We been taking care of this family since your grandmother married old man Blaisdell, and Carter was doin' it before that. Mrs. Blaisdell don't want your daddy shot. They're just two people facing off at each other. Now, how 'bout you, young man? Would you like something to eat?"

"No, thank you. Agatha, how long has Carter known my grandma?"

"Since she was about twenty years old. He tol' me what a pretty little thing she was then. She's still a handsome woman."

"You moved here to Vinton from Boston, didn't you?"

"Yes," Agatha said, "when Carter sent for me. Him and Mrs. Blaisdell first met in eastern Tennessee. She was alone except for a little son she had. Didn't she ever tell you this? His name was John. He died real soon after that. Smallpox epidemic. Carter buried the poor child for her. She needed looking after, so he took up with her and followed her into Kentucky and, eventually, here. Here's where she met Mr. Blaisdell."

"Why—?"

"That's enough," Agatha interrupted him. "You got more questions about your grandma you ask her. I'm talking out 'a place."

Tony smiled. "Did you and Carter go to college together?"

"Heavens no! I been working all my life. But I met him in Boston when he was in school," Agatha nodded. "Before that, his daddy was a slave in South Carolina. Him and his mama took the name of the owner, Foote. That's why my husband's last name is Foote. Carter saved the old white man's son from drowning. He was so grateful he sent Carter along with his son to get an education. Them two boys had become friends. Anyway, yeah, Carter and me got married just after he graduated from college."

"How come Carter didn't stay there—in the east?"

Agatha tilted her head as she considered. "He got the itch to see his folks again. I had steady work for a white couple, so I tol' him to go ahead, that he knew where I was. He packed up and headed south. This was after the war. He said he found the plantation, but it was all messed up—nothing like it had been. The owners were gone, God knows where, and his folks were dead. We don't even know where they're buried. Carter wandered for awhile, fought to keep himself from being accused of crimes he didn't commit and away from white man's justice, didn't fit in anywhere else, and was about ready to head back east when he found your grandma." She suddenly laughed. "And that, young man, is all you're getting. Like I said, ask your grandmother."

14

Tony did not go to bed. In his room he threw on his clothes and tiptoed down the stairs. Grandmother Grace and Uncle Daniel were still in the study. Tony crept past the slightly ajar door and eased himself out the front, shutting the main door softly behind him. His one advantage was that Grandmother Grace never looked in on him once he had gone to bed, and he knew his mother wouldn't get up to check on him.

The person Tony feared for was Lon Shirley, who likely might be hiding his father by this time. He hoped to get to Lon before Sheriff Buckner or Deputy Parker did. Perhaps the two of them could convince his father to leave or hide out somewhere else in Osanamon County before the officers descended on him.

Tony ran down the driveway and ducked into the trees to put on his shoes. He stuck to the edge of the trees until he was well along the road before coming back into the open, paused to look back at the big dark house and kept walking fast, staying in the middle of the road until he came to Vinton's Main Street, which had lights at each corner now.

He stayed in the shadows of the trees, the houses and the storefronts that were darkened. He knew it was past midnight, and hoping not to run into someone departing one of the taverns in the business district, he turned off Main onto a parallel street and approached the poolroom from the backside, sneaking past the rickety old stable where Lon kept his horse.

The back door was locked as he had expected it would be. No lights showed on the second floor above the poolroom, the area that served as Lon's living quarters. Tony picked up a handful of pebbles from the alley, watching the half-open window and the curtains inside moving with the night breeze, and started throwing them.

A light came on, and Lon Shirley's grizzled head poked out, looking down at him.

"Hey, what the hell! Tony, is that you? Stop throwing rocks at me. What are you doing here at this time?"

"My father in there?"

"No, he's not. What'd I do? Forget and lock the door on him?"

"Let me in," Tony hissed at him.

Lon's head disappeared from the window and in a few seconds Tony heard the back door being unbolted. He went inside quickly, and Lon shut the door.

"Explain yourself, young man. You should be home in bed."

"I had to wake you somehow."

"I wasn't asleep," Lon said. "I was laying in the dark

thinking. Old people do that sometimes. So what's your big hurry?"

Tony followed Lon upstairs, talking as he did. He told the man of his father's abrupt visit to Blaisdell House and the fact that his father had somehow got hold of Deputy Orville Parker's handgun.

Lon looked disgusted, and somewhat comical because he wore only his trousers and socks, his suspenders hanging loosely at his sides. He said, "He's not here, Tony. You can bet Sheriff Buckner's looking for him, too."

"I was afraid you was hiding him and might get yourself in trouble."

"I ain't in trouble, boy. Relax and breathe a little. Your ol' man's the one in trouble. But I guess I should've expected that."

"What will they do to him when they find him?"

Lon shook his head. "Lock him up, probably. I never seen your daddy since earlier tonight—before him and Parker got together. And that's the truth. But your daddy was here while I was down in the poolroom locking up. I can tell 'cause some things are missing: an old blanket, extra coat and his knapsack. I can guess where he's headed. He wants to lay low and plan things out, though he ain't very good about doing it."

Tony said, "And he's got the deputy's pistol, too."

"Why would he keep Parker's gun? That's another dumb thing to do. Hell, I got more guns right here—if that's what he was after. Few years ago he had a girlfriend here in town. Everybody knew it. I don't know how she could hide him though."

"You mean Annie Pyle," Tony said.

"Ain't you the bright one. First thing, Parker and Buckner will look for him at Hopper's rooming house—where he used to go to see that woman. For all I know, they might've caught him there. I ain't heard nothing more."

"Damn it, what can we do, Lon?"

"Quit your cussing," Lon snapped. "You ain't old enough to cuss, and you don't know all the words yet. Relax while I get my clothes on."

"Okay, what're we going to do?"

"I'm gonna assume they haven't caught your daddy yet," Lon said, dressing as he talked. "I'll take you home and then I'll go find him."

"How can you find him if the sheriff can't?"

"Because I know a couple places to look."

"I remember what you told me once," Tony said as it dawned on him. "McGuire's Lake."

Lon pulled on his heavy shoes. "He might be there. He camped out there sometimes when he got restless. If he is, I'll tell him to stay 'til we get this mess straightened out. That's if he ain't too damn stubborn to listen. I'll go to your grandmother and try to get her to use her influence."

"Lon, he wants money from her to let her keep me."

"The damn fool," Lon said.

Tony said, "I'm coming with you. Nobody will be looking for me 'til after daylight anyway."

"You're crazy. Let your Granny find out you're gone and she'll have the sheriff after me in earnest."

"Lon, we can be back from the lake before daylight. I want to go."

Lon stared at him before replying. "By God, I might be stupid, but okay. There's a chance Dave might listen to you better'n me." He tugged at his long-sleeved undershirt to adjust it, and then reached for his plaid shirt. "You know, Tony, just 'cause he's your dad don't make him right. There's nothing wrong with being a banker."

Tony shook his head. "Seems like everybody but me knows I'm going to be a banker."

"Your grandmother loves you."

"So what?"

"Just saying," said Lon. "You think it's some accident you get your way with her more'n anybody else?"

Tony watched Lon buttoning his shirt using only the fingers of his right hand. His crooked left hand and misshapen left arm was hitched to his side. The hand and arm that had been broken long ago and never healed properly had always fascinated Tony. He had noted that whenever Lon gripped a pool cue he always slid the shaft across the seam between two knuckles of his left hand. Tony remembered hearing stories in the poolroom that Lon had been a terrific pool player a long time back.

Another story was that Lon had some woman somewhere, maybe over in Elston which was about twenty miles away, but that could have been just plain bull, a way to get at Lon. Tony had asked him once if that particular story was true, and Lon had stared him down. Tony figured he didn't want to talk about the woman, if there was one.

Tony said to Lon, "You like my father a lot, don't you, Lon?"

"He can be a damn fool," Lon said, adjusting his

suspenders. "Who the hell knows about people? Your mother never really got to know him either, and that was too bad."

"She never leaves the house," Tony said. "How did he meet her? They won't tell me."

"Right after her daddy, ol' man Blaisdell, died, Louella seemed to perk up. Came to town a few times on her own for shopping. He met her outside a store down the street. I think it flattered her that he showed an interest. He walked her home that first day. She snuck out to meet him after that. But she took sick again just after you were born. And there was a battle there, between your grandmother and your daddy as to where you should be."

"Grandmother Grace says he's always making trouble for everybody. She said he don't want to work for a living."

Lon grinned. "Hell, neither do I. That's why I run a poolroom." He snapped his suspenders and reached for a jacket. "Get back to the stable and saddle Old Bill. I'll bring a couple blankets and anything else we might need and be right with you."

15

Grace Blaisdell awoke with a start from a bad dream. It took her a second to realize she still was seated in the soft chair in the study, beneath the portrait of old D. J. Blaisdell. She had a blanket on top of her, tucked to her chin, not remembering how it got there. She must have dropped off after Daniel left the study to go back to his and Ruth's bedroom. Two brandies had been one too many. The blanket covering her had been either Daniel's or Agatha's doing.

Grace had been young again in her dream, back when she was a child and first introduced to Jess Simson. What in hell made her dream of that unhappy time? Old Jess was a loser if ever there was one. He never saw a bottle he couldn't love or a fight he wouldn't relish, and he couldn't win at either.

He had been thirty-five years old when Grace's father had sold her to him. She had been fourteen, not quite fifteen. That was in 1859. My God—Jess Simson! Absently, Grace again touched the scar below her eye.

Old Jess hadn't really wanted a wife. In fact, he was incapable of making love to a woman if he had one. But he bragged that he was a hell of a lover as well as a hard, manly drinker. An image he wanted so as not to feel left out since all his buddies claimed experience with many women, single and married.

Later Grace realized Jess Simpson never really had anyone who cared about him. He imagined being the butt of people's jokes for remaining a mid-thirties' bachelor. So the one time he got lucky betting on a horse race and won close to six hundred dollars, he decided to shut up his critics.

Right there in that small town in eastern Tennessee old man Hardison had a passel of children, including one very comely almost fifteen-year-old daughter named Grace. Hardison was an itinerant farmer living, as did other scattered members of his family, from hand to mouth. So when Jess Simson approached him with an offer of four hundred dollars, two things were traded in the deal. One, Hardison literally sold his daughter Grace to Jess—justifying it by saying it was in the Bible that a man could sell his daughters—and he had to throw in a half-blind mule that could pull Jess's old wagon. Also, Hardison had to swear on his Bible that he would never tell of the transaction. As far as anyone else was concerned, Jess had wooed the young miss and convinced her to marry him. Humiliated, Grace was literally dragged before a self-proclaimed, traveling minister who performed some meager ceremony for three bucks.

Then she and Jess had begun their unconsummated marriage. There was no wedding night or honeymoon. Jess had gotten drunk with his friends and stayed away almost a week from the small shack he had finagled. When he did appear, he announced that he and his wife would be heading west where he would endeavor to find work.

Out of money by this time, Jess loaded his meager possessions and Grace's single dilapidated cardboard suitcase into his wagon and they set off. When Grace had started to protest in her bitterness, Jess slapped her hard and told her to shut up. Her parents had not bothered to see her off or to say goodbye to her.

In no time Grace learned what it was like to hear her stomach growl with hunger.

They landed in a town called Crawford with a ramshackle sort of Main Street. Jess found an afternoon's work sweeping out a saloon and washing mugs for the sum of forty cents. That he spent on liquor. Grace did much the same kind of work, cleaning out the single general store, dusting, and straightening the stacks and racks of clothes for thirty cents. Jess took it from her and went back to the saloon. Grace sat in their rickety wagon and wept as night drew close.

She was startled when a stranger approached her. He was well dressed for a traveler, if that's what he was, mounted on a chestnut mare with a finely-tooled saddle. He tipped his hat to her.

"Hello, there," he said. "My name's Clive Gibson. Don't mean to intrude on your privacy but I couldn't help noticing you look mighty unhappy for a pretty lady."

Grace blinked at him through her tears.

"You might think I'm spying on you, but I'm not. I saw a man with you," Clive said. "Your father—brother?"

"My—my husband," Grace murmured, looking downward.

Clive Gibson drew a long breath and stared off toward the saloon. "So," he said. "Looked like he took some money from you that you didn't want to give up. Needed a drink, huh?"

Grace sniffed and nodded.

Clive got down and tied his horse's reins to the wagon's wheel. He smiled again at Grace and, without a word, went into the saloon.

Grace sat in the wagon, feeling miserable, alone, and—probably—laughed at.

Another hour passed, the sun was low in the western sky, when Clive Gibson emerged from the saloon with Jess in tow. Obviously, Jess Simson had had more than a couple of drinks. He and Clive were laughing together like old friends.

Clive helped Jess into the wagon, tied his own horse on at the back, and climbed up to sit beside Grace. Jess was slumped in the back. Clive drove the mule to the livery stable at the end of the street and had the stable-hand feed and water both animals. Afterwards he paid the man, climbed back up, took the reins and drove Grace, and Jess out of town.

"Your husband found hisself a job," Clive said.

Grace looked at him quickly, her eyes wide.

"Few miles from here," Clive said, "I got a interest with another fella in a forty-acre piece of farmland. I don't farm it myself when I can hire it out. There's a house on it. Not much of one, but it's pretty good shelter, which looks like what you both need. Jess is gonna farm it for me for a percent of the profits. He claims he knows how, so we'll see. Family that used to be there up and moved away suddenly."

Grace tilted her head quizzically at him. She felt uneasy about riding in the dark along these unfamiliar pathways.

"Don't talk much, do you? What's your name?"

"Grace," she said, softly.

"Nice name. You're a handsome woman, Grace. Anybody tell you that? How old are you?"

She shook her head and didn't respond to the question about her age.

Clive craned around and said, "Jess, look in my saddle bag there. See what you find."

Grace heard Jess scuffling around behind her.

"Hey," Jess said. He scrunched up between them holding a bottle of whiskey by its neck. He had a big grin on his face. The full moon was up now.

"Help yourself," Clive said.

Cradling the bottle, Jess slumped back into the rear of the wagon.

"Wish you hadn't done that," Grace said softly to Clive.

He grinned at her and shrugged.

"Are you a farmer, Mr. Gibson?" Grace asked meekly.

"I own interests in several farms, plus other things," Clive said. "I don't call myself much of anything. Maybe you could say a businessman. I do a lot of things, Grace—some legal, some not so. Some people call me a gambler because I don't like to stay in one place. They say I'll do anything to make me some money, which is probably true. I own a few things down in New Orleans, including part of a shipping company. I have to stay on top of my possessions. One of the reasons I'm here in Tennessee is to get somebody to farm my ground.

Your husband lucked into it. With you here, I might make more trips back than I normally would."

Grace frowned, not knowing how to take his statement.

"How about you?" Clive asked.

"What?"

"Are you very much in love with your husband?"

Grace didn't reply. She felt the question was somehow offensive.

"Uh huh," Clive said. He was a handsome rogue when he smiled.

A few miles outside the town, Clive guided the mule off the road onto a narrower, muddy lane that was little more than wheel ruts. He was in no hurry. It was darker between the trees. At one spot where the rickety wagon bounced, Jess Simson cursed from the rear.

"Careful, Clive," he said, cheerfully. "We don't wanna spill none of this good stuff."

Grace looked around with some trepidation at her husband. "You done enough drinking today. You don't need no more, Jess."

"Shut up, woman!" Jess snapped.

Clive Gibson grinned. "Leave him alone, Grace. I could tell the minute I saw Jess he's a man that needs his whiskey."

Grace said, "I don't want him feeling bad when we get to the farm."

Clive changed the subject. "Hey, we're gonna go right alongside the river for a while. See it there through the trees? Look how the moonlight shines on it. Been a lot of rain here lately. That's why this old road's so muddy." The rumble of thunder brought his eyes up toward the dark sky. "Gonna rain again real soon."

"Is this the only road to the farm?" Grace asked softly.

"It's a short cut." He saw her craning around. "No need to look at your husband. He's a happy man now." He raised his voice. "Ain't you, Jess? Ain't you happy?"

Jess mumbled something.

"When you finish that bottle, you should find another one in that saddlebag."

"Oh, please, Mr. Gibson," Grace pleaded.

"Clive, please."

Jess drained the bottle. The road was close to the edge of the high riverbank, and Jess threw the empty bottle out over the bank. It splashed into the water below. "That takes care 'a that," he said to Clive Gibson.

"Grab the other one, Jess," Clive said, his voice muffled by a crash of thunder following a flash of lightning.

They could see the slants of rain on the other side of the river.

Clive motioned ahead and flipped the reins. "Clump of trees up there on the left," he said. "We can pull up there 'til she blows over. These summer storms don't last that long. And I saw you got blankets in the back."

16

When they reached the trees, he drove the wagon off the road into the small depression under the overhanging branches. Then he helped Grace down and had to lend a hand to Jess when the man stumbled leaving the wagon bed. He pulled out a rolled blanket and tucked it under one arm.

"Over there. Beneath that big tree."

The first heavy raindrops struck the leaves above them.

"Should we get under the wagon?" Grace asked.

"There will be water all under there in a second," Clive said. "You don't want your dress all muddy. If we sit on that root over there, we can hold the blanket over us."

Grace followed the two men, Jess staggering, to the large projecting root and sat between them. It rained hard outside their meager shelter. Clive had removed his wide-brimmed hat and tucked it behind him.

From inside his coat he pulled another bottle of whiskey. He passed it over to Jess, who looked surprised but took it.

"Helps keep the chill off," Clive said. He grinned around at Grace. "I imagine you guessed that I've been a whiskey drummer, too. Still do it occasionally. That's why I got the samples."

Grace, huddled in the middle, started to protest, but one glance at her husband told her it was hopeless.

When the rain let up, Jess never noticed. He had passed out leaning against the trunk of the tree, and the bottle had slipped from his hand. Clive Gibson stood up, carefully lifting the wet, heavy blanket. He dropped it on the ground behind the tree and spread it with the toe of his boot. Grace was shaking Jess, pulling at him until he fell off his seat and lay on his side, snoring, with his legs drawn up.

"We got to help him," Grace pleaded to Clive. "Help me get him back to the wagon."

Clive nudged Jess with his toe. Jess blubbered and snored. "He's out all right," Clive said. He picked up the bottle, looked at what was left inside and recorked it.

"That was mean, what you done to him," Grace said dully.

"His fault. Nobody forced him to drink my whiskey." Clive looked at her, studying her tear-streaked face. "Take it easy, Grace. We got plenty of time."

Grace saw the way he was looking at her, letting his eyes move from her face down her body. This tall, big-shouldered man frightened her. He took a step toward her.

What it was that drove Grace she never fully understood. Anger or panic, or both. The next thing she knew she was lunging toward him, reaching for him, her fingers curled into claws, raking at his face with her nails. Clive cursed and grabbed her arms, forcing them to her sides, as he pulled her close against him. Then he smiled and kissed her on the mouth, following the twisting and turning of her head.

"Ah, you do want to play, Grace," he said. "That's a good girl. Jess never plays with you, does he?"

He kissed her more than once, pressing in on her, until he felt her relax. When her lips parted, he tried to kiss her open-mouthed. When she could feel his lower lip between her own, she bit him savagely.

Clive jumped back and swiped a hand across his mouth. He worked his lip with his tongue and spat blood. Then he laughed and shook his head.

Grace turned to run, but Clive had her arm and spun her around. Very deliberately, letting her see it coming, he backhanded her in the face and knocked her tumbling over the large root. Her eyes gleaming with hatred, Grace gasped for breath.

Clive stood over her. "We don't have to do it this way, Grace," he said, quietly. "Now we got it out of our systems. Be good now. You'll be glad you did."

He looked around at Jess, who was snoring peacefully, before he unhooked his belt and pushed his trousers down. Grinning, he displayed himself to Grace, and she closed her eyes. Clive took off his coat and folded it carefully to place it on the root.

Then he went down to her, hovering above her briefly as he touched her ankles, knees, and legs, then lifting her dress and fighting her undergarments down to her feet. He gazed at her, touched her, felt her, stroked her.

Grace sucked in her breath and held it, her eyes tightly shut.

When he entered her, it was white searing pain. Her mouth opened and she gasped, her face contorting. She remembered nothing, thought of nothing, knew nothing. The first pain had blotted everything else out. But it was oddly changing. Her back started arching, and she was feeling more than any pain. Much more. Did the gasping she heard come from her—or him—or perhaps both?

Grace was not even sure when he left her. Her eyes opened to the branches moving overhead, dripping water, and she heard a more distant sound of thunder. She lay there, looking straight up.

Clive stepped up beside her with his hands on his hips. He was dressed again, even to his hat, but scowling as he looked down at her. She had not covered her nakedness. He extended a hand to her. "Get up, Grace. You don't wanna catch cold on the wet ground."

Grace let herself be lifted to her feet. She swayed unsteadily. Clive held her until she could walk. She turned her back to him as she tried to find and adjust her clothing. "If I was a man, I'd kill you," she said with her back to him.

"Would you, Grace? I don't think so. What if I give you a gun?"

He went to the wagon for his saddle roll and brought back a Navy model .40 caliber pistol. He handed it to her butt first.

"You have to cock it first," he said.

Grace exerted more energy than she would have imagined,

using both thumbs to draw back the hammer. She pointed the pistol at Clive's chest.

"Do you want to?" he asked.

Grace swallowed and felt her tears burning her eyes. She lowered the gun.

Clive took it, lowered the hammer, and put it away. He came back for the wet blanket. "Got dry clothes you can change into?"

Grace nodded dumbly.

"Do it while I get your husband in the wagon."

Clive managed the unconscious Jess Simson into the back of the wagon. Then he watched Grace finish dressing. She looked at the dress she had taken off.

"This is ruined."

"There's a mercantile store back in town," Clive said, meaning the store where Grace had earned some money. "They stock women's clothes. I'll buy you a couple new dresses and deliver 'em to you at the farm. You should'a told me."

Grace looked at him bitterly.

"You were bleeding back there. I didn't know you were a virgin. Never even thought it. Looks like Jess ain't much of a man, is he?"

"You hurt me," Grace said.

"I hope you believe I'm sorry. I'll make it up to you."

Shit, Grace Blaisdell thought angrily in her study as she snapped herself back from the past.

Why dredge up all that old stuff?

17

"Old Bill" was what Lon Shirley called his horse. Tony didn't know how old the big gray gelding really was, but Lon had owned him and kept him stabled in the old shed behind the poolroom ever since he could remember.

Old Bill gave the boy his usual disdainful look when Tony bridled him. Lon had said once that there must have been a mule somewhere in Old Bill's background because he was such a smart and stubborn horse. Tony doubted that Old Bill had anything close to the brains of a mule, but he never argued with Lon about it. He never trusted the horse either. Tony had never trusted any horse since the time his Uncle Dan took him riding and he fell off and broke his arm. And right now Old Bill appeared not to think much of the idea of carrying the two of them into the woods in the middle of the night. Actually Old Bill didn't care much for being ridden anytime.

Lon came down, adjusting his clothing, and Tony noted

that the man carried his shotgun. Lon was wearing his denim jacket and carrying a frayed corduroy jacket under his arm. He went back for a saddle roll that was bulky with an extra blanket, a lantern and a bulging canvas bag. He tossed the corduroy jacket to Tony as he fashioned the worn and cracked leather sheath to the rear of the saddle and slid the gun in.

"I hope we're not going to shoot him," Tony observed, meaning his father.

"Sometimes, with Dave Hunter, I'm never sure," said Lon.

Tony sniffed the jacket before putting it on. "It smells."

"No doubt, and a little big for you," Lon said. "But you'll need something. It'll be cold before morning." He gave Tony the canvas bag that had a strap on it. "Hang that over your shoulder. Make yourself useful. You can carry the lantern, too."

Tony looked inside the bag. "This is what took you so long?"

"Nothing but a bottle of water and a few sandwiches for your daddy."

"Does he know about your sandwiches?"

"Shut up and tighten the cinch." He waited until Tony did. "Now tie this roll on there."

When they were ready, Lon used his good hand to pull himself into the saddle. Tony doused the other lantern in the shed and followed Lon outside. Lon waited while Tony closed the stable door, then pulled him up behind him. Tony held onto Lon's belt as they rode, but he could have stayed on without holding. Far from a racehorse, Old Bill liked to take his time, which was fine with Tony.

Tony realized they must have made an odd sight if anybody was awake to see them on the streets of Vinton—the graying man, leather-skinned and dressed in faded denim with the old straw hat level on his head, the slender boy holding onto him, wearing the oversized man's jacket with the grub bag slung across his back and the unlighted lantern in his hand, atop the plodding big gray horse bobbing its head with each step.

They were on Second Street, headed west out of town. After three blocks there was no more brick or tarred road, only the dirt street rutted by automobile, wagon and bicycle wheels. At the edge of Vinton, they reached shantytown.

Here the streets were narrower and the shacks, all single-story, were crowded together. Some people out here lived in mounded tents stretched over wood frames. There were no sidewalks, spacious front yards or tall trees, and only a few of the shanties had small porches. The porches had clotheslines strung between the uprights, some with clothes and sheets still on them to be left overnight.

Bundles of firewood were stacked on some of the porches. Most of the dwellings had chimneys because the occupants generally had wood burning stoves for the cold weather and cooking. There were a number of chicken coops between the houses, the coops in close because an earlier experiment of having them out back near the open field didn't work. Too many foxes and invading predators found easy pickings.

Occasionally a dog rushed out and barked. There was a sour smell from a nearby dump, and when the wind was right, the ripe outhouse odors were smothering. These residents shared outhouses. Rows of three or four-seaters had been constructed behind the dilapidated housing.

Lon tried to guide Old Bill around the mounds of horse manure that lay in the streets. Old Bill didn't seem to mind stepping right through them. Most of the time, in the dark, you couldn't see them until you squished into them anyway.

Tony wrinkled his nose. The only times he had been near shantytown were when Lon had taken him duck hunting at the lake and they had cut through this part of town.

They could have skirted shantytown by staying on the main road, but Lon wheeled Old Bill over to take the shortcut and pick up the road at the other end. Tony was curious until it suddenly came to him.

"This is where she lives," he said. "That woman my father was seeing. Do you think she's hiding him?"

"What?" Lon shot back at him.

"I know about my father and that woman. I heard the gossip. You don't have to treat me like a little kid."

"You think you're anything else?" Lon snapped. "You don't know nothin'. This is a short cut."

"But she lives out here someplace," Tony said. "You're not sure yourself that he ain't with her."

"She's married now," Lon said.

"So what?"

"Quit trying to grow up too fast. You should listen to your grandmother."

18

They rounded a corner, and Lon reined Old Bill to a stop.

Tony saw people clustered in the street ahead though there were no streetlights in this part of town. Lamps or candles were lit in some of the shanties here and there and other people stood in their doorways looking toward the street. Some of the nearest onlookers carried lanterns or candles. They had gathered around something that held their attention.

Tony leaned to one side to try and see around Lon's broad back. He recognized both of the automobiles in the street. One was the sheriff's station wagon with a crude gold star painted on the front door. Along with several other kids, Tony had examined it the day the sheriff got it. It had been parked on display outside the police station. Tony had seen how the bench seat in back had a steel bar in front of it so the lawmen could handcuff prisoners.

The other automobile belonged to Wyler, the undertaker,

with his business name scripted on the side. A horse drawn hearse, manned by Wyler's young assistant, waited on the other side of the undertaker's car.

Two men came away from the group carrying a body on a blanket or a stretcher. A slender white arm dangled from beneath the blanket. Tony touched Lon's arm, and Lon nodded. The men carried their burden to the rear of the hearse, another man following with a lantern. The man with the lantern let the back down so it formed a bed, and the others laid the body on it.

Tony's breath caught. "They got him, Lon," he whispered. "He's dead."

Lon dismounted and put up his hand to restrain Tony. "You stay here. I mean it! Wait right here."

Tony craned to watch as the assistant chucked the horses and the hearse pulled away. It was followed by the undertaker's car with Wyler at the wheel and another man with a black bag who Tony recognized as Doctor Sanders, the younger of the two doctors in town. Through a break in the crowd Tony saw Lon talking to Sheriff Buckner.

A woman, who Tony didn't know, had taken up station next to Old Bill. She clutched a ragged shawl around her shoulders that covered her threadbare nightgown. Tony leaned down and asked her what had happened.

She looked at him. "You should be in bed. What you doin' out this hour?"

"You got to tell me," Tony said.

In the dim light she frowned at him. "I heard a woman got shot."

Ahead, Lon had asked the same question to Sheriff Buckner and got the answer.

"Annie Coaker," Buckner said, "Ivan's wife. Where'd you come from, Lon? What the hell you doin' out here?"

A tall, black-bearded man who had been standing to one side and a little behind the sheriff pushed his way between them. The scowling man was Ivan Coaker. He glared at Buckner.

"Let's get after him, Sher'ff," he said.

"Easy, Ivan. Who do we get after?"

"The son of a bitch that kilt my wife," Ivan said. "We're wast'n time while he's gett'n way."

"We'll get him, Ivan," Buckner said. "You just let me handle it."

"Handle it then! You're standin' here talkin'."

"How'd it happen?" Lon Shirley asked the sheriff.

Buckner lifted the revolver he was holding in his hand. "Looks like she was trying to run from somebody. Whoever it was used this. It's Orville's gun, Lon. The killer fired three shots at her. Two hit 'er in the back, and one missed."

"Yeah, in the back," Ivan Coaker snarled. "Annie's dead, Sher'ff, and I aim to see that bastard the same way. Clifford and me'll go after im."

"That's right. That's what we'll do, Sher'ff," another man said.

Buckner cocked his head at Ivan Coaker. "And where will you start looking? Who will you look for?"

Deputy Orville Parker joined them and said with a smirk, "Look for Dave Hunter. He was the one that hit me from behind and stole my gun. He shot her."

Buckner scowled at him. "We don't know that for sure."

"It was him," Parker insisted.

Ivan Coaker spat into the dirt and nodded to his brother who had stepped close. "We'll get im, won't we, Cliff'rd?"

"Goddamn right we'll get im," his brother said. Both men were hard featured and looked very much alike although Clifford was the shorter of the two.

"Better cool 'em down, Sheriff," Lon said to Buckner.

Ivan turned on Lon. "I know he's a friend of yours. And maybe the sheriff's in no hurry because he thinks old lady Blaisdell won't like it."

"Watch it, Ivan," Buckner told him quietly. "I want to be sure before we hunt a man for murder."

Ivan looked at the faces surrounding them. "Me an' Cliff'rd's not 'fraid. Who else'll go with us?"

Half a dozen hands went up tentatively. Deputy Parker started counting the hands.

Buckner shook his head. "Wait a minute, men. Let the law take care of this." He looked at Ivan. "I mean it, Ivan. You start a riot or try to lead a mob and I'll lock you and your brother up."

Ivan Coaker muttered something to his brother, and Clifford, frowning at the sheriff, nodded.

"Rest of you folks go back to your homes," Bucker said loudly. "There ain't no more to see here. If I need anybody to deputize, I'll let you know."

Several of the crowd broke away and started for their shanties. The women seemed most willing to go. Several of the men stayed, mumbling among themselves, watching Ivan and his brother.

"Nobody actually saw Dave shoot her, did they?" Lon asked the sheriff.

Buckner scratched his chin and nodded toward a barefooted man standing nearby in his nightshirt and trousers. He had put on his pants in such a hurry he had forgotten to fasten his fly, and part of the nightshirt stuck out like a flag. Buckner said, "Phipps heard her scream and heard the shots. He lives right there. By the time he got out of bed, she was laying here in the road face down. She didn't say nothin' before she died. Phipps didn't see no strangers, but by that time all the others were running around, too. One of 'em was smart enough to send for me and the doc."

"Where was Ivan?" Lon asked.

Ivan answered for himself. "Me an' Cliff'rd waz fishin' at the river. We do it lots 'a times—take a jug with us and run our lines at night. We heerd the shots and run back fast as we could. I wish'd I'd been here. I'd'a nail'd the son of a bitch."

"Right," Clifford said, emphatically.

"And we ain't no closer to catching him, Sheriff."

"I guess nobody saw Dave Hunter shoot her," Lon said. "So you don't know it was him."

Ivan said, "You heerd Orville say that he'd stole his gun. That's 'nuff."

Buckner looked from Lon Shirley to Tony seated on the back of Old Bill. "What're you doing here, Lon? And with that boy?"

"We might be goin' fishing, too," Lon said.

"Or hunting maybe?" Buckner asked. "Does his grandmother know you got him?"

"Of course," Lon said.

"They know where Hunter is, Abe," Orville Parker said to the sheriff. "Hunter's hiding along the river somewhere, and Shirley's takin' the kid to him."

"We don't know he's hiding along the river," Lon said.

Sheriff Buckner nodded. "If you do know where he is, don't hold out on me."

Lon nodded. "I ain't trying to make your job harder, Abe, but I know Dave Hunter. He didn't shoot the woman. He didn't have reason to."

"What the hell, Sher'ff," Ivan Coaker snapped. "All of us knowed he was chasin' after her 'fore we got married. He was fuckin' her."

"Or, the other way around," Lon said. "There was others, too. It don't mean Dave Hunter killed her."

Ivan made a move as if to go for Lon, but Buckner got between them. "That's enough—from both of you! I don't care what used to be unless it's got something to do with who shot 'er in the back."

"He done it all right," Clifford Coaker said. "He wanted to fuck 'er again, and she said no. So he shot her."

"That makes sense," Deputy Orville Parker said. "It was her idea for it to be over, and he didn't like it. He comes out, finds out she's alone in there, and tries to start something. She runs from him and he shoots her."

"Could be the way it happened," Buckner admitted.

Lon shook his head. "And he just leaves Deputy Parker's gun behind?"

Buckner asked, "Where would you look for him if you had a mind to?"

"It's a big county," Lon said.

"Sure, it's a big county. I don't want to have to deputize a whole lot 'a men and send 'em out. They'd be armed men, Lon. Suppose I ain't with the ones that find him? It'll be better for your friend if you tell me where to look."

Lon spread his hands in an "I don't know" fashion.

Buckner handed Orville Parker his pistol. "Put that away and keep a good hold on it from now on. One more job tonight, Orville. Then you can rest that head of yours." He motioned toward Lon's horse and Tony. "You take Lon's horse back to his place. You know where he keeps him. Don't lose your gun on the way. Lon and the boy can ride with me. Both you Coakers, too."

Ivan Coaker scowled. "Ain't we goin' after Dave Hunter now?"

"Let me worry 'bout that."

"You ain't plannin' to lock us up?" Ivan growled.

"We'll talk, that's all," Buckner told him. "I'll bring both of you home. I want some things understood between us."

"We got a right to go after Hunter. He kilt my wife."

"I'll tell you what your rights are," Buckner said.

"The sher'ff's puttin' us off, Ivan," Clifford Coaker said.

"Shut up, Clifford," Buckner snapped.

Lon heard Clifford giggle. He looked over to see Deputy Parker helping Tony down from the horse.

19

Grace Blaisdell, with her bathrobe snugged around her, stood in the foyer with Sheriff Buckner, Lon Shirley, and Carter and watched Tony climb the stairs. She waited until he was inside his room with the door shut before she turned to the sheriff. "Is he in trouble, Abe?" she asked.

"No," Buckner said. "Him and Lon was together, goin' fishing they said. I just brought him home. Sorry to wake you."

"I wasn't asleep."

"There's something you should know. Daniel ought to be here, too."

"Mr. Daniel is in the garage," Carter said.

"Ask him to come in please," said Grace. Carter belted his robe and went out through the kitchen. Grace said, "I didn't know Tony had left the house."

"He wants to know what's going on," Lon Shirley said. "You can't blame him for that."

"I'm not blaming him for anything, but it was against my wishes." Her eyes flicked over to the sheriff. "Thanks for bringing him home, Abe."

Buckner touched the brim of his hat.

Lon gave Grace a quick little smile, a sudden quirk at the corners of his mouth. She pursed her lips, though her emotion was unclear, and glanced away.

"Can I get you something to drink, Abe?" she asked.

"No thank you, ma'am."

Carter and Daniel came through the kitchen into the foyer. Daniel was dressed in rumpled clothes, not old in age, but worn and in need of cleaning. His wrinkled white shirt was open at the neck. There was dirt on the elbows of his suit coat and his shoes. He blinked at Sheriff Buckner.

"Where were you, Daniel?" Grace asked.

"I couldn't sleep. I walked because I had a lot to think about, but maybe didn't realize how weary I was. Guess I had too much brandy because I fell asleep out near the garage. Carter had to shake me to wake me up. What is it, Abe? Have you found him?"

"Not yet, Daniel," Buckner said. He looked at Grace and Daniel. Carter, listening, stood in the background. Looking at countenances, Lon shuffled his feet. Buckner drew a breath and went on, "Dave Hunter's in serious trouble now. It looks like he killed a woman tonight." He focused in on Daniel. "It was Ivan Coaker's wife."

Daniel's jaw dropped before he clenched his teeth. Carter looked at Lon. Lon watched Daniel. Grace stood stoically.

"That's how it looks," Buckner continued. "Annie Coaker

was shot with my deputy's pistol. The gun you said Hunter had with him when he came here."

Now it was Grace's turn to register a look of disbelief, or horror. Her eyes flicked over to Daniel, who looked away from her.

"Are you all right, ma'am?" Buckner asked.

"Yes. Do you have an eye-witness?"

"Nobody actually saw Dave Hunter do the shooting," Buckner admitted, "but there's men right now that want to go looking for him. I don't know how long I can hold 'em back. I want to bring him in peacefully."

Daniel looked confused. "Why would he?"

"I'll find that out when I catch him," Buckner said. "Orville thinks she didn't want nothing more to do with Hunter, and he didn't like it."

"Orville?" Grace queried. "Orville Parker?" She cast another quick glance at Daniel. "I heard Orville Parker was seeing the girl, too. Where did you find the gun?"

"In the middle of the street. He dropped it and run after he shot her." The sheriff blew out a long breath. "Lots'a people kill on the spur of the moment, Ma'am. They wouldn't do it if they had to plan it carefully. Sometimes they make mistakes. Hunter made his when he dropped the gun. There's no doubt it's Orville Parker's gun."

"Where—where was Annie's husband?" Daniel asked.

"Him and his brother was at the river. Fishing and drinking—drinking mostly. They heard the shots. Now they intend to go after Hunter. You can guess what Ivan will do if he finds him. But I want Hunter before he gets hurt or hurts somebody else. Can you help me?"

"What can we do?" Grace asked.

"If he contacts you, convince him to give himself up, for his own sake. Get hold of me no matter what time it is. But don't take no chances."

"We will do that," Grace said.

"Good. I'll wire the sheriff in Elston in case he shows up there. In the meantime I'll send out my deputies for a search. I got some people outside, so I better go now." He looked at Daniel again. "I wanted to be the one to tell you."

"Thank you for that, Abe," Grace said. "And, Abe—I hope you don't have to hurt him."

"Same here," Buckner nodded.

Carter went to the door with the sheriff and shut it behind him. He stood, looking at Grace.

"I'll stay up if you need me to," he said. "I can keep a lookout."

"Go back to bed, Carter. He's not a danger to us."

Carter departed through the kitchen toward his quarters at the rear of the house.

Daniel sat down heavily on the third step of the stairway. He stroked his chin where the bristles were beginning to show, rubbing his hand over his mouth and downward as though in shock. He stared straight ahead.

Lon Shirley stepped close and touched him gently on the shoulder. "You okay, Daniel?"

Not looking at Lon, Daniel gave a short, curt nod.

Grace came close to his other side. "You can't change what happened."

"Ruth?" he blinked, "I know what she'll make of it." Then he nodded to his mother. "I'll be okay."

"Ruth's staying overnight in town again," Grace said to Lon. "Carter followed her in to make sure she's safe. The Reverend Jones probably talked her into spending the night there because he, also, is concerned for her safety."

Daniel nodded absently. "Her daddy's got a spare bedroom in the back of the church. She'll be okay there. I should be the one to tell her about Annie."

Grace looked at Lon again. "Goodnight, Lon," she said. It was a soft command.

Lon nodded, went out the front door and shut it behind him.

Grace returned to her son. "Daniel, is there something you need to talk about?"

"Nothing we haven't covered or already talked to death," Daniel said, staring straight forward.

"You left me in the study," she said. "Did you see the deputy's gun when you went for your walk?"

"I didn't look," Daniel said. He lifted his brows. "I know what you're thinking."

"I'm not thinking. I'm listening to you. Look at me. Do you believe that Dave killed Annie?"

He looked at her. "I don't know. Maybe. Dave's often hot tempered."

"Would he be foolish enough to go to the Coaker house after her?"

"If he thought he could get her by herself without the Coakers around," Daniel said. "But that's just plain stupid."

Grace absently touched her fingertips to her lips as she thought. "Maybe this will make things better between you and Ruth. Even the worse tragedies can have some good consequences."

"You mean with Annie dead. Hell of a price to pay for my marriage."

"I think we all should go to bed now, Daniel. It's been a long night."

Daniel arose and stood staring at the floor. "I'll be up in a moment."

Grace shrugged and went up the stairs. At the top she turned and looked down at him. He hadn't budged.

Grace crossed the upstairs hallway until she was outside Tony's door. She turned the knob gently and went inside.

"You're not asleep, are you, Tony?" It was more a statement than a question.

"No," he replied.

She stood framed in the doorway, the only light coming in through the open window, before shutting the door. Tony was in bed with the covers drawn up. His clothes were piled on the floor. Grace crossed and sat on the foot of the bed and looked at her grandson.

"I should be angry with you," she said, "but I'm not. Why did you feel like you had to sneak out?"

"I knew he was in trouble," Tony said. "I was afraid Lon would be in trouble if he hid him. I had to warn Lon that he had a gun."

"How did the sheriff find you?"

"Lon wanted to look for him. He didn't want me to go, but I insisted. We were on our way by shantytown when we saw all the people and knew something had happened. That's how the sheriff saw me."

"Then you know what's going on."

"I didn't see the woman that got shot," Tony said. "They moved her before I had a chance. Everybody thinks my father shot her. Lon don't believe it. I don't know—it was the same gun."

Grace was silent for a moment. "Tony, I don't like to give your orders, but I have to now. As long as your father is free, I don't want you seeing Lon Shirley again."

Tony's fists tightened on the covers. "No! Please, no!"

"I've made up my mind. You don't understand everything just yet. It's for your own good."

"But I've got a job with Lon. I got to go to work tomorrow."

"I'm sorry I must disappoint you. I'll send him word you're not coming."

"You promised."

"I have to take that promise back now. Things have happened to change it. I have to do what's best for the family. Your welfare and future are more important to me than a little summer job."

Tony turned his face into the pillow, trying not to cry out his disappointment.

Grace said, "You will have a job. You'll be earning your own money, only it will be more now, Tony. There's a time in life you have to make a move. You have to see that time and do it." Her voice softened. "Move too soon, or wait too long, and everything could be lost. Do you understand?"

Tony didn't answer.

"Tomorrow you will meet me at the bank at noon. Carter can bring you in. I don't want you coming to town by yourself.

We'll eat in town and then I'll buy you a new suit. At the bank you'll be watching and learning all you can from now on from your Uncle Dan. Until school starts, we'll go together in the mornings. It's a real beginning for you, Tony."

"I want to work in the poolroom."

"You'll change your mind after awhile. I won't be here forever, and Daniel and you will be the ones to take over. It could be a lot worse," Grace said, kindly.

"I told Lon I'll be back tomorrow."

Grace lightly touched his cheek. "He'll see where your place is. When you're a grown man, the poolroom will not be right for you."

"It's right for Lon."

Grace chuckled. "Lon is—different," she said. "But you can't always have fun. It might be fun for all men to stay little boys, but the good ones have to grow up, shoulder their responsibilities."

"My name ain't even Blaisdell," Tony said, bitterly.

"We can't help the name," Grace told him. "But you have your mother's blood in you and therefore her mother's blood. Mine, Tony. Good blood has determination. Mine has been tested, laughed at, gossiped about, and yet has always come through. There was a promise I made to myself a long time ago."

"What?" Tony asked.

He suddenly sensed the change in his grandmother's mood.

"Someday, maybe," Grace said and rose to stand beside him. "I'm tired now, and you need to sleep."

20

Clive Gibson returned to the falling down shack on the forty-acre piece of land several times over the next few months. That's how he and Grace embarked on a passionate love affair. Plus there was a genuine appreciation for each other between them.

Grace always looked forward to seeing him. She had heard that war between North and South was imminent, but he never wanted to talk about it with her. He wouldn't answer her questions about what he might be doing once the war started.

As for Jesse Simson, he looked forward to Clive's visits too. Clive always brought whiskey for Jess, and that would keep Jess happy, and nearly unconscious, for days. He brought nice dresses for Grace, among other presents, and slipped them to Jesse's fifteen-year-old wife. Once Jesse was out of the way, happy with his bottle, Grace would try on the dresses, modeling them for Clive. He brought books and helped her read literature, history and philosophy. Clive complimented her on her brains as well as her beauty. They then would wind up on the old bed or sometimes on a grassy knoll away from the shack. Whenever Clive left, he always slipped Grace some money.

Grace was in love with this rugged individualist and knew it. Being in love was a new experience for her. When Clive was absent, she fantasized about him and longed for his return. She hoped and prayed that sometime soon Clive would take her away from this place and show her some of the finer cities down south, like New Orleans or Charleston, of which she'd only heard.

Jesse never questioned his wife's pregnancy, assuming that sometime when he was drunk he had fathered the child growing in Grace's belly. To his few drinking acquaintances, he bragged how he had really pumped her up with a kid and how he hoped it would be a boy so he could teach him all kinds of things.

It did turn out to be a boy. Jesse panicked and drank himself into a stupor. Grace had to deliver alone, managing outside in Indian fashion, and had to cut and tie the cord by herself. Then she washed the child before the two of them collapsed on the old bed, but not until after she had shoved Jesse's inert form off onto the floor. He continued snoring. Grace cried because she wanted Clive to come back. Any kind of life with Jesse would be intolerable.

Crops failed, and Jess cursed his bad luck and whatever had given him the idea he could ever farm that damned piece of land. He started cursing Grace and the infant as burdens to him.

In disgust, Jess hitched the mule to the small wagon and went into town alone after pushing Grace down and demanding to know if she was holding out money on him. She told him that if he touched her again she would hurt him bad.

Jess had enough change for one drink in Sloan's saloon. With any luck he would be able to talk acquaintances into buying him more. Unfortunately, already being owed money by Jess, they weren't having any. He brooded and nursed the single drink.

Goldie Bennet, one of the bar girls, came over and smiled at him, asking him what the matter was. Jess took her arm and pulled her down onto his lap. She giggled and hitched her shoulder when he kissed her on the neck. "Now you quit that, Jesse Simson," she said.

A man got up from the bar and came over to look down at them. "Leave Goldie alone, Jess," he said. "You got a wife. Go home an' take care of her."

"Be quiet, Billy," Goldie said.

Sloan saw what was developing and called to her, "Hey, Goldie, you work here or don't you? Stick to the paying customers."

"I don't like his hands on you," Billy said to Goldie, then to Jess. "Leave her alone, Jess."

Jesse rose as though he was about to turn and leave the bar. Then he hit Billy suddenly, catching him by surprise, sending him sprawling over the next table, spilling beer on the two men there. They both got up and started for Jess. Jess hit the first one quickly and staggered him. The other grappled with Jess and took a punch in the gut. Goldie screamed. Sloan came around the counter clutching an ax handle.

He used the handle on Jesse, against the side of his head. Jess slumped against the wall but stayed on his feet. Blood trickled down from a gash on the side of his head above the hairline.

"It's over, Jess," Sloan told him. "Better stop right there."

Jesse finally decided and staggered outside. Head down, he drove the mule and wagon out of town.

On Sunday Grace greeted Sheriff Joe Williams at the door of the shack. "Where is he?" Williams asked with a sigh.

Grace stepped back to allow the sheriff inside. "On the bed."

Williams stepped in and nudged Jess until he stopped snoring and opened his eyes. The sheriff took a toothpick from his mouth and stared down at the other man.

"Ira Murdoch is pissed at you, Jess. You broke his nose in that bar fight."

Jess grunted a sharp laugh but didn't sit up.

"He's swearing out a complaint against you," Williams said. "Sloan and Billy Mays back him up. You started it."

"And I would'a finished it if Sloan fought fair."

"Fighting you ain't his job," Williams said. He resumed chewing on his toothpick. From across the room the baby started crying, and he glanced in that direction. "You gotta go before the judge, Jess. Probably get a fine."

"Hah!" Jess said.

"We don't have money," Grace said.

"County will make it so Jess can work it off. No other way, Jess."

"Hah!" Jess said.

But that's what he did. Jess was sentenced to work a month for the county according to the court's directions. He wound up on a farm owned by a man named Healy, who was the judge's brother. Another customer of the same court worked alongside him. That man's name was Ira Murdock.

They were pitching hay from a wagon to a barn loft where Healy's son was stationed to arrange it. Ira Murdock was chuckling.

He said, "You got in trouble over Goldie Bennet? Boy, that's a good one. She don't even like you, Simson."

"What the fuck you know?" Jess snarled, his grip tightening on the pitchfork.

"I know what she says," Ira continued, laughing. "She says you can't git it up if you wanted to. You're as harmless as a neutered dog."

"I'd shut up if I's you," Jess said.

"No dick Jess Simson," Ira laughed. "That's a good one."

Jess cursed, dropped his pitchfork, and punched Ira Murdock full in the face, knocking the man off the wagon. "Damn you, Murdock," Jess said. "There ain't no man can lick me, and you know it. Stay on your ass where you belong."

But Ira was up, grabbing Jess around the ankles and dragging him from the wagon. They landed on the hard ground and rolled over before scrambling to their feet. Jess smashed his nose and knocked Ira down again. Ira got up, swinging wildly, and Jess knocked him down a third time. Ira pulled himself to his feet slowly, shaking his head, and they circled each other. When he backed against the wagon, he whirled and grabbed the pitchfork.

Jess dodged the first thrust, rolling under it, and came up close to the wagon where he could seize the other fork. Ira jabbed at him, but Jess batted the weapon aside. Squaring off, they circled and feinted at each other. The boy in the loft was yelling at them.

Ira bore in, sobbing a curse, thrusting, and Jess parried the stroke and drove his fork straight into Ira's belly. The three long prongs went in easily, nearly lifting Ira off his feet as he was impaled on the fork. When Ira screamed, Jess released his grip. Ira fell, his scream choking off, both legs churning and hands clawing at the thing imbedded inside him.

Jesse stared in horror, then saw the boy, open-mouthed, looking at him from the loft. There was only one thing to do. Jess fled into the woods and kept running.

By the time other men arrived, Ira Murdock had bled himself to death and Jesse Simson was history in that part of the country.

Grace Blaisdell drew a deep sigh.

She was standing outside her grandson's bedroom door in the darkened upper hall of the big house. The memory had rushed back to her, and she hoped she'd never had to tell Tony about those days long ago.

But it had been a passage for her. All gone. Ma and Pa, and then Jesse, but losing Jesse was a good thing. "It's all gone for us," she had told her infant son at the time. "Just you and me, John," she told him though he didn't understand her. "The two of us now. Just you and me against all the rest."

21

Daniel Blaisdell met the two men by the converted barn to a garage behind the house. Daylight was barely breaking the eastern sky. One of the wiry men had climbed to the second floor and tapped on Daniel's bedroom window until it awakened him. Ruth had not come home yet.

Ivan and Clifford Coaker both grinned as he approached them.

"If you got business with me," Daniel said, curtly, "I have an office for that. Don't come sneaking around this house."

Clifford nudged his brother and giggled. "He's got hisself 'n office. Hear that, Ivan?"

"I don't think he wants to conduct this business in his office," Ivan said and spat off to the side.

"Get to it," Daniel snapped. "What do you want?"

"Oh, couple a things. Mostly what's rightfully ours," Ivan said. "We want you to get our money for us."

Daniel urged them into the shadows as they talked. "What money?"

"You know what money," Ivan said. "Annie's money. She's got money saved in your bank. It belongs to me now, 'n I want it."

"You know that for sure?"

"I done found that little bank book you give your customers. She's got over four hundred dollars. That counts the fifty dollars she added to it yesterday. I want it."

Clifford's grin showed his rotten front teeth. "That's a lot'a likker money."

"You get the picture, Mr. Blaisdell," Ivan said.

"Clearly," Daniel said. "I can't get it this minute. Judge Parks will have to okay it, and I'll have it for you."

"Like when?" Ivan asked, stopping Daniel from turning away. "What the fuck's a judge got to do with it?"

"Like when Judge Parks says," Daniel replied. "He'll determine next of kin for any kind of inheritance. It'll be after the inquest which is a formality."

Clifford giggled. "You knowed that money's there because you done give some of it to Annie yourself."

Daniel peered at the brothers. "What makes you think that?"

"Come on," Ivan said. "You can play dumb for other people."

Clifford nodded vigorously. "We knowed 'bout you and Annie before Ivan married her."

"She told you? Or did you hear rumors? Either way you're both full of shit," Daniel said evenly.

"Everybody knows," Ivan said. "And we got letters you

writ to Annie. Here, I'll show you one." He pulled a crumpled sheet of paper from his pants pocket and handed it over. "See? You tellin' us that ain't your writin'?"

Daniel swallowed, but he couldn't deny it. She had encouraged him to communicate with her because they both were lonely people. "Yeah, I wrote her notes telling her I appreciated her friendship. We didn't do anything about it."

"Depends on how it reads to you," Ivan laughed. "Go on, keep it. We got others. Couple hundred more dollars, and you git 'em all. Guar-an-teed. That's the second thing we want. As fer Annie's savings, that money's mine now. It belong'd to my wife and she's dead. So what's hers is mines."

Daniel nodded. "I told you the court must settle your wife's estate."

Ivan's eyes narrowed. "Es-*tate*? She ain't never had no es-tate."

"A legal term," Daniel said. "But that's how it's done. Nobody has any claim on your wife's possessions, so you will get the money she saved. Might take a week or two."

"Week?" Ivan exploded and grabbed Daniel's shirtfront. "What the hell you mean?"

Daniel seized Ivan's arm and twisted it until the man, his face contorted in pain, released his grip and sank to one knee. "Don't ever touch me again, Coaker, or I'll kill you."

Ivan stumbled back, confused. He hadn't expected that violent reaction from Daniel.

Clifford came up and brushed Daniel shirt where Ivan had grabbed him. "He didn't mean nothin'. Don't take it serious like. We knowed you'll do right by us. So will the others."

"Shut up, Clifford," Ivan snapped. "A week or two? What about for the letters?"

"Yeah, advance us enough for a jug," Clifford added.

Daniel extracted from his pocket a couple of dollars and pushed them into Ivan's hand. "This is all you get for extortion. Business between you and me is finished. The rest of the money's safe where it is. Looks like you'd be more concerned about your wife's death."

Clifford grinned. "Oh, we are. We're so concerned we're gonna do the sheriff's job for him."

"Clifford, I tol' you to shut up," Ivan said. "We don't wanna be telling Mr. Blaisdell ever'thing."

"Aw, Mr. Blaisdell don't have no love for Hunter," Clifford said. "Hunter was chasing after Annie, too. He might even tell us where he is, if we ask him real nice."

"The two of you put together don't make you man enough to threaten me," Daniel said. "Leave it to the sheriff."

Daniel started to turn away toward the house again.

"Wait a minute," Ivan said. "We ain't all finished yet."

"Something else you want?" Daniel asked, facing them again with a threatening look on his face.

Ivan blinked but squared his shoulders. "I mean a little whiskey ain't gonna square it with us. Annie kept a lot of letters. You keep that in mind, Mr. Blaisdell. They could turn up in the wrong hands if you don't do right."

Once more Clifford giggled. "All 'a this is out'a the goodness of your heart." He snickered and put his hand to his mouth. "You being such a big man at the bank an' all. I bet your mother'd pay if she knowed."

Daniel's cupped right hand shot out and struck Clifford

in the throat. Clifford gagged and staggered. His brother had to catch him from falling. Ivan eased Clifford down to a sitting position while Clifford gasped for breath. Daniel's direct look at Ivan was more than a mild threat.

He said carefully, "You approach my mother about anything, and you'll be hurting more than you think possible."

"Okay, okay," Ivan grumbled. "You don't hafta get mean over a few love letters. But you git to work, Mr. Blaisdell, on getting us the money we got coming."

Daniel nodded slowly, feeling his face flush. "What I wrote to Annie was before she got married."

"Well, there ain't no dates on 'em. Might look like you writ 'em since then."

Clifford gasped, regaining his breath and voice. "We got 'em in a safe place."

"I think we'll do business," Ivan said. He spat on the ground between them. "Meantime, me an' Clifford's gonna look for Hunter."

Clifford, helped to his feet by his brother now, stumbled a bit as he stepped forward and rubbed the toe of his boot into Ivan's spittle before looking at Daniel. He kept a careful distance back. "See ya real soon, Mr. Blaisdell," he said, hoarsely. "Oh, by the way, in case you wondered, you was seen in shantytown just before Annie got killed. Friend of ours sure it was you. Said you was riding a bicycle."

"We didn't say nothing to Sher'ff Buckner," Ivan said. "Not yet. I mean it's just possible you murdered my wife. But the deputy's gun that Hunter had makes us pretty sure it's him. We just givin' you some information."

22

When Daniel returned to the house and stepped into the kitchen, Grace, already dressed, said, "What did they want?"

"You saw," Daniel said. The kitchen window had a view of the barn/garage. Or else Carter had told her. "What would they want, Mother? Money, of course."

"Did you give them money?"

"I bought 'em a drink to get rid of them." Daniel stood with his lips pursed. "They'll want more."

"What money do they think you owe them?" Grace asked.

Daniel snapped out of it. "Annie's account money. Her savings. She had quite a bit."

"And you explained to them how that will be up to the court."

"Yes." Daniel helped himself to a cup of Agatha's coffee on the stove. "I'll handle the Coakers."

"Be careful with them." Grace drank her own coffee as Agatha came into the kitchen and took their breakfast orders. When Agatha left their presence, Grace said, "It's not something else you're not telling me about you and Annie Coaker?"

"Annie's dead," Daniel said. "Leave her in peace."

"Are you handling it all right?"

Daniel uttered a short laugh. "Sure, Mother."

They ate breakfast in silence, Daniel being privately surly. Grace looked at him from time to time. Carter came into the kitchen and nodded to them before drawing himself a cup of coffee. For a couple of seconds his and Grace's eyes locked.

Daniel excused himself from his half-finished breakfast and left the room, going upstairs to get his tie and suit coat.

"Thought you might be interested to know," Carter said, "your grandson has left the house."

"Well, hell," Grace said and massaged her forehead with thumb and forefinger. "You didn't try to stop him?"

"You think I'm going to physically manhandle that boy?" Carter nodded toward the window and the outside. "Those Coakers, they're not good men."

Grace nodded. "Daniel believes they'll try to cause us some trouble."

"You don't need to worry about it, Miss Grace," Carter said. "Daniel or I, either one, can take care of the Coakers. But it'd be nice to know what they're up to. Maybe I'll scout around and hear what I can."

Grace half-smiled. "Don't go near shantytown. Somebody will shoot you."

"Don't worry 'bout me," Carter said.

"No," she said. "It's you who always worries about me."

Ever since they first met, she thought.

Forty years ago.

It was 1865, and Grace, all of twenty years old, was struggling to keep herself and her five-year-old son, John, alive and occasionally fed. She traveled from village to town asking for menial work for pennies or food. At nights they camped in the woods. Their clothing had become rags.

Clive Gibson had left her some money, but not a whole lot. The man who had inherited the farm on which Grace lived told her she had to leave. He cared less about the small child she had. In fact the man, she had forgotten his name by now, gave the impression that he was not at all unhappy Clive had died. He wanted to sell the property.

So Grace Simson and young John had hit the road looking for some kind of salvation.

John, trembling and chilled and wheezing every breath, was very sick the night she met Carter Foote. Two men Grace had never seen before came out of the woods and approached her meager campfire. She had looked hopefully at them.

It was quick to see that those men were ruffians. They warmed their hands at her fire and passed comments to each other about "a cute little thing." Grace finally asked them if they would leave.

They laughed and grabbed her, forcing her to the ground. She pleaded with them not to hurt her child. One of the two held her arms while the other dropped his pants and fell upon her. She struggled valiantly but without success. Finally, sobbing, she reconciled herself to her fate.

That was when Carter Foote arrived. Coming out of

the darkness of the woods. Grace caught only a glimpse of him from the corner of her eye, and, at first, thought he was another companion to these two. She saw in the firelight that he was a young Negro man, tall and broad shouldered. She sobbed.

The Negro seized the man on top of Grace and, with one quick motion, wrenched and snapped his neck. The second man scrambled up and clawed at a rusty revolver in his belt. He got the pistol free and pointed it at the black man, who was approaching him.

He pulled the trigger but nothing happened. The weapon misfired. The man dropped the gun and started to flee, but he never made it.

The Negro's huge fist descended on the back of the man's neck, and Grace heard the sound like a large limb cracking. Her attacker crumpled in a heap. The big black man reached down and helped Grace to her feet, steadying her.

"You all right, Miss?" he asked in a deep voice that bore an eastern accent.

Grace couldn't respond. She was sobbing wildly. Finally, she managed, "Please don't hurt me."

The black man steadied her and let her cry it out. Finally he asked, "Do you know them?"

She managed to shake her head.

"Okay." He seated her gently. "You wait right here by the fire. I'll take care of it."

"Please—don't—don't leave me," Grace cried.

"I'll come back. I promise."

The Negro tossed the lighter of the two men over a

shoulder and dragged the other by his shirt collar. He took them into the woods.

Grace couldn't stop shaking. Finally she remembered her son and went to his side. He was trembling harder than she. She embraced him and held on.

What were they going to do now? She had no idea. What was going to happen to them?

Several minutes later the big Negro emerged from the woods with a large backpack in one hand and a bundle of clothing in the other and approached the fire. He dropped his bundle and backpack and touched Grace's shoulder, and she pulled away from her son. The Negro knelt over the boy, studying him in the firelight.

"He—he needs help," Grace said in a small voice.

His shiny dark face somber, the Negro did not reply.

"Where can I go for help?" Grace asked.

The black man stood up and shook his head. "He's your son?"

"Yes."

"He's having a hard time breathing, Miss. Like he's drowning."

"Drowning?" Grace had never heard of such a thing on dry land. "No! No! He's not! He'll be all right."

"I've seen it before, Miss." The Negro looked like he wanted to pat Grace's head but refrained from it. "It's the consumption. He'll get weaker and weaker, and—I'm sorry, Miss. I don't know if a doctor could help him now. And I don't know where there's a doctor."

"Somebody's got to help him," Grace cried. "He can't die."

"We all do, from something or other." The Negro shrugged. "I guess he might pull through."

"He's not dying," Grace said, adamantly.

The Negro said nothing. He squatted on long legs near the fire.

Grace breathed rapidly, frantically. "Did—did you kill those men?"

In the firelight, the Negro nodded.

"You buried them?"

"I don't have a shovel," he said. "They're in the creek over there." He pointed into the darkness before motioning at the bundle of clothing and single pair of boots. "That's their stuff."

"You took their clothes?"

"Seemed like a good idea," the Negro said. "You never know when extra clothes can come in handy. That's one good pair of boots. The other fella, he had some real worn out shoes on. They're still on him."

"It—it seems cruel," Grace said.

He shrugged. "They don't mind now. They had a few coins in their pockets. I took that too. It bothers you?"

"I just—" Grace stopped.

"You're a pretty little lady," the Negro said. "Don't worry, I won't hurt you. I just feel sorry for you and your boy out here alone. Where are you going?"

Grace shook her head. "I don't know. It don't matter. I got to get some money and food somehow. And I got to find a doctor for John."

"What's your name?"

"Grace Simson." She almost said "Gibson" because

she felt herself more married to Clive than she ever had to Jesse.

"Your husband?"

"Gone."

The Negro breathed in and out and nodded, the firelight dancing in his eyes.

"What—what's your name?" Grace asked.

"Foote," he said. "Carter Foote."

"You from these parts?"

"Not any more. My folks were slaves. The white family was pretty good. Their son and I are the same age. I saved him from drowning once. His folks repaid me by sending me to college with him, up in Massachusetts."

"I thought you sounded educated," Grace said. "Are you married, Mr. Foote?"

"Please, call me Carter. Yes, I am. My wife and I have jobs working for a white family in Boston. After the war, I came back down south to see if I could find my folks. The old plantation was in ruins. I don't know what happened to the family. I found another former slave who said my folks are dead." He shrugged. "Nobody knows where they're buried, or even if they are."

"Are you going back to Boston?" asked Grace.

"Eventually. Right now I'm just wandering, seeing how things look in this part of the country. It looks like we're both lost souls."

"I'm scared," Grace said and choked back a sob. "I'm scared for John."

Carter Foote nodded. "Suppose—if you want—I stick

with you for a little while? You won't owe me. But if we're both traveling—? You do need looking after, Miss Grace."

"Yes, we need help," Grace said softly.

In her kitchen now, she stared at the doorway through which Carter had exited.

"And you're there—as usual," she said softly to her departing friend.

She stopped reminiscing when her daughter-in-law Ruth entered the kitchen and sat sullenly at the table. Ruth looked like something was bothering her, but she wouldn't talk about it. Grace didn't press her.

23

It was just getting daylight when Tony had awakened, but he had no idea what time it was. He dressed quickly, hopeful of getting away from the house before his grandmother or Carter saw him and getting to Lon Shirley. He knew Lon would go back out into the woods looking for Dave Hunter regardless of what the sheriff had told him. Tony felt he had to be with Lon.

He almost made it out of the house before he realized Carter was behind him in the foyer. Tony exhaled and mouthed a "please" at Carter. One of Carter's gray brows lifted, but he didn't say anything. He turned away as though he had not seen the boy.

Outside, Tony had to duck around the garage and hide in the trees because he saw the Coaker brothers approaching on foot. He recognized them from last night. He watched them move on toward the house, and when they were a good distance from him he hurried back onto the road and jogged toward town.

Once there, Tony cut around the block behind the bank to avoid being seen as much as possible. He entered the back door of the poolroom after checking to make sure Old Bill was still stabled in the alley. He found Lon racking the balls on both tables prior to opening the front door for business. Lon looked at him and saw that he was out of breath.

"I expected you, but I didn't know when," Lon said. "Figured you'd be really pissed off at me if I left without you. Go find Benny Smith and bring him here. He should be over in front of the hotel about this time."

Tony did as ordered and brought the middle-aged, broad-smiling man to the poolroom. Benny came anxiously. He often took over for Lon when Lon had to leave for some reason. Benny wasn't very bright, but he enjoyed the responsibility. And nobody ever tried to cheat Benny though they always had to help him make change. Nobody cheated Benny because nobody wanted to be seen as cheating Lon.

Benny went behind the counter and stood grinning. Lon told him he could have two bottles of pop and make himself a sandwich if he would look after the place until they got back. Benny nodded vigorously.

"I was afraid you'd gone without me," Tony said. "Want me to saddle Old Bill?"

"Not yet," Lon said. "I been thinking about last night. Some things I want to find out before we go."

"Like what?"

"Just questions," Lon said. "I want to see a couple people. I can do this without you if you want to stay and help Benny."

"I'm going with you."

They took the alley beside the poolroom and the next cross alley for a block and a half. Lon took them through the back door into a tavern called *Bagget's*.

A man of indeterminate age looked at them from behind the bar. He spoke to Lon, and the greeting was returned.

Lon motioned to the stairs leading up. "Henry, I need to speak with your pa," he said. "Won't take long."

"Last room on your right," Henry Bagget said as he watched Lon and Tony climb the stairs.

There were several rooms on the upper level. Tony heard a woman's giggle from behind a closed door. "What's going on?" he asked.

"Maybe better you don't know yet," Lon said, and then reconsidered. "Oh, hell, Henry and Harvey got a couple women works for 'em. Sometimes the women have men friends. Nobody's supposed to know that, though everybody does."

Tony hurried to keep up with Lon. Lon went to the last room, knocked and waited.

"Why are we here?" Tony asked in a whisper.

"This old man probably knows more people in Vinton than anybody else," Lon said.

The invite came from inside.

Mr. Bagget sat on the unmade bed with a mug of coffee. He wore long johns and was barefooted. His hair was gray and unruly, and he needed a shave.

"Lon Shirley," he said by way of greeting and looked at Tony. "I seen this kid around. He's a Blaisdell, ain't he?"

"This is Tony," Lon said, "Dave Hunter's son. Grace Blaisdell's grandson."

"Okay," grinned Bagget, looking at Tony. "I tossed your old man out'a here more'n once when he got drunk."

"I ain't surprised," Tony said.

"And your daddy killed a woman last night."

"Don't think so." Lon sat in a rocking chair and leaned forward. "You know a lot, Harvey. I was telling Tony how you know everybody in this town and everything that happens."

"Well, not everything," Bagget chuckled, but he obviously was pleased by the compliment. "You don't come in much, Lon."

"I don't drink much," Lon said, "and I keep pretty busy at the poolroom. Harvey, I need to ask about someone."

But Harvey Bagget was looking Tony over. "You know how to fight, kid?"

"A little. I don't fight much."

The old man chuckled again. "Boys ought to fight. Good for 'em. They can't get to be men if they don't fight. Boy, I had plenty fights when I was a youngster. I remember when some men sported guns on their belts. I taught my boy Henry how to fight."

"Great," Tony said because he didn't know what else to say.

"You had to be tough when I was young. I don't know if Henry can break up a fight the way I used to. He keeps a pistol under the bar now." The old man sneered at the idea. "Anyway, who do you want to know about, Lon? If they hang around in Vinton, I'll know 'em."

"Tell me about Annie Coaker."

The old man grunted. "Used to be Annie Pyle. You know she worked here for a little while. We had a kind'a financial arrangement. Barmaid, and—maybe a little more once in a while if you get my drift."

He grinned as he scratched his nose. "Anyhow, she up an' quit me—got a room over at Amanda Hopper's and helped Amanda fix meals for the guests and clean up the place. Of course, we know what Amanda's girls do for men who got money." He winked. "But Annie was never satisfied with any one thing or one person. Orphan girl when she was little. She stayed at Amanda's five, maybe six, years 'til she married Ivan Coaker. Even then, she'd go back to spend some nights there because she couldn't stand shantytown. Who could blame her?"

"Why did she quit you, Harvey? Were you wanting too big a cut?"

Bagget grinned as he picked his nose with a bony finger and then scratched his head. "I treated her nice, Lon. But I asked myself the same thing, so maybe I didn't handle her right. I got a sense for trouble coming. Trouble is more'n I need at my age. No, I just think Annie got higher ambitions."

Lon smiled. "Were you and your son both screwing her?"

Now Bagget laughed. "You asked that in front of the boy? Hah! Well, hell, you know Annie was no angel. She had her share of men and then some. But my major business is this saloon. Henry wanted her to stay, and they had a fight about it, I guess, and she told him to go to hell." He chuckled again. "Occasionally some clean-cut guys visited Annie. You know, the traveling salesmen type, and even a banker or two."

The last statement was delivered pointedly. Bagget grinned at Tony.

"Why did she marry Ivan?" Lon asked.

"Hell, who knows? Maybe he's the only one that offered to go that far. Or maybe she liked getting beat up every so often. Some women do. Ivan would do things like that. Get a little liquor in him and he can do anything."

"Even kill his own wife?"

"Only if it benefited Ivan."

"I never knew Annie close and personal," Lon said. "But I couldn't imagine her marrying Ivan Coaker and moving into that shack at shantytown with him and Clifford. That's hard to get clear in my head."

"Well, how do you figure women? Annie was a wild one. My bet is she wouldn't have stayed at the Coakers too long. Like I said, she went back to Amanda's lots of nights. First good opportunity and she'd be gone without a backward glance." Bagget looked at Tony again. "This boy's daddy was one of Annie's men."

"Long time ago," Lon said.

"Few years," nodded Bagget. "Oh, one more thing. I did hear she had this special boyfriend. She had him before and after she married Ivan. Maybe Amanda Hopper knows. Ask her, Lon, and then tell me. Annie talked more to Amanda than anybody else. I think Annie looked at Amanda like some kind of big sister or mother she never had."

"What about Clifford Coaker?" asked Lon. "Think he was screwing her, too?"

"Maybe. The three of 'em lived in the same shack sometimes. But I doubt it. Ivan used to say he'd never take seconds. It don't make sense that she'd have anything to do with Clifford. He's dumber than Ivan. Tell you the truth, Lon, I never picked Ivan as the marrying kind neither. Him and Clifford liked living together down there in shantytown and doing just what they pleased. They drink up most of their spare change in here. But there's no doubt Annie took a step down when she left Amanda's rooming house to marry Coaker."

"They weren't married long, were they?"

Bagget got busy picking his nose again. Tony looked away.

"Couple months is all," the old man said. "Some rumors say she was pregnant, so she might'a thought she had to get married. Ivan could've been the way out. There ain't too many unmarried men around."

"You don't believe that. Ivan being kind enough to marry her to take her off the hook?"

"No, if she *had* to get married, then it was Ivan's kid."

"You got no hint of any married man who might'a been Annie's lover?" Lon asked.

"Hah! This boy's daddy." Bagget pointed his bony finger at Tony. "But he didn't knock her up 'cause he wasn't in town 'til yesterday. So maybe it was his uncle." He looked steadily at Tony as he spoke. "I hear your daddy came back and wanted to take up with Annie again last night. When she refused, he shot her."

"You heard wrong," Lon said, standing up. "Come on, Tony." He gave Tony a little shove toward the door, stopped and looked back at Bagget. "Harvey, don't be making cracks to the boy, not if you want to stay on my good side. You can say what you want to me because I know bullshit when I hear it. Understand?"

"Sure, Lon. No harm meant."

Tony followed Lon from the room. As they went down the stairs, he asked, "What was that all about?"

"You heard," Lon said.

"Only that she had another boyfriend."

Lon looked at Tony and tilted his head toward a nearby chair and then went to the bar and leaned over toward Henry Bagget. Henry just looked at him and paid no attention to Tony.

"Henry," Lon said, "how well did you know Annie Pyle?"

"She worked here awhile. Stayed upstairs. Then she left."

"She something special to you?" Lon asked.

Henry Bagget snorted and looked both ways before replying. "I ain't got nothin' to say 'bout that. You're asking if I fucked her. Ain't your business, Lon. She was willing so long as she got paid."

"How does your wife feel about it?" Lon asked.

Bagget's eyes narrowed. "Don't go bringing my wife into this, Lon Shirley. We'll have a major disagreement if you start that shit."

"So she doesn't know." Lon slapped his palm down on the bar. "Hard to keep a secret in a town like this." He grinned at Henry Bagget. "Was it you who knocked her up?"

Bagget gave a scoffing laugh and turned away.

When he rejoined Tony, Tony asked, "We going now?"

"Right," Lon said. "Couple more stops I want to make before we leave town. Sure you want to do this with me?"

"You bet."

24

The county jail sat directly across the street from *Wyler's Funeral Home*. Lon and Tony climbed the stone steps, crossed the jail porch, and went inside a wide double-door.

Tony detected the peculiar smell inside the corridor. It seemed like a combination of worn saddle leather, human perspiration and urine odors. There were long wooden benches against each side under the chipped, peeling walls, and three people, two women and a man, sat on one of the benches. The women looked ashamed to be there; the man bore no particular expression. Tony didn't know their names though he had seen the man on Main Street a time or two.

This was his first time inside the county jail, and he remembered that someone had told him that the cells were in the basement below. He followed Lon to the door that was standing open with the words *County Sheriff* painted on it.

The only man in the room was a young deputy named

Urban Meyer lounging with his booted feet propped on his desk. He was picking his teeth with his fingernail.

"Abe Buckner around?" Lon asked.

"Nope," Meyer said.

"Will he be back soon?"

"Can't tell," Meyer said, inspecting the fingernail he was using as a toothpick and wiping it on his uniform pants.

"Is Deputy Parker with him?"

"Nope."

"This his day off?"

"Nope."

"Any special reason?"

Meyer grinned. "Headache. Big one says Orville. Abe made him go home to bed."

"And you don't know when Abe will get back?"

"Nope."

Lon said, "Since you're in a talking mood maybe you can tell me. Is there any chance it wasn't Parker's gun that killed Annie Coaker?"

"Nope."

"How can you be sure?"

Meyer picked his teeth some more and flicked something away. "Abe said the gun had been fired. He smelt the burnt powder. It had three empty chambers. Doc Sanders took out the bullets. Said they looked like .38's."

"Would Parker have any reason to kill the woman?" Lon asked.

Meyer shrugged.

"Was he fucking Annie?"

"Who wasn't? Orville bragged that he got some, but who

knows? Annie might've turned him down. If you mentioned her, he'd start sulking a lot, but I doubt if he'd shoot her."

"Maybe," Lon said. "Did the doc say Annie was pregnant?"

"Funny, but he never mentioned it. If she was, it wasn't Orville's. No, I don't think Orville killed her. After he got his gun stole, he was with Abe practically all the time. Dave Hunter killed Annie."

"Nope," Lon said and nodded to Tony. He looked at Meyer. "How 'bout you, Urban? Were you screwing her too?"

Deputy Meyer broke into a huge grin and laughed. His expression turned mocking. "Lon, you know I'm a married man."

Tony turned back toward Deputy Meyer from the doorway. "Why are these people out in the hall?"

"Them?" Meyer said. "Probably got relatives downstairs. I'll get to 'em in a little while." He stuck his stained finger back into his mouth.

Tony caught up with Lon outside the building. "So what are you doing?"

"Keep up," Lon told him. "You're younger'n me." He spoke as they walked. "The gun's got me bothered, Tony. Been on my mind all morning. You said your daddy had the gun when he came to the house. Okay, but then what happened to it?"

"Uncle Daniel threw it out the door to him."

"So? What did your daddy do with it? If he threw it away, or dropped it somewhere, how did the killer find it?"

"Maybe he did kill her," Tony said, reluctantly.

"No, that's the idea the law's starting with. I'm starting the opposite. I say he didn't do it. But that damn gun's got me messed up."

"Well, if my pa didn't take the gun," Tony said, "it had to be somebody else in the house. Uncle Dan or—or Carter."

"I don't like it," Lon said and fell silent.

Their next stop was *Amanda's House—Rooms and Fine Dining—Daily or Weekly Rates,* by reputation the better of the two such businesses in Vinton, on Fourth Street. Everyone knew it was a nicely disguised whorehouse. It was very quiet inside, and a young waitress, cleaning girl gave them a long look. She told them they only serve breakfast, lunch, and supper to guests who stay at Amanda's.

Lon identified himself and asked to speak with Amanda. He and Tony sat at a table in the empty dining room. Amanda, a short stocky woman with gray hair, came from the kitchen and nodded to Lon. Lon introduced her to Tony.

"Your pa's in a peck of trouble," Amanda said, taking a third chair at the table. She motioned the young waitress closer. "Eat anything yet?" she asked.

"I didn't," Lon said. He nodded toward Tony. "He probably had a big breakfast."

"Not me," Tony said.

"You fellas get the ham and beans," Amanda said. "You need something."

Lon held up two fingers to the young girl. "Two orders."

"And two coffees and a glass of milk," Amanda added.

"He drinks coffee," Lon said.

"Three coffees," Amanda told the girl. "Lon, you ain't

come to see me for a long time. Not since Susie and Ida moved away."

Tony glanced quickly at Lon. Lon caught the look, and his face reddened.

Amanda chuckled. "What's on your mind, Lon?"

"Annie Coaker."

"Oh, oh. Poor Annie. I was shocked—sad—but not surprised. She liked to take chances."

"Tell me about her," Lon said. "She worked for you."

Amanda gave the same account of Annie's early life that Tony had heard from old man Bagget. The coffees and ham and beans came. Between mouthfuls of food Amanda said, "I had the same kind of childhood with no ma or pa. Only I got lucky and met my husband early."

"How long did Annie work here, Amanda?"

"Five years, up to just a couple months ago. I can't brag about her work habits, but the men, especially the men, didn't complain. Annie didn't care much for the routine cleaning and washing. Of course, I knew she wouldn't stay around forever. Hell, she even got religion. She wanted out of here, meaning Vinton, and into a good life. Who's she gonna find here to give her that? I can't help feeling sorry for her."

"What chances did she like to take?"

"Men," laughed Amanda. "She wasn't particular if they flashed money."

"Then why did she marry Ivan Coaker? He sure as hell didn't flash any money at her."

"Truth is, she never told me why. But you can bet she had her reason."

"Was she pregnant?"

"If she was, I couldn't tell," Amanda said.

"But you let her come back and stay here when she wanted to get away from Ivan."

"We were friends."

"Ivan didn't care?"

"Not as long as she gave him money for drinks."

"Did she still work for you after she married Ivan?"

Amanda glanced at Tony. "You mean cleaning tables, rooms, cooking or washing?"

"You know what I mean."

Amanda shrugged. "We had a sort of business arrangement. I don't see nothin' wrong with that. What made you think Annie might've been pregnant?"

"Hearsay," Lon said. "Unless she was trying to trap some man. Did she have a special boyfriend?"

"She hinted at it," Amanda said. "I figured she had somebody maybe from Elston, or somewhere else out 'a town, but she wouldn't say who. Men would show up and ask for her specifically."

"Who asked for her more than anybody else?"

Amanda shook her head. "Nobody I can put a name to. You know, could be she got to the age where she just figured she ought to get married. Some of my girls do that. Usually they run over to Elston and try to hook a guy. Maybe Annie did, too."

"But not Coaker," Lon said.

"You got it," said Amanda.

Lon drank some coffee, framing his thoughts and questions. "She wasn't here every night, was she?"

"No. Most nights though. Few nights she wasn't."

"And those nights she stayed there in shantytown with Ivan and his brother in that stinkhole?"

"Hard to imagine," Amanda said. "I see what you're driving at, Lon. You're thinking she was meeting some guy, slipping away somewhere and spending a lot of time with him. It could've been a married man—you know, with a secret place for them. Annie would do something like that if it was profitable for her. I know a little bit how she thought and what she wanted."

"Amanda, I think you might know who her special boyfriend was."

Amanda drank some coffee and looked away. "I'll tell you what I told Sheriff Buckner. I don't know. Take it or leave it. That boyfriend she's said to have? He must've bargained with her on something. She wasn't going to stick with Ivan."

"How do you know?"

Amanda nodded slowly. "If I didn't know these girls pretty well, I'd be a poor excuse for a mother substitute." She looked at Tony. "Maybe your daddy came back to town sooner than you realized."

Tony shook his head. "He don't have money."

"But, of course, your uncle is one of the richest men in Vinton."

"Don't be suggesting that," Lon said.

Amanda laughed. "Just mentioning married men who'd want to keep it quiet."

"There's a few others," Lon said. "Deputy Orville Parker for one."

"Hah!" Amanda said. "Even Sheriff Abe Buckner if you want to make a list. They've all visited my establishment one time or another. They have their special girls. What are you trying to do, Lon?"

Lon finished his meal and pushed the bowl aside. He drank coffee.

"Amanda, you keep a pretty good eye on your girls. You got to know some of the men who visited Annie."

"Sorry, Lon. That's one thing she didn't confide in me, and I don't spy on 'em. Last time I saw Annie—it was just a couple days ago—she had on a new dress. It had to have cost a pretty penny, more money than she got from this place."

"Ivan couldn't have bought it for her," Lon said. "He never had two dollars to scratch together."

"One of my roomers said he ran into Ivan Coaker only a few days before him and Annie got married. Some of Ivan's friends were joking with him, and Ivan got pissed off and claimed he never had no intention of ever getting married. To me, that means Ivan wasn't doing her no favor by marrying her. But maybe he was doing himself a favor."

Lon nodded. "Getting paid to marry her. I can see it, Ivan and Annie both gouging the same person."

He paid Amanda for their meals and coffee and put on his straw hat before motioning Tony to the door.

"Come again, Lon," Amanda called. "You'd like a couple of my new girls."

Lon said, "This boy's father didn't kill Annie. I'd like to find out who did."

"That's Abe Buckner's job," Amanda said.

25

Tony breathed out an exasperated sigh of impatience.

He said, "We're doing a lot of walking and not much learning."

"Oh, I think we've learned some things," Lon said.

"Yeah, like either my pa or Uncle Dan took the deputy's gun and killed the woman. Where we going now?"

Lon pointed ahead. "I'm going to speak to the man standing by his flowers."

"That's a church," Tony said.

"And he's your Aunt Ruth's daddy."

They approached the thin man who was dressed somberly in black with a clerical collar and stood watching them. The sun was hot and he stood with jacket over arm. There was a small silver-cross pinned to the pocket of his black shirt. Outside the white church with the stained-glass windows was a large sign that read: *Congregation to Repel the Apocalypse*. Beneath that: *The Time Is at Hand, Revelations* 1:3.

"Lon Shirley, the pool baron," the preacher said with a little smile.

Lon nodded. "I see you've changed the name of the church. Reverend Jones, have you met Ruth's nephew Tony Hunter?"

"Nephew by marriage," Reverend Caleb Jones said and shook hands with Tony. "I've heard Ruth speak of him. It's a pleasure, young man."

"Thank you," Tony said. He noticed the little smile crescents around the minister's blue eyes and the specks of white in his dark, closely cut hair.

"Well, you got a good flower bed started," Lon said to the preacher.

"Thank you. One of my small pleasures in life."

Lon pointed. "What's that?"

The Reverend Jones stepped over and pulled an object from the ground. He showed it to Lon and Tony. It was a crucifix in the shape of a dagger, the bottom of the cross coming to a sharp point, the point now smeared with moist dirt.

"A friend of mine, a Catholic priest in Rochester, New York, gave this to me. He says it was blessed by an archbishop, and supposedly it's some kind of ancient fertility symbol. My friend knew of my interest in flowers and things of beauty and thought maybe it might help my flowers grow. I'm sure he meant it jokingly, but it is a beautiful little object and I never could bring myself to get rid of it."

"Does it help your flowers grow?" Lon asked.

Caleb Jones shrugged with a smile. "Who knows? I'm not one to criticize another's beliefs." He looked off to his right and left before focusing on Tony again. "I don't see you in church on Sunday," the preacher said kindly. "Or you, Lon Shirley."

"Never had much use for church," Lon said, "but I never spoke against it."

"You see your share of sinners in the poolroom."

Lon laughed. "I see my share of sinners any time I walk down the street. You're going to have some nice looking flowers there, Reverend."

"Thank you. And how are the Blaisdells?"

"Okay," Tony said. "Aunt Ruth says you're a holy man."

That brought a chuckle from Reverend Jones. "I should be a lot holier than I am. We all should. Are you gentlemen simply taking a stroll?"

"Actually I'm looking for information about the woman who was murdered last night," said Lon. "You heard?"

The minister's expression changed to downcast. "Yes. Annie Coaker." He sighed. "*That* is a real shame. Poor, poor woman. I thought there was hope for her. I pray for her soul."

"Amanda Hopper said she got religion."

Jones nodded. "Oh, I see. Yes, Annie came to church a couple of times, but I'm afraid our Sunday congregation didn't look fondly upon her. I encouraged her to read the Bible and tried to teach her. If she truly changed, it wasn't obvious to me. She wouldn't let me counsel her. So I wouldn't say she *got* religion."

"Did she tell you about any special men in her life?" Lon asked.

"No, but if she had, I wouldn't share it with you. Whatever she said in confidence remains that way. It has to."

"I understand," Lon said. "Just like I had to ask."

"Why?" Jones asked. "Talk is that this boy's father murdered Annie."

"We don't believe it," Lon said. He took off his straw hat and wiped his brow with his sleeve. "I don't suppose you noticed any special men in your congregation paying attention to Annie?"

Jones uttered a short laugh and shook his head.

"Thank you, Reverend."

"I can tell you this," Jones said. "I saw one particular man being very familiar with Annie. In fact, it was in shantytown where some of my parishioners live and where I often take a walk. I seek lost souls wherever I can. The man was Bagget."

Lon raised his brows. "Harvey Bagget, that old cuss?"

"Henry Bagget, his son," Jones said. "Henry and Annie were talking out in front of Ivan Coaker's shack. Didn't see Ivan or his brother, so I don't know where they were. Probably in Bagget's saloon drinking. Anyway, Henry was pushing up close to Annie and talking to her. I couldn't hear what. They were both smiling. Then he patted her in a very familiar way in a private place."

"On her ass, you mean," Lon said.

"Precisely," Jones said. "I'm only relating this to you because Bagget made a snide remark to me about my faith. They both saw me, saw that I was shocked, and stepped apart. I was going to ask Annie about it if she ever came back to church but never got the chance. I only hope she got to confess her sins before she died. All we can do now is pray for her."

"That's your business, Reverend. Thank you." Lon nudged Tony. "Come on, Tony, let's go."

Reverend Jones called after them, "It would be nice to see you—either or both of you—in church on Sunday."

Lon didn't look around. He hustled Tony down the street.

Tony had a thought. "There's something else, Lon. I saw Ivan Coaker and his brother going to the house this morning."

Lon stopped him with a hand on his shoulder. "You don't know what for?"

"I guess to see somebody. It couldn't have been Grandma."

"I don't think she'd have anything to do with 'em."

"Maybe Uncle Dan. Aunt Ruth said she saw Uncle Dan and Annie talking inside the bank yesterday."

"The bank," mused Lon. "Uh huh. I bet Annie's got money there and the Coakers want it. Or—" he frowned. "Or they might've seen something last night and was trying to get money from your uncle. It could even be that he owed them for something else."

"You mean, like paying Ivan Coaker to marry Annie?"

"You're too smart," Lon said. "But if the sheriff finds out, that's how he'll look at it."

"It had to be Uncle Dan, I guess," Tony said glumly. "Where're we going now?"

"Now you can saddle Old Bill," Lon told him. "We'll take that ride."

26

When the horse was saddled and ready, and they once again had their bundle of supplies, they rode, Lon in the saddle, Tony behind him, once more through shantytown.

It looked different in daylight. The stench was even stronger beneath the warming sun and an intermittent breeze whipped dust around some kids playing in the street. The individual shanties appeared dingier than Tony had realized or given thought to before.

Many had no windowpanes, some no doors with only sacking or a long-discarded blanket tacked over the uneven doorframes. Few had any kind of porch or stoop. The ones that did had individual clothing and bedclothes drying outside. A smattering of shacks had bicycles, rusted and dirt-caked, propped against their fronts. Ragged settees, probably discarded several times over, and broken chairs had been haphazardly placed along the street edge. Some older folk had laid claim to them, to pass the time smoking and talking.

The neighborly chatter ceased as Lon and Tony plodded past on Old Bill. The people watched them warily as they did most strangers who came through shantytown.

They dismounted at one of the shacks near the end of the street, and Lon spoke with two women who were outside gossiping. The women pointed out one of the shanties, and Tony followed Lon to the door. A man whom Tony recognized from the previous night, unshaven and wearing a stained undershirt tucked into his trousers, came to the door in his stocking feet.

Lon smiled at him and said, "Mr. Phipps, I'm Lon Shirley. I was here last night talking with the sheriff. Do you remember me?"

"We never formally met, but I seen ya 'round places," Phipps said, scratching his whiskers. "What can I do for ya?"

"It's about what happened. What you saw."

"What's the use?" Phipps said. "Can't help that poor woman now. And I already told the sheriff ever'thing. You a relative of Annie Coaker?"

"No. I'm a friend of the man they think shot her."

"Ah." Phipps' eyes narrowed. Then he grinned. "Thought for a minute you might be Annie's rich uncle. 'Cept you don't look very rich."

"Did you see her rich uncle?"

"Naw, but that's what she tol' my sister. My sister seen Annie in a fancy dress that I guess Annie was showing off. She said her rich uncle bought it for her and there would be plenty more, but she couldn't let her husband see it." Phipps frowned. "Look, I didn't know Annie very good. She didn't live here that long. I just heard stories 'bout her, that's all.

She was prettier than most women round here, but she didn't deserve getting' shot in the back. So 'cuse me if I don't give a damn for the bastard who shot her. You said you're a friend of his."

"I know the man they're accusing," Lon said.

Phipps grunted, scratched his chin again, and said, "There's a difference?"

"All I'd like to hear about is exactly what you seen and did. It won't take long."

Phipps sighed. "I couldn't sleep, but my sister was snorin' away, and it was pretty late. First thing I heard was a bicycle fall down. I thought it might have been the wind. Or somebody coulda bumped into one. There ain't much light here at night. Anyway, I didn't worry 'bout it. Maybe half the folks here got bikes. For all I knowed it was somebody comin' home drunk and fallin' over one. Guys that go an' fish at the river usually take a jug with 'em. I knowed a fella who's got a still in the woods, but I won't tell you his name."

"Did you hear an automobile?" Lon asked.

"Not 'til the sheriff come. Then the undertaker."

"Did you hear the shots right after the bicycle fell?"

"Not right after," Phipps said. "I probably dozed a bit, but I couldn't get in a deep sleep. Then I heard Annie scream, and then the shots. Three of 'em right in a row. My sister was scared to death. She kept tellin' me not to go outside while I was puttin' my pants on. I told her to stay where she was, that it probably some fool shootin' off a gun in the street. I didn't tell her about the scream 'til later."

"And you're sure it was Annie that screamed?" Lon asked.

"Who else could it be? I fired up my lantern and run out to see. I think I was the first person to get to her. I tried to turn her over, and my hands got bloody, so I let her lay like she fell. One of the boys got on his bike and went uptown. Ivan and Clifford came runnin' up from the river in a few minutes, both of 'em pretty drunk. Ivan just stood there starin' at her. No way to tell what he was thinkin'."

"How often did you talk to Annie?"

"I didn't. My sister tried, but Annie wasn't too friendly with other women. Sis thinks it because of the rumors that Annie had lots of men. I told all this to Sheriff Buckner."

"Okay," Lon said. "You heard somebody trip over a bicycle, later the scream, then the shots—in that order. And that's what you told Buckner?"

"Yep." Phipps again scratched his chin whiskers. "One other sound I heard that I didn't mention 'cause it wasn't important."

"What?"

"Just before I got to Annie and seen she was dead, Fiedler's dogs set up a yowling down at the end of the block. I was cussing them damned dogs. It happens once in a while, wakes people up, but Fiedler won't get rid of 'em."

"So it could've been somebody running away from the crime," Lon mused.

"Or running to it," Phipps said. "Now, if that's all—?"

"Please, one more thing, Mr. Phipps," Lon said. He motioned toward the street. "Will you show me exactly where she was when you found her?"

Phipps sighed again, went out into the middle of the street, down a short way, and pointed. Lon and Tony went with him. A couple of kids stopped playing and watched them.

"Right here," Phipps said.

The dust had covered any traces of blood or marks from the body.

"Which way was she headed when she fell?" Lon asked. "They were moving the body by the time I got here."

"Facin' this way." Phipps squatted down to trace an arrow in the dust with his fingertip. "Like she was runnin' away from somebody and right toward the middle of the street. The sheriff said she might'a been turned around when she got shot."

"Not likely," Lon said. "She was hit square enough to be killed." He knelt on one knee and looked around at the Coaker shack behind them. "I'd bet she was knocked forward by the bullets. She was running from her house and, if she fell exactly forward, the shots came from in front of it, maybe even the front door."

"Meebe. Word goin' around is that Hunter knew Ivan and Clifford wasn't home, so he tried to get in and molest Annie. She run from him, and he shot her."

Lon rose to his feet. "Then what did he do?"

"He run, naturally," Phipps said.

"Which way? Along here past the body? Somebody could've seen him."

"No, I guess he ducked around the back of the house. But the gun was out here in the street. One of the women found it. I held it 'til the sheriff got here."

"The killer probably threw it out here into the street," Lon said.

"Or dropped it when he was running," said Phipps. "That's what the sheriff thinks." He wiped his hands on his undershirt. "Hey, fella gets liquor in him, gets horny, he don't have much clear thinking about what to do. If it was me, I would'a took the gun and got rid of it somewhere else. I mean, providing I was sober enough."

"Come on," Lon said. "I'm curious about what's behind that row of houses. Let's take a walk around there."

"You won't see nothin' but dirt and weeds back there," Phipps told him, "and some junk. That patch of ground belongs to the town now. Maybe someday they'll clear it and let somebody build something on it. Some of the families got little gardens they plant at the edge, but that don't amount to much. Most folks use it for a dump."

"How was Annie dressed?" Lon asked as the three of them went around the Coaker shack at the end of the street.

"Just her nightgown," Phipps said. "It was kind of pulled up in back. I straightened it out as best I could before the sheriff got here."

They stood looking at the open area, a field speckled with drying water pools from the last heavy rain and now overgrown with grass and mounds of trash beyond a row of reeking outhouses. Some of the people had even constructed clotheslines back here. It made Tony wonder if they could ever get the smell out.

The open area appeared to extend about a quarter of a mile to the woods, and beyond the wood line was the river. There was a foot-worn path, not a street, behind the shanties, and another path off toward the river. The path behind the shacks was bare ground, covered with a layer of dust, and in a few places there were depressions that had been mud holes and were still damp. It was rough, uneven ground that Lon stooped to examine.

"Kids play much back here?" he asked.

"Not with the smell and all this junk," Phipps said. "Would you? Most of 'em play in the streets. Anyways, there's snakes in that field."

"Do they bring their bikes back here?"

"Them who's lucky enough to got one, maybe. But I wouldn't. Sure wouldn't leave one back here very long. You'd be askin' for it to be stolen. That's transportation, mister. Get a bike out in that field and tear it up and you've lost something."

Lon traced a track in one of the muddy indentations. "Somebody's been here on a bike recently, could be earlier this morning—or even last night." He followed the track and pointed to a shallow spot that had been water-filled and was still darker than the surrounding ground. The overlapping imprint of bicycle tires was unmistakable. "Right here, behind these houses," he said. "Don't know which direction the rider was going."

Phipps shrugged. "Well, it's unusual."

Lon straightened up and walked down the block along the edge of the field and behind the outhouses. Tony and Phipps followed, Tony occasionally holding his nose.

They came to a large pen, a wire enclosure, across from the footpath behind the outbuildings of one house at the end of the block. Two of the three brown and white dogs inside the pen got up and stretched. Tails wagged. One came to the fence and pressed his nose into it. Tony scratched the dog's nose, and the tail wagged faster.

He looked at Lon and Phipps. "Seems like nice dogs."

"Them's Fiedler's dogs," Phipps said. "They're okay, but he don't work 'em enough."

"The dogs that barked last night," Lon said. "They're not barking now."

"For one thing you ain't sneaking up an' surprising 'em. For another, they knowed me."

"But these are the ones you heard?"

"Yeah, I did," Phipps said. "Only they wasn't barkin' exactly. Howlin' was more like it, kind of in-between and high and sharp. I heard 'em do that once before when I was standing right here talking to Fiedler. That time they was giving it to a nigger coming along here on his way to the river. Fiedler told me they always do that when a nigger gets close."

Tony blinked. *Carter*, he wondered. Lon nodded, looking out across the field at the wood line.

Phipps said, "Niggers don't live right here close. They're over in the far corner a few blocks away. They keep to themselves and we like it like that." His eyes narrowed. "Hey! You ain't suggesting some nigger come over here and shot Annie Coaker? Because, if you are—?"

"Don't even mention that," Lon said.

"Yeah. The boys would sure burn 'em out fast if that's the case."

"It was some animal in the brush," Lon said, "that set the dogs off. How long you been living near the Coakers, Mr. Phipps?"

"Five years."

"Didn't it surprise you when Ivan and Annie got married?"

"Damned right," Phipps said. "My sister seen him passin' by a couple weeks ago and congratulated him. Ivan got hot an' told her to mind her own damned business. Guess he figured all the guys at the saloon would be kiddin' him. Ivan don't take a lot of kiddin'." He scratched his whiskers and laughed. "When Ivan got married, I think it hurt Clifford most of all. There for a week or so Clifford stayed fallin' down drunk. Him and Ivan even had a fistfight out in the street one night. It didn't last long 'cause Clifford never could beat Ivan. Ivan begged him not to get up, but Clifford kept getting' up and Ivan kept knockin' him down. Finally he had to pick Clifford up and carry 'im inta the house."

"Annie spend a lot of nights here with the two brothers?"

"Now there's a funny thing," Phipps said. "Seemed like she'd be here occasionally, but that's all. It's said she went to downtown most nights to meet her old friends. I heard it was at that roomin' house."

"Thanks for your help, Mr. Phipps," Lon said and nudged Tony. "We can go to Old Bill now."

"Maybe I oughtn't to tell you this but I will," Phipps said. "Ivan and Clifford got together a bunch of the fellas this morning to go huntin'. They all got guns, but they ain't huntin' rabbits or squirrels."

Tony was glad to get away from the rancid odors behind the shanties. In the street it wasn't a whole lot better. He took deep breaths and hoped the stink didn't stick to him.

27

The man did not look like a lawman, though he might have been.

He could be a traveler who had just happened onto the campsite. All Dave Hunter could see from his position in the woods outside the clearing was the man's back, the light he carried, and the rifle he cradled in one arm. Travelers usually don't carry their rifles at the ready.

It was dark now, and the man set his lantern, balancing it, on the log where Dave had been sitting earlier. The man knelt beside the smothered campfire and poked gingerly at it with a stick. He extended his fingers, palm down, over the ashes to test the heat.

Dave frowned. He could rationalize the lantern, and even the rifle, but testing the warmth indicated that this man was either looking for someone or wary of someone returning to the encampment.

Dave had selected this campsite before noon. It was still

better than a half mile through the woods to the lake. Not being a skilled woodsman, Dave wasn't sure where he might find some food, and he was very hungry. He had thought about but neglected to take Lon Shirley's shotgun. He didn't want his friend thinking he was stealing from him. And it was more than likely that Lon would seek him out here and bring something to eat. If he didn't, Dave would raid a vegetable patch of some farmhouse when it got dark again.

Last night Dave had slept in the woods within two miles of Vinton but had built no fire. He had barely kept warm enough wrapped in Lon Shirley's old overcoat. When he had awakened this morning and stretched out the stiffness, he hoped to view more rationally all that had happened.

Main thing was it would not be easy to get around Deputy Orville Parker. That man would carry a long grudge because Dave had embarrassed him in a fight and taken his gun. He knew Orville would love to shoot him on sight even though the deputy undoubtedly had his gun back by now. But this armed stranger at his recent campfire puzzled him. If the man was a robber, Dave didn't want to walk out there. He had nothing worth stealing, but robbers had been known to shoot victims for no reason. And he still had a score to settle with Grace Blaisdell.

Dave had thought considerably about Grace, her son Daniel, her daughter Louella, and Tony during the day. He had come to the conclusion that he would approach the family again, this time with less anger.

Did he really want Tony traveling with him? It was a question he had labored over for hours. He didn't feel particularly like a father. And it was a fact that Tony was better off living with his grandmother Grace. When it got right down to it, Dave wasn't sure what he really wanted.

But it wouldn't hurt to squeeze some money out of Grace Blaisdell.

Reluctantly, he realized that Daniel had told him the truth. If he wanted to stay in the area, he's have to get a job and make something of himself. If there are no jobs in Vinton, there might be opportunities in Elston, the bigger city some fifteen miles away. But as far as the town of Vinton was concerned, it would definitely take Grace Blaisdell's influence to pull Orville Parker off his back. So he needed her for more than just cash.

Dave peered out from the bushes. Who the hell was this armed stranger at his campsite?

In the glow of the lantern Dave watched the man carefully now. The man couldn't see him because beyond the lantern's arc of light nothing would be visible to the naked eye in the dark forest. If the man was a traveler, he might replenish the campfire and settle down for the rest of the night. In that case, Dave would wait until he was asleep and then sneak in and relieve the stranger of his rifle. A rifle would come in handy out here in the woods, especially in seeking food.

Dave tensed.

Now the man in the clearing was standing and looking about, his eyes moving past the spot where Dave was concealed. But when the man was facing him, Dave could see that he also had a pistol tucked in his belt in front. It was too much firepower for an ordinary traveler.

The stranger cupped one hand to his mouth and gave a long whistle before he picked up the lantern and started waving it. A second later there came an answering whistle from somewhere to the other side, then yet another from a different direction.

Dave backed deeper into the woods and turned in the direction of the lake. He did not wait to see how many there were or whom they were after. He suspected they might be Orville Parker's friends after him.

28

Lon Shirley had a good fire going in an open area near the edge of the lake. When he looked around at Tony, he saw that the boy was lying on his side with his head resting on his arm, possibly asleep because his back was to him. Lon covered him with his corduroy jacket and went to the supplies they had piled by a tree. He lay down and smoked his pipe, using his saddle as a headrest.

They had been in this location since late afternoon and had not seen anybody. Twice they had walked a distance around the lake without finding signs of Tony's father. Lon had insisted they return to this location to wait. It was near good grass on the other side of the trees where Old Bill was hobbled. Tony had asked how long they were going to wait.

"We have to give him a few hours," Lon said. "If he don't see our fire and come looking for us, we'll go back to town and try again tomorrow. It'd be mighty uncomfortable to stay out here all night if we don't have to."

"Maybe we're a long way away from where he is."

"No, I think he'll be along. This is right close to where your daddy and I went fishing a couple times. He'll remember that. Another sandwich?"

Tony took a sandwich from Lon's canvas bag and ate it. Lon sat and smoked.

"How'd you two meet?" Tony asked.

Lon chuckled. "Long time ago. Your daddy's a lot younger than me, you know. Anyway, I got a wild hair up my butt and decided to see more of the country. I locked up the poolroom, left Vinton and for a few months rode the rails. Your daddy jumped on at one of the junctions and we shared the same car. We got to talkin', I guess. I came back to Vinton, and he sort of tagged along."

"You told me once that he saved your life."

Lon nodded as his smile spread. "Pretty much. He warned me about the yard dicks the railroads hired to keep guys from riding for free. I'd never seen 'em, but he told me they could be mean. We ran into some later. The train was stopping for water, and we jumped off to cut through some woods to get around on the other side of the yard. We stopped for a drink at a well behind the depot, and that's when I seen 'em. They carried clubs and poked around through the cars. I watched 'em drag one guy out and beat him 'til he was unconscious. Then one of 'em saw us at the well and stood watching us. I didn't know whether to run or not, but your daddy told me to just stand still."

"Then what happened?" Tony asked eagerly.

"The dick must've figured out what we were up to because we were dirty and had bedrolls strapped to our backs.

Your daddy said, 'If they start this way, we'll start walking. Otherwise just stay where you are until the train starts to move. Then we make a run for it.' I told him I didn't know for sure I could make it onto a moving train with my arm the way it is, but he said he'd help me."

"Did they go after you?"

"When the train started up again," Lon nodded. "It got to moving pretty fast and I was scared. But I knew that's what your daddy wanted so they couldn't drag us off. I thought the whole damned string of cars was going to be by us before we'd move. Dave put the water bucket down real careful, all the time with that one guy watching us with his arms folded like he hoped we'd try for the train. Your daddy said, 'This is it, Lon Shirley. Go for the ladders. We got to make it, so follow me. Now!"

Tony's mouth hung open while he waited for Lon to tamp and relight his pipe. "Come on," he said irritably.

Lon said, "He took off, and I was right behind him. I couldn't let myself look at the train because I'd have sworn sure as hell it was going too fast for me to make it. A fast runner I never been. That dick shouted to his friends, and they came running after us. I didn't look back. I kept my eyes on your daddy. He picked a car with the door partly open and jumped up and caught hold of one rung and held on. I saw it was getting away from me and I heard him yelling 'Faster!' I gave it all I had when I made the jump. My left arm was pretty useless for holding on, but I got a grip—barely—with my right hand. My fingers started slipping. Your daddy leaned out and grabbed my wrist in one hand and held me. I wouldn't'a guessed he was that strong. He held onto me until I got a better hold and could hook my right arm around the ladder. Once I got my feet planted we were okay. Those yard dicks were still yelling behind us, but they'd give up the chase. Tony, if your daddy hadn't grabbed me when he did, I might not be here now."

"So that's why you owe him," Tony said. "Did he stay in Vinton until he met my mother?"

"Until he married her," Lon said. "Or I should say 'til right after you was born. Your daddy met your momma at the bank—where else?—said she was the prettiest little girl he'd ever seen. And she was pretty, too, but always frail lookin'. She'd just got out of school and started right in working at the bank to please your grandma. Old man Blaisdell was dead by then, and your granny was in the office every day until your Uncle Dan took over."

"It's strange my mother would marry him," Tony said.

Lon shrugged. "Maybe not. Probably the only chance she ever had to do something unexpected. She had her life laid out for her, but your daddy's life was different. He was a wild cuss, but that could be what attracted your momma to him. Anyway, they eloped across the river to Kentucky and got married. By the time your grandma found out, it was too late to stop it."

"Was she happy then? My mother?"

Lon thought about it. "I honestly don't know. Your daddy was not smart. He worked for me to make a little money but never kept any. Your mother got more sickly. I let 'em have my room up above the pool hall, but I could see she wasn't a healthy person. And your daddy wasn't always true to her."

Tony nodded, his brow furrowed. "Grandmother Grace said it was another woman, the one that got shot."

"She was mixed up with your pa. The night you got born I had to go get the doc. I don't know where your daddy was. Anyway, it wasn't easy birthing you, but you've never made things easy for anybody," Lon added with a chuckle. "A few days later, soon as your mom was strong enough and with the help of your grandma, she gathered you up and went back to Blaisdell House. That's where she's stayed ever since. Your daddy got pissed off at that and took off on his own again. He stayed away."

"What does he really want?"

"I don't know," Lon said. "I doubt if he knows."

Tony thought for a minute, then asked, "Lon, you never told me. Did you ever get married?"

"No, sir. Who'd take a sinner with a crippled arm like me?"

"Never wanted to, huh?"

"I never said that." Lon was thoughtful for a moment. "It just never worked out."

"I guess," Tony snickered. "You're right, who'd want to marry you anyway?"

After that they had not talked, and now Tony napped on the ground while Lon smoked and rested back against the saddle. Lon looked over at the boy and smiled. He listened to the sounds of the frogs and crickets and an occasional splash out on the lake, remembering the first time he had brought Tony here to hunt ducks.

Five years ago when Tony had been seven, it had been very cold that morning in the late fall before the sun was up.

It was a Saturday because Tony wasn't skipping school. His grandmother wouldn't hear of that, and Lon didn't want him to. They had ridden out on Old Bill while the first lamps were being lighted in the farmhouses along the road. Lon had allowed Tony to carry the unloaded shotgun.

Lon could still see the way it had been that morning, the first light above the trees at the far end of the lake. It was fun because Tony, sleepy-eyed and drowsy, looked awe-stricken all wrapped up in the outdoor winter coat his grandma had sent for, as he stood back and watched Lon unwind the mooring chain of one of the boats on the lake as though something big was happening. It didn't take a lot to impress a young boy.

Tony was amazed that boats were available. Lon explained that hunters left their boats at the lake year round and never minded anybody using one as long as he cleaned it out afterwards and tied it securely. It had been purplish dark overhead and the stars still were bright.

"Get in," Lon had told him and helped him do it. "I'll push us out."

Then they were gliding out on the dark water, the wind-driven waves slapping the bow of the boat, and Tony was huddled deep in his coat trying to keep warm.

"Take the other paddle," Lon said. "You won't think about the cold if you're working. Just push with it. I'll guide us."

"Where we going?" Tony's teeth chattered.

"The other side," Lon said. "You can't see the brush yet, but it's a natural blind." Ahead of them the bare branches of the trees were outlined in the growing light. "Look up and to your left." He pointed out three V-shaped formations of waterfowl in the sky. "They're going away now. There will be plenty more. They're leaving the fields on the other side of the river. The river is straight ahead of you, but you won't be able to see it."

It was much lighter by the time they moved the boat in behind the brush. Lon pointed out various birds to Tony and made him listen to sounds. Then he explained to him about using the shotgun and about gun safety. Tony became engrossed enough to forget his shivering.

Suddenly Lon had shushed him and pointed out two approaching wedges. Tony was fascinated with the tight formations, the way they seemed to move their wings in unison. Then Lon took an old duck-call and put it to his lips. Tony thought he heard the ducks answering Lon's call. And when the nearest wedge broke, circling lower, the tone of the duck-call changed and Lon was chuckling to them. They dropped faster than Tony had thought they would, made a sweeping pass and came back before they set their wings and splashed into the water.

Lon grinned at Tony and winked. "You got to talk to 'em," he whispered. "See the different colorings? Looks like four drakes and six hens." Then he shouted: "Hey!"

That sound had set them off in a sudden flurry and beating of wings as they lifted. Lon raised his shotgun, bracing the butt into his right shoulder, one eye shut, resting his cheek against his thumb and the barrel of the gun across his crippled left forearm. Two shots exploded, causing Tony to flinch and clap his hands over his ears. Two of the ducks fell solidly into the lake. The others were going away as Lon reloaded.

"You talked too loud and scared them," Tony said.

"I wanted 'em up," Lon told him. "You don't shoot 'em on the water."

"Why don't you shoot some more?"

"They got up fast, did you see? I was afraid I might hurt one and not bring it down. You don't want to hurt things if you can help it."

"You shoot good," Tony said. "Do you ever miss?"

Lon laughed as he took the paddle to move them out to where the ducks were floating on the water. "Sometimes. It's like playing pool, or anything else. Everybody misses sometimes."

"How many more you gonna kill?"

"Two's enough this morning, young man. You're cold, so we'll go home. I'll have Mrs. Coulter clean and cook one up for me. The other we'll give to Carter and Agatha, and you and your family can have duck to eat."

Yes, it was a good memory. It had been another couple of years and a few more times hunting together before Lon had allowed Tony to shoot the shotgun. Now the boy was getting to be a good shot.

Lon grunted and smiled again as he looked at the dying fire. He would have to rebuild it again if they were to stay here much longer.

29

Lon's pipe was out and he sat up straight to tamp it and search his pockets for another match. The heat from the fire now felt good to him. There was a chill in the air, the sky was overcast, and it was darkening rapidly. When he looked at Tony again, he saw the boy was asleep, huddled in the heavy borrowed jacket. Lon decided it was time to take Tony back home; he couldn't keep him out here into the night.

He lit his pipe and blew out the match. But when he dropped the matchstick he thought he saw something in the woods off to his left—a brief flicker of light, only it had disappeared quickly. The cracking of the fire covered any sounds.

Lon peered into the darkness. It could have been his imagination or could have been caused by the glare of the match flame against his eyes. It also could be Dave Hunter coming to them. He waited and looked.

Then he saw it again, briefly.

Lon knocked the ash from his pipe and shoved the pipe into his jacket pocket. He moved beside Tony and shook the boy's shoulder. Tony awoke with a start. Lon motioned him to be quiet and whispered, "Over there."

Tony raised himself, his eyes following Lon's pointing finger. "Where? I don't see nothing."

"Near that dogleg at the end of the lake," Lon said softly. "Twice I seen it. First time I wasn't sure."

"Is it a light, Lon? It might be one of the farmers that seen our fire and wants to have a look."

"Or somebody hunting," Lon said. "I thought I heard voices."

"Yeah, there's a light," Tony said, excitedly. "I saw it that time."

"Well, it ain't your daddy," Lon said and stood up. "He wouldn't be out here showing himself with a light or talking to somebody." He coaxed the boy to his feet. "You take our shotgun and go back there in those trees. Hide yourself and wait for me. Keep your eyes open."

"Don't you need the shotgun?"

"There's more than one out there," Lon said. "I don't wanna be holding a shotgun if two or three guys come on me. It's too late to avoid 'em. They've seen our fire. Go hide yourself, and protect the gun. Do what I told you."

Tony pulled the old jacket tighter to shield his arms and neck and, carrying the shotgun, slipped back into the darkness of the woods. He stopped where he could still see Lon in the small clearing. It was very dark where Tony was hidden, and somebody would have to be practically on top of him to see him.

The oncoming light turned into a steady dot coming toward Lon's dying firelight. A man's voice called out and another answered. Two men, one holding a lantern high, emerged from the woods. From the opposite direction came two other men, one with another lantern. All four men were armed. They converged on Lon by the dying fire.

A hand fell on Tony's shoulder, and he froze in sudden panic. Then he heard the voice behind him, asking his name: "Tony?"

Tony's knees wobbled. It had to be his father.

Tony expelled his breath and twisted about. "Yeah, it's me."

"You okay, kid?" the whispered voice asked. "What the hell you doing here?"

"Lon and me, we were looking for you."

"Keep yourself hidden, boy," his father said. "I'll lead 'em away."

"I've got Lon's shotgun," Tony said. "You want it?"

"No," his father said, quickly. "Somebody'd sure get killed. I heard 'em say my name. What are they hunting me for?"

"You don't know? They think you killed Ivan Coaker's wife."

"What? Annie Pyle's dead?"

"Annie Coaker," Tony said. He could barely see Lon in the clearing surrounded by four men. He couldn't hear what was being said. "Last night."

"Stay where you are and don't come out," his father whispered.

Dave Hunter deliberately crashed loudly through brush

as he left Tony behind. The four men at the campfire spun away from Lon Shirley. One raced into the woods in the direction of the sounds ahead of the others shouting, "I'll get him!" To Tony it sounded like the whiny voice of Clifford Coaker.

"Wait, Clifford!" That was his brother Ivan's voice.

But Clifford didn't wait. He had grabbed the lantern from another man and charged ahead. To Tony it looked like a game unfolding in front of him. But then he couldn't see anything once Clifford was swallowed up by the forest darkness. The last three men, one with the other lantern and two with rifles, broke away from Lon Shirley and followed Clifford.

Tony left the shotgun out of sight, propped against the base of a tree, and rushed out to Lon in the clearing.

"I told you to stay put," Lon told him, sharply.

"Lon, I saw him—my daddy!" Tony gasped. "He was coming in from that direction."

"He's leading 'em away from us," Lon said and cursed.

Tony started toward Lon's lantern. "Let's go!"

Lon restrained him. "No, you might get shot out there. We'll stay here. Where's the shotgun?"

"Big tree over there. I didn't think you'd want it stolen."

"We're better off unarmed," Lon said.

There was a sudden outcry of shouting from the woods where the pursuers had followed Dave Hunter. It had to be difficult going in there in the dark. Lon gripped Tony's arm and held him close by the campfire light that was fading fast now. More shouts were heard before shots were fired.

Suddenly, there came an agonized scream.

In another couple of seconds it was followed by a voice

calling for help, moaning loudly. It was Clifford Coaker's voice crying for his brother.

Tony looked at Lon and saw his big friend's lips tightly pursed with a scowl on his face. The cry for help came again.

Ivan Coaker's voice shouted: "I'm coming, Clifford! Hold him! I'm coming!"

Two rifle shots cracked out. Those were followed a moment later by a third and fourth.

Then for a minute or two there were no sounds except for a human moaning.

The crashing in the brush grew louder as the men approached. One man, supported by two, was groaning pitifully.

"Be careful with him," Ivan said. "He's hurt. My brother's hurt bad. He's losing blood."

"Yeah," a skinny man supporting the wounded man said, "he got his own knife shoved in his gut. Damned fool."

"Don't you call my brother a fool," Ivan snapped. "Pull it out!"

"I ain't gonna pull it out. You do it."

Ivan withdrew the knife from Clifford's belly, and Clifford screamed shrilly.

The skinny man turned loose, and Clifford Coaker slumped to the ground with another soft cry.

"Don't stand there! Do something! Lon, do something."

Lon looked down at Clifford. "What can I do? He needs a doc before he bleeds to death."

Cursing, Ivan looked around from his kneeling position over his brother. "Where's that goddamn kid? Where'd he go?"

"He's hiding from you. I told him to."

"Jesus Christ! Stabbed with his own knife," Ivan cried. "Clifford! Clifford! God, he's hurt bad."

"I'd say so," the other man concurred. "Bleedin' like a stuck pig."

"Goddamn it, Slim, we gotta get 'im to the doctor," Ivan choked. "Hep me. You hold on, Clifford."

"Long way to town," the skinny man called Slim said. "What about Hunter?"

"I hit him," Ivan said. "I know I did. I seen him plain when he stood up and I shot him."

"Well, we didn't see a body."

"It's out there somewhere," Ivan said. He glowered at Lon. "Where's your horse?"

Lon pointed. "Over there."

"I'm taking your horse. I gotta get Clifford to town to Doc Sanders."

Lon nodded. "He might not make it getting' jostled around on a horse."

"Well, goddamn it, he can't walk back."

"And we sure can't carry him," the man called Slim said.

Ivan rose to his feet and addressed the skinny man. "Come on, Slim. Saddle that fuckin' horse. Me an' Hurd will bring Clifford."

"I tol' you when we started we shouldn't be walking all over these fuckin'woods, 'specially in the dark," Hurd said.

Ivan seized his shirtfront, then released his grip. He said, "Quit bitchin' and stay here, Hurd, where you can watch this one-handed son of a bitch. If he tries anything, you shoot him. Hell, shoot the boy too."

"That's pretty dumb even for you, Ivan," Lon said, calmly. "Hurt the boy and you'll have the Blaisdell's after your ass."

"He's got a point," Hurd said.

Slim came back leading Old Bill by the bridle. "Okay, let's hoist him up."

Clifford screamed in pain when they lifted him. Slim and Hurd balanced him on the horse until Ivan could swing up behind. They shifted Clifford until Ivan had his arm firmly around his brother's upper chest, cradling him. "You fellas walk home," Ivan said, "and bring my rifle. I gotta get Clifford some help."

A few minutes later it was just Lon and Hurd and Slim in the clearing. The firelight was all but extinguished, and Hurd turned up a lantern.

"You like trying to kill a man?" Lon asked.

"Shut up, Lon," Hurd grumbled. "It wasn't your wife that got shot in the back."

"Yours neither," Lon said. "I can see how you got your blood hot for the hunt. How do you know it was Dave Hunter Clifford run across and not some stranger that knifed him? By the way, Clifford looks bad. It's a stomach wound. Worst kind I'd imagine."

Slim looked at Hurd. "What we doin' standin' 'round here?"

"Well, Ivan said to stay here with Lon," Hurd said.

"That's a genius idea," Slim said. "We're out here in the dark about to freeze our asses off while Ivan's on his way to town. You know how long that's gonna take him?"

"Long time."

"Piss on this," Slim said. "I'm just about for goin' home."

Hurd heaved out a long sigh and nodded.

Lon said to them, "You men can relax and put down your weapons. I won't hurt you."

Hurd frowned, but set his rifle aside. He helped Lon pick up more dried twigs and work them onto the last glowing embers of the fire.

"Slim," Lon said, "Ivan will forget all about you once he gets his brother transported to town. Besides, the boy's here, too, watchin' us right now. You want to 'splain to Miz Blaisdell how you kept her grandson in the woods at gunpoint?"

"Fuck it, Lon," Hurd grumbled. "I ain't gonna shoot nobody, and I ain't gonna get in over my head with the Blaisdells. I'm going home, Slim. It's a long walk. Far as I'm concerned, you can do what you want."

"Now you're being smart," Lon said.

After Hurd and Slim had tramped off, Hurd carrying Ivan Coaker's rifle, Tony emerged from the wood line bringing Lon's shotgun. He said, "Lon, they took Old Bill. We'll have to walk back."

"That's right," Lon said. "Tony, you stay here and feed the fire. Keep yourself warm. I'll take the lantern and have a look around."

"I'll go with you."

"No. I mean it, son. You stay right here. Our deal was you'll do what I tell you. Your daddy might be long gone."

"Or he might not," Tony said in a whisper.

"That's true, too. Anyway, you stay. I'll try to track him. Won't be easy in the dark. We might have to wait 'til morning. In that case, I'll come back and we'll start walking."

30

It seemed longer to Tony, though it probably was not more than half an hour, when Lon returned to the clearing with a hard-set expression on his face. The man squatted beside the fire and warmed his hands. He didn't look at Tony.

"Well," said Tony, "did you find him?"

Lon gave him a pained look. "I got bad news for you, boy."

Tony drew in a breath and waited.

"Ivan didn't miss," Lon said. "Your daddy got shot in the back. I found him. He was already dead."

Tony expelled his breath. He didn't know exactly how he was supposed to feel. It wasn't as though he had been close to his father. If he felt anything, it was numbness.

"What—what did you do?" Tony asked.

"Covered him with some brush and my coat," Lon said, looking away. "I'm sorry, Tony."

"Me, too," Tony said. "I didn't know him, Lon."

Lon stayed by the fire for several minutes, staring into it or off into the darkness of the woods.

Finally Tony asked, "What'll we do?"

Lon looked at him as though surprised by the question. "We'll do it tomorrow when it's daylight."

"What?"

"I'm not taking him to town to be displayed as a murderer who got caught," Lon said. "I made up my mind to that." He rose a bit unsteadily. "We better go back now. We'll go home."

"And just leave him?"

"Won't matter," Lon said. After he checked the amount of oil and got his lantern lighted and brightened again, he looked at Tony, who sat in the clearing with his borrowed coat drawn up about him. Tony raised his head from his arms. "Sure you're okay?" Lon asked. "You don't have to do this with me. In fact, it might be better if you don't."

"I'll be with you tomorrow," Tony said and rose to his feet. He looked at his friend. "You'll freeze without your coat."

"No, we'll move fast enough to keep warm. Keep that coat tight about you. I don't want you catching cold."

With the lantern held high, Lon kept ahead of Tony leading them in the direction of the old dirt road that circled the lake. Once there they quickened their pace until they climbed the incline to the main road. Then they walked silently, side by side.

Two and a half hours later they were at the porch of Blaisdell House. Carter Foote opened the front door before Lon had a chance to knock. Carter saw their expressions and said nothing. He stepped aside to allow Tony and Lon entrance.

From the library study came Grace Blaisdell wearing her housecoat, slippers, and a nightcap. Daniel was right behind her. Grace had opened her mouth to say something curt but stopped. She tilted her head at Lon Shirley.

Lon stepped around Carter and said, "Got to tell you something, Gracie. Daniel, too."

They huddled at the library entrance. Tony stood at the bottom of the stairway with his head bowed. Carter, sensing the seriousness of something, eyed him with compassion.

Grace came to Tony and touched his shoulder. "Tony, you go to your room and try to get some rest. You'll be going with Lon tomorrow morning."

Tony looked at her quickly. He had expected almost anything but that. He had thought she would rail at him for being out late and would make demands. He blinked at her.

"Go on, now," she said, softly.

Tony took off Lon's coat and went upstairs. Below, Lon watched him and picked up the coat. He looked at Grace and Daniel.

"I have to round up my horse now," Lon said. "Should we say ten o'clock?"

Grace and Daniel nodded.

Tony didn't sleep right away that night although he was physically exhausted. He kept turning the events over in his mind and felt himself torn between sadness and anger. It was hours later that the exhaustion overtook him. He passed out.

31

The sun was bright outside his windows when he awakened, and someone, Agatha probably, had laid out fresh clothes for him, all except for the shoes. Tony had no idea what time it was so he used the upstairs bathroom, one of two in-house, dressed quickly and came down to the kitchen alcove.

Grandmother Grace and Uncle Daniel were having coffee. They had finished breakfast, and Agatha had removed the dishes. Tony saw Carter in the kitchen, helping Agatha, and Carter nodded to him.

"Water or milk with your eggs?" Grandmother Grace asked him.

"I'm not hungry," Tony said as he sat at the table. He looked at the two adults. "I've got to get to Lon 'cause he might be gone by now."

"He won't be," Daniel said. "He's waiting for us."

Us? Tony's question was in his eyes.

"You're taking the car," Grandmother Grace said. "I'll

ride into town with you and open the bank." She waited as Agatha placed a glass of milk in front of Tony. Hungry or not, he drank it quickly. She said, "Daniel, you can tell me what there is to tell me later."

Daniel nodded as he set down his coffee cup and pushed it aside. He dabbed his mouth with a napkin. He had his suit on, and white shirt, but no necktie yet. Tony noted that he wore outdoor boots instead of his usual shiny shoes. The shoes were on the floor beside his chair. He said, "I'll bring the car out front."

After Daniel left, carrying his good shoes, and Carter followed him out to help crank the engine over, Grace asked Tony, "Are you feeling okay?"

Tony nodded.

"Sure you won't eat something?"

He shook his head.

Finally, he said, "Grandma, I want to work for Lon this summer like you promised."

Now his grandmother nodded as she sipped coffee from her cup.

"Please?"

She nodded again and gave him a brief smile.

"Lon told you about—him?"

"Yes," she said.

"Does my mother know?"

"She's resting this morning. I'll talk to her later today."

"I didn't know if I should," Tony said.

"Not unless she wants to talk with you about it," Grandmother Grace said. She reached out and laid a hand on the boy's arm. "Tony, I didn't want this to happen to your father. I hope you believe that. It was not my intention to cause him harm."

"They were cowards," Tony said, bitterly. "He was unarmed and they shot him anyway."

"That's what a mob does sometimes."

"We only seen four of 'em," Tony said. "And Clifford Coaker got stabbed with his own knife. I hope he dies."

"Don't say that," Grace snapped. "There's enough death all around without wishing for any."

From the distance, they heard the car engine cranking and coughing to life.

Aunt Ruth, dressed in white chiffon, came into the kitchen alcove and took the chair vacated by Daniel. She wore her expensive black walking boots with the two-inch heels. That was a pretty good indication she would be going into town to see her father. "Good morning," she said without enthusiasm.

"Do you have plans today, Ruth?" Grace asked.

Ruth nodded as Agatha brought her a cup of coffee and stood by. "I'm going to see daddy." She shook her head at Agatha. "No breakfast for me, Agatha, but thank you."

"Give the reverend our regards," Grace said.

Ruth nodded and sipped her coffee. "Has Daniel left for the bank already?"

"He's outside with the car, waiting for us."

A horn blew out front of the house.

Ruth rose and left the kitchen area.

She went out the front door and down from the wide porch to the driveway. Daniel, curious, watched her approach.

"You're up early," he said.

"I'm going into town."

"We can squeeze enough space for you to ride in with us."

"I'll go by myself," Ruth said. "So? Is the whole family going to that woman's funeral?"

"What I heard," Daniel said, slowly, "is that Annie will be buried tomorrow, not today. Since Doc Harris is retired, he's allowed her to rest in his parlor so she won't have to be laid out at shantytown."

"How are you holding up, Daniel?"

"Fine. Why wouldn't I be?" He tilted his head at his wife. "Ruth, are you angry about something again today?"

"Nothing but the usual," she said, looking off. "I wonder how many wives are deceived by their husbands."

"Damn!" Daniel expelled his breath and shook his head. "Ruth, anything between Annie and me was over before we married. I told you that a thousand times."

"And you're just as convincing now as ever," she said, sarcastically.

"What do you want from me?" he asked quietly.

Ruth thought about it a moment. "I want your salvation, Daniel. I want the salvation for our marriage. But until I can trust you—"

"What do I have to do for you to trust me?" he asked.

"I want you to sincerely ask forgiveness from God," she said. "I want you to return to my father's church with me. I want you to pray with him—from your heart. Then I want you to show the other women in this town that you have only one wife. That you cherish her and will never fail her again."

"Anything else?"

"You're being cynical," she said. "I should've known."

"Am I the only failure?" Daniel asked.

"Probably not, but you are my husband."

"Only in name," Daniel said. "I had no idea that on our wedding night you planned to shut me out. You've shut me out ever since. We either give our marriage a chance, or we don't."

"You're in no position to make ultimatums to me," Ruth said.

"What if I agree to talk with your father?"

"That will be a start," Ruth said. "He feels you need counseling."

Daniel reached over and pressed the bulb that honked the horn on the car. He did it twice. When he looked up, his wife was stepping upon the porch to take a seat in one of the porch swings.

32

Grace got out of the car on Main Street directly in front of the bank. She watched Tony as he scrambled out and ran toward the poolroom to get Lon Shirley. She said to Daniel, who was behind the wheel, "You don't have to rush, you know. Lon will know what to do. Have you everything you need?"

Daniel nodded. "Shovels—blankets—we'll be all right. I'll be back soon as possible, Mother." He paused. "Thanks for understanding."

"That's the easy part," Grace said as she turned toward the bank, tapping her ebony walking stick with each step of her right foot.

Once inside, she noted that their two clerks had already set up for business, and she stood at the front window until she saw Tony and Lon Shirley get into the car. Daniel drove off. Grace craned to the side and saw the smiling, buck-toothed man, Lenny Smith, in the doorway of the poolroom.

She took off her hat and scarf and riding coat, hung them on a coat tree, greeted the clerks, and went back into the office. With a sigh she sat behind the desk and propped the walking stick up against it.

One of the clerks stuck his head in the office. "Somebody out here wanting to see you, Mrs. Blaisdell."

"Asking for me specifically?"

The clerk nodded. "He wouldn't tell me his name. Said you'd want to hear him out. He looks like a bum."

"That pretty well describes everybody in town," Grace said. "Have him come in."

The man who entered the office was Ivan Coaker. His body odor reached Grace as soon as he was inside and had shut the door. She wrinkled her nose but said nothing.

Ivan Coaker took off his cap and held it in both hands in front of him. "Miz Blaisdell? I'm Ivan Coaker."

"I know you," she said.

"Can I sit down?"

"If you're capable," she said.

Ivan took the visitor's chair across the desk from her. He reached into his shirt pocket and pulled out some crumpled papers. "I figure we can do some business."

"You want to make a deposit?"

"I ain't got no money. Not 'til I get what you're keeping from me."

"Okay, what kind of business?"

"Take a look at them letters," Ivan said, mildly gloating.

Grace fingered them apart, there were two, and lifted one sheet to read. Written by Daniel, she knew. She recognized his handwriting. There was no date on the letter, and no envelopes.

"You know what them is?" Ivan asked.

"Looks like letters written to your late wife," said Grace.

"That's it," Ivan said. "Your son, Daniel, wrote 'em to Annie when she was alive. I brought a sample for you. There's others I keep in a safe place."

"Looks like one friend talking to another," Grace said, mildly. She stared at Ivan Coaker until he averted his eyes. "You want to return these to my son?"

"No!" Ivan blurted. "I mean, not exactly. I'll sell 'em to you, Miz Blaisdell. All of 'em."

"Why?"

"I need money," Ivan said. "Doc Sanders patched up my brother Clifford last night. He says I owe him twenty dollars for the stitches an' all. Clifford's wound might be infected. The doc plastered him with hammered silver foil an' hopes it works. Clifford's laid up for awhile."

"What happened to your brother?"

"He fell on his knife an' stuck hisself," Ivan said. "So, we need some money."

"You want a loan from the bank?"

"No," Ivan said, scowling. "I wanna sell these luv letters to you. I done figured you don't want no big scandal 'bout your son. We can keep everythin' on the quiet."

"How much?"

"I figure one hunnert dollars ought'a do it."

"Uh huh," Grace said with a hint of amusement. "Mr.

Coaker, I'll give you a single dollar for these two, and another dollar if you bring me the rest."

"What?"

"That's my offer. You can buy a couple of drinks."

"Hell," Ivan scoffed, "I might give these to the newspaper editor. Think how they'd look on the front page."

"Our newspaper is a two-sheeter published once a week. I know the editor very well. We do business together. But you go right ahead and take them to him."

"What?" Ivan said, again.

"Ask him for money. Or you can take them to the paper in Elston. It's a daily. Also, you could just nail these to doors along Main Street here and see what happens. Your choice, Mr. Coaker."

"Now that ain't fair!" Ivan exploded.

"I just reduced my offer. Fifty cents for the letters. You don't take it, that's your privilege."

"You're lookin' down your nose at me. I don't like it. You ain't so smart."

"Smarter than you," Grace said. "Mr. Blaisdell when he was alive, God bless him, saw to it that I had some good tutors. He wanted me to speak well if I was to run this bank someday."

"You done insulted me," Ivan said bitterly.

"Here's another possibility," Grace said. "Let me think for a moment. When is your wife's funeral?"

Ivan scowled at the desktop. "She's in a wood coffin over at the undertaker's. He wants twenty-five dollars to bury her, an' that includes diggin' the hole an' filling it in. See? I need money for lots of things."

"I'll do this for Annie," Grace said. "I'll pay the undertaker's fee for those letters."

Ivan was suddenly interested. "You will?"

"Yes. You planning on a headstone of any kind?"

"No, that'd be an extra ten or fifteen. He said he could do a wood one with her name an' dates engraved on it for four bucks. 'Course, the wood won't last a long time."

"I know," Grace said. She remembered a small wooden cross of tied-together sticks that Carter Foote had stuck in the ground where he had buried her first son, John. He had dug the grave with his own hands. It was someplace in northern Tennessee. She realized she'd never be able to find it again if she wanted to—if there was anything left to find. She said, "Even a temporary marker is better than none."

"You mean you'd pay for the marker too?" Ivan asked.

Grace nodded. "This is a one-time offer, Mr. Coaker. Take it or leave it."

Ivan, frowning, made a tentative, slow reach for the letters on the desk.

Faster than he would have thought possible, he caught the blurred motion as Grace raised the walking stick and cracked the knob sharply down on the desk close to Ivan's hand. He recoiled so sharply that his chair was pushed back a couple of feet. His eyes wide as saucers, he jerked his hand back, cradling it in his other hand.

"I thought we was bargaining," he said.

"You thought wrong," Grace told him and propped the walking stick up against the desk again.

A clerk stuck his head in from outside. "Everything okay, Mrs. Blaisdell?"

"Just fine, thank you." She gave him a small dismissive wave of her hand, and he withdrew. "Am I to take it that you don't want my offer, Mr. Coaker?"

"No, I ain't said that," Ivan wailed. "How 'bout payin' the doc for my brother Clifford, too?"

"No. That's between you and the doctor."

"When will I get Annie's savings money?"

"When Judge Parks declares the inquest is over and frees her assets. It will be soon, perhaps today or tomorrow, or even next week. I'm still waiting for your answer, Mr. Coaker, and I'll give you exactly three seconds."

"Okay, okay," said Ivan loudly. "Christ, I heard you can be a bitch."

"I'll give you the money for Annie's burial now," Grace said. "If I learn that you used it for anything else, anything at all, I'm taking it out of your wife's assets. I will be checking with the undertaker. And there's one more thing I want from you."

"What's 'at?"

"A proper funeral for Annie. You arrange it with the undertaker. Set it up for tomorrow morning—say, ten o'clock at the cemetery. You get the word out so that everyone who knows her can attend if they want to. I'll help by having the newspaper put out a special flier. It can be posted in a number of places, especially in the saloons."

Ivan appeared in shock. "You mean you'll take the money you give me out of what I got coming for Annie? You can do that?"

"Of course." Legally, she couldn't, but she figured that Ivan Coaker wouldn't know that.

She rose and stepped out of the office, leaving Ivan sitting and craning around. When she came back, she counted out twenty dollars on the desk in front of him and watched him seize it and jam it inside his shirt pocket. She said, "Remember what I told you. And you'll bring me the rest of the letters."

Ivan nodded, got up and backed to the door.

"One more question for you, Mr. Coaker," Grace said.

Ivan groaned as his shoulders sagged.

"Are there other letters? Letters between Annie and other men besides my son?"

"Well, now I don't see that's none of your business," Ivan said and ran out.

Grace knew she'd never see the other letters, if there were any. She found matches in one of her desk drawers, pulled close a metal can that served as a wastebasket, and set fire to the papers that Ivan had given her. The ashes went into the can.

She swung around and looked upward at the portrait of the late Darwin James Blaisdell and smiled.

"Some things you taught me well, D. J. Some things I had to learn on my own, but you did your best and you did right by me."

And by Daniel, she thought.

33

In 1868, in northwestern Kentucky, Carter Foote had carried an injured boy into their makeshift camp that consisted primarily of a campfire and a few worn blankets they had accumulated in their travels northward from Tennessee. Their two backpacks with extra clothing, shoes, and a few utensils were stacked in the clearing.

The young Grace had been left to tend the camp, making coffee and cooking beans, while Carter had said he would scout around and see if he could find any meat. By this time Carter had acquired a rusty old rifle that was ball and cap, vintage Civil War, and a powder pouch and handful of balls. He had to be careful if he shot game because most likely he wouldn't be able to replenish the ammo.

He had the rifle slung on his shoulder and the boy in his arms. Grace, surprised, rose from the fire to look.

"He's alive but hurt bad," Carter said, lowering the boy to the ground. "Three men beating on him to rob him. They took his shoes and shirt and whatever he had in his pockets. He had a friend about the same age. The friend's dead. They beat him to death with clubs."

Grace nodded. In their journey it wasn't unusual to see the work of outlaws and highwaymen. She peered at the unconscious, but shivering, young man. Then she recoiled with a gasp. His left arm had been badly broken, and bone fragment was sticking out, pale yellow in the flickering firelight. She looked at the pinched, pain-ridden mouth.

"He's just a boy," she said.

Carter nodded, placing his rifle aside. "Nearly a dead boy. He won't last 'til morning."

"What—what about the three men?" Grace asked.

"I shot one in the leg, and they took off."

She nodded to herself. "Did you bury this boy's friend?"

"Covered the body with leaves and branches. I figured I'd better get this one back here to get a better look. We got to keep him warm, too. He's chilled."

The boy was, indeed, shivering violently even though he was unconscious.

"That arm is awful," Grace said.

"I know."

"The bone is sticking out."

"Probably infected by now," Carter said. He heaved a long sigh. "Bring some blankets here, Miss Grace."

She did. Three blankets, none of which were very clean even though she had washed them at a stream a few days earlier. Carter, kneeling beside the injured boy, was studying him intently.

"Carter, can you do anything for him?" Grace asked.

"He needs a doctor, and there ain't one probably in miles," Carter said. "We can't carry him, that's for sure. He's a big boy. Anyway, moving him would kill him for sure." He sighed again. "I got to try to straighten that arm."

"Can you?"

"I don't know. All we can do is try."

Carter surveyed the young man some more, from different angles. Then he knelt again at the boy's left side. "I got to do this," he said, "because you won't be strong enough to pull hard. But the pain might kill him by itself. Miss Grace, you got to sit on him—actually sit on his chest with all your weight and keep his right arm down. I'll straddle his legs to hold them while I work It won't be pretty."

"I'll keep my eyes shut," Grace said.

She was wearing men's pants and work shoes, clothing they had picked up somewhere. She maneuvered herself until she was directly above the boy's chest and then sat down. She leaned her weight to the side to try and hold the right arm stable.

Carter took his position facing her, not looking at her but looking intently at the boy's left arm. He drew a deep breath, gripped the injured arm above the wrist and pulled quickly and hard.

Grace clenched her teeth when she heard the bones grinding together.

The boy screamed and tried to thrash about. It took all of Grace's strength to push him down and come close to holding him. Though his eyes were still tightly shut, she had never heard such a cry of pain before. Then he went limp.

The lad had sweated so heavily that Grace could feel the dampness of his perspiration through the seat of her pants. Slowly, she removed herself from the boy's chest and knelt on the other side of him. Carter was tearing one of the blankets, the oldest and most frayed, into strips. He would hold them in his teeth and tear the strips into thinner strips.

"Miss Grace," he said, "you wash away the blood, real easy like, and use this piece here for a bandage. We'll tie it on. Then I'll tie this arm to his side. After that, all we can do is hope for the best. I don't think he'll wake up right away. We have to keep him warm."

"Maybe not ever," Grace said. "He looks so young, and—" She stopped, not sure what word she wanted. Innocent? Handsome? Helpless? She shook her head and went to the fire for hot water.

During the night the boy started moaning and stirring, though still unconscious. Grace sat up and watched him. He shivered violently, but his face was feverish to her touch. She took her own blanket and pressed it over him. Carter had already done the same with his blanket. Not even all the blankets were keeping the boy from shivering.

We have to keep him warm, Carter had said. Grace looked over at Carter. He was on his side, facing away from them, his knees drawn up and arms folded across his chest against the night chill. She fed more branches onto the fire, but it wasn't helping the boy. What to do? There had to be something. She reached under the blankets and felt the boy's chest. It was clammy. He groaned loudly.

Body heat? She had heard somewhere that it was the best

way to break a chill. The way the boy looked now he might be dead within a few hours. Grace made her decision.

First she unfastened the cardboard belt the boy wore that was holding up his ragged workpants. Pulling downward she drew off the pants and placed them closer to the fire. The boy wore no underwear. For a couple of seconds Grace simply looked at him. His body was well sculpted, and he could have been a handsome young man if not for his gruesome injury and the discomfort he now was suffering—that is, if he was feeling anything at all. She couldn't guess what he might be feeling.

She stripped off all of her clothing. Naked, she slipped beneath the blankets and pressed against the shivering young stranger. She put her arms around him, careful to avoid his severely damaged arm, and pressed herself as tightly as possible to him. He moaned and quivered against her.

She held him like that for a long time.

For a while she dozed. Then she was aware that his shivering had subsided somewhat, though not entirely. He still appeared to be unconscious. He was beginning to sweat, and so was she, their combined body heat doing that. She continued to hold him, shifting her body ever so slightly only to avoid cramping her own arms, hips, or legs. It must have helped because she dozed off again.

For several nights in a row, Grace did exactly the same thing. She clutched the boy to her naked body. Carter knew but never said a word. It was three or four days before his breathing had softened somewhat, though he still twitched and groaned in his sleep.

On the fourth night something else happened.

Grace hugged him, both of them naked beneath the heavier blanket, until she fell asleep. When she awakened, she was aware of something else. Though the boy appeared to be sleeping and breathing easier, he also was undergoing an erection. His penis was hard and pressing into her belly. Grace's first impulse was to withdraw quickly, but something stopped her. She stroked the boy's sweaty back and felt his prodding. It was the first hard penis she had felt probing at her since her last meeting with Clive Gibson.

Moments later she adjusted herself on her side facing him and parted her legs. As though his penis had its own mind and determination, it pressed between her legs. Grace sucked in her breath, not sure how she should be feeling. One thing she didn't feel was disgusted, or that she was doing anything wrong. Her legs parted wider, and she used one hand to guide him.

It amazed her how easily he slipped inside her. And how good it felt. She pressed hard to him and began a rhythmic movement to work on him. He moaned and rolled his head slightly but still appeared to be unconscious. Grace doubled her efforts. She fantasized that once more she was making love to Clive.

It had been a long time for her since she had had sex. For years now she had clung to the memory of Clive Gibson, whom she had grown to love, and thought sometimes that there would never be another man for her. But this boy, right now, was making her feel so very good.

Her release came first and she gasped. A second later she felt his release, his semen rushing into her body. She held on tightly, eyes shut, teeth clenched, and then gradually relaxed.

She felt herself smiling. When she looked at the boy's face she saw that he was awake. At least his eyes were open, and he had a confused look mingled with gratitude on his face. His lips trembled, but he couldn't say anything.

Grace helped him remove from her and then promptly got up to tighten the blankets around him and go for a canteen of water. She brought it back and let the boy sip from it. She recapped the canteen and patted his cheek. He was sweating heavily now but didn't appear to be chilled.

Under the moonlight Grace went to the stream nearby, since she and Carter always tried to camp near water, and washed herself. Near the campfire she put on her clothes, wrapped herself in another ragged old blanket and went to sleep. She had a smile on her face.

As the boy slowly recovered, though he didn't have full use of his left arm and it was warped and twisted, he traveled with Grace and Carter as they moved northward to the Ohio River. They stopped at small towns and fair-sized ranches to ask for work and usually got some, though it never amounted to much and certainly not enough to keep them in one place. Grace washed clothes and bedding for pennies, Carter was a handyman with tools and could build or repair most anything needed, and even the boy was strong and willing and able one-handedly to muck out stalls and toss bales of hay. Generally, they worked as a team.

But more than that, Grace and the boy maintained an on-going love affair, almost nightly sleeping together under the same blankets and enjoying sex at least once each night. When she caught Carter smiling at her one time, she remarked, "It don't mean anything. He's much younger than I am."

"About nine years," Carter said. "Means nothing. My wife, Agatha, is two years older than me."

Grace rationalized away any embarrassment she might have felt about making love with a teenaged boy. People had to do what was necessary for themselves and for each other.

By the time they reached southern Indiana and the small town of Vinton in Osanamon County, circumstances had changed for Grace. She discovered that she was pregnant. She had found a job selling women's clothing, and Carter had been hired by one of the local farmers to put a roof on his house. The boy was taking what odd jobs he could and wound up working in a dilapidated poolroom for an arthritic old man who could barely get around. Grace never told the boy about the baby growing inside her. Carter knew, but she made him promise he would never tell.

A stroke of good fortune came her way when she met another man, one much older than she. He was Darwin James Blaisdell, president and owner of the *Vinton Bank and Trust Company*. She went into the bank in hopes of starting a modest savings that would help her when the time came to have the baby and caught the eye of the old man who interviewed her personally. Before she left his office, he was calling her by her first name.

He said, "Grace, I think you are the prettiest girl I've ever seen."

Grace had blushed and returned to her job. But old Mr. Blaisdell found numerous reasons to shop where Grace worked. He kept smiling at her, and Grace had the impression that he wasn't one to smile very often. Also, she heard rumors about him but put scant credence to them.

Supposedly, the old man, never married, often drove his buggy the fifteen miles to the bigger town of Elston and to a particular whorehouse he favored there. But word had filtered back to Vinton that Mr. Blaisdell couldn't perform with women. He would pay the girls just to watch them undress, then drive back to Vinton even more lonely and desolate than before. It seemed to please him when he could find an excuse to talk with Grace.

One afternoon he asked her to take a walk with him. She wasn't sure why she accepted, but she did. On that walk he opened up to her and confessed his weakness.

"Grace," he said, tearfully, "I want to get married. I want a family. I want one son and one daughter, at least, if possible. Maybe being married, having it sanctified, will make me more of a man. I hope so." He put his hands on her shoulders and looked at her solemnly. "I'm a rich man, Grace, and I don't want everything to die with me. That might be selfish of me, but I don't feel that way. You're beautiful, and I need a comely wife. Will you marry me, Grace?"

She was so stunned she couldn't reply.

"You'll have everything you want," he said. "I promise."

Finally, through tears of her own, Grace said, "Mr. Blaisdell, I must confess something to you, too. I am with child."

He blinked at her. "And you love the father?"

"Love? I guess so, but he doesn't know. I can't marry him. I never could. But I don't want to deceive you."

Mr. Blaisdell thought it over as they resumed their walk.

"All right. Nobody needs to know. This can be our child if you'll have me. Now I have a request. If the child is a boy, I want him named Daniel after my father. If it's a girl, I want her named Louella after my grandmother. Is that satisfactory?"

Grace nodded, and then stopped him. "My good friend, Carter Foote, and I have traveled a long way together. He's always looked after me. If he'll stay, I want to keep him."

"Of course," Mr. Blaisdell said. "Consider it done."

"I'll ask him to send for his wife. She's back east. Will you agree?"

"Absolutely."

Grace wiped away tears as she nodded. "Then I will be happy to marry you, Mr. Blaisdell."

He laughed. "You better start calling me D. J. Everybody else does."

34

Daniel drove the car in as close to the lake as he could manage it, found a turnaround and parked it headed back toward town. He, Tony, and Lon Shirley carried the blankets into the woods. Lon guided them to where he had covered his friend's body with leaves and branches to keep predators away. They could see the lake with a slight haze hanging above it nearby. Lon and Daniel pulled away the branches and coverings and stood quietly for a moment.

Tony approached and stood beside them. He looked solemnly down at the man who was all but a stranger to him, not sure how he should be feeling, then deciding to just let it go and not worry about it. But still an ambiguous sorrow weighed heavily inside him.

He stood and watched, putting his faith in Lon and Uncle Daniel.

Finally, after a long moment of silence, each person handling it in his own way, Lon Shirley lifted his face to look out from under the brim of his hat at the brightening lake. The sun had started burning through the mist. "We can give him an appropriate burial now," he said.

Daniel looked at him. "We can take him in with us. Mother and I will see that he's buried properly."

"Properly to your mother is not the same as properly to me," Lon said. "Trust me, Daniel. If they never find him again, they'll never know, or claim they know for sure, what he did or didn't do."

"I trust you, Lon, but it doesn't seem right."

"Aw, to hell with right," Lon snapped. "This is not only for Dave Hunter. It's for me, and Tony here, and all of us who considered him a fairly decent man. Do you want to help me?"

"Yes," Tony and Daniel said together.

Lon squeezed his eyes with his thumb and forefinger. When he took his hand away, he was smiling. "I was thinking how Dave liked it here at the lake. He thought he was a better woodsman than me. Told me once that when his time come he'd like to be buried somewhere in the woods, not in a town cemetery." He looked at Tony. "Tony, walk down the lake a piece and find us a boat. Bring it here. You know how to handle a boat. Daniel and I will move him down to the water."

A little ways down, Tony found two rowboats moored to the same gnarled stump. It looked like neither boat had been used in quite a while. They were dirty and muck-filled, and one did not look solid. Tony selected the sturdier boat and raked out the soggy leaves with his hands. He washed his hands and one paddle in the water before he untied the boat and pushed it out.

Lon and Daniel waited for him with the wrapped body in a lakeside clearing. The two men helped Tony ground the boat. Tony still felt strange and oddly detached.

His father's body had been wrapped completely in the blankets they had brought from town. The bundle was tied at both ends. It looked ungainly and lumpy, not at all like a human form. Tony shuddered and averted his eyes.

Lon said, "I'm sorry, Tony. We put rocks inside the blankets to weight it. There's no use looking at him now. You can wait here on the bank for us."

"No, I want to help," Tony said.

Daniel started to protest, but Lon simply nodded. "Take that end, Daniel," he said. "Easy now. We'll put him in the boat."

Tony watched them move slowly with their burden. Lon took off his shoes, socks, and trousers so that he could wade out and lay it gently inside. He came out, wiped his legs and feet with a spare blanket and put pants and shoes back on. Then he held the boat steady with his strong right hand while Tony and his uncle Daniel gingerly stepped into it. Lon shoved hard to push the boat out before he jumped in. He balanced himself before he was seated, then took the paddle from Tony.

Daniel saw him struggling with it one-handed, so he reached out. "Let me paddle," he said. "I won't run us in circles."

Lon laughed. Even Tony smiled.

Daniel took the paddle and moved them out onto the

lake. The mist had practically disappeared, and Tony could feel the warmth of the sun on his face.

Lon gave directions. Tony realized, having been here on the lake with him before, that he was pointing them out toward the deepest part. Daniel worked effortlessly and smoothly.

"I hope nobody's out here today," Lon said.

Tony heard squawking and watched two large crows circling above the trees on the far bank. Ahead of him Lon's head lifted too as he saw the birds. Lon nodded at something he was thinking. Then he said, "We're almost there."

They were silent for a few minutes. "Okay," Lon said. The word was barely spoken. Tony realized they were in the middle of the lake.

Daniel stopped paddling and allowed the boat to drift. He looked around at Tony. "If you got some goodbyes to say, now's the time."

"No goodbyes," Tony said.

"Or a prayer."

"I don't know one that fits," Tony said.

"Goes for me, too," Lon said. "Let's get it done."

"I guess we all should've known him better," Uncle Daniel said.

Lon was all business now. "Ready? You lift his feet, Daniel. I'll take this end."

Together the two men heaved their bundle over the side where it splashed heavily. The boat rocked wildly until Lon and Uncle Daniel steadied it. When Tony looked over, there was nothing to see in the dark water. The bundle was gone.

Daniel took up the paddle again, guiding them back

toward the clearing. As they neared it, he said, "Look there."

Tony squinted in the brightness, able to see someone standing in the clearing.

"It's the sheriff," Lon said.

Sheriff Abe Buckner, in uniform, stood waiting at the edge of the lake. He watched Lon and Daniel beach the boat then step ashore and give Tony a hand in getting out.

"Morning, gentlemen," Buckner said. "Surprised to see you here, Daniel."

Daniel shrugged. "It's a good morning to be out on the water."

"Fishing?"

"We were scouting out some good places to fish," Lon said. "What're you doing here, Abe?"

"See anything interesting?" Buckner asked. "Something I might care about?"

"Looks like it might be a sunny and hot day."

Buckner grunted. "Ivan Coaker came riding in hell for leather with his brother last night. He kicked Doc Sanders' door in and dragged the doc out of bed. Made him take care of Clifford right then. A neighbor heard the racket and got me this morning. Afraid the doc was being killed."

"What happened to Clifford?" Lon asked.

"Got stuck with his own knife," Buckner said. "He's hanging on. Ivan wouldn't talk to me 'til I threatened to stick him in jail. He says he found Hunter here at the lake last night. You and the boy, too. He said he shot Hunter after Hunter knifed Clifford."

Lon said, "Ivan's not so good a shot as he thinks."

"You saying he missed. He swears he hit him." Buckner looked at Tony. "What do you know, son?"

"It was too dark for me to see," Tony said.

"Ivan might swear to anything," Lon said. "It was a dark night, Abe."

"Ivan says there was other guys that saw Dave Hunter, too."

"Did he tell you they had guns and were shooting?" Tony snapped.

"I don't like it myself," Buckner said. "Lon, I want Dave Hunter. If Ivan did hit him, you ain't doing him a favor by lying to me. Hunter would need a doc, too. Where is he?"

"I ain't hiding him, Abe. I wouldn't do that if he was wounded. We did see him. He's gone now."

"Gone?"

"A long way away. He won't be back, Abe. But you can keep looking if you want to."

Sheriff Buckner shook his head. He said to Uncle Daniel, "Dan, what do you know?"

"I never saw Dave Hunter last night," Uncle Daniel said. "No one's proved Dave committed any crime except punching your deputy. I'm afraid that's all you'll get from us."

Buckner took a cigar from his breast pocket and savagely bit off an end. "Hell, give me a match."

Uncle Daniel produced one and lit the cigar for him. He tossed the match back into the water where it hissed briefly.

"If Clifford should die," Buckner said, "You can bet Ivan won't stop looking for Hunter. But I don't know. Clifford's a strong one. That ride in would've killed almost any man."

He studied Lon's face. "Tell me, Lon. Would it do any good to get some fellas together and search this area?"

"No," Lon said.

Tony spoke up. "I oughta' put the boat back where I got it. Lon taught me to do that."

"Lon teaches you lots of things, don't he?" Buckner said. He looked again at Uncle Daniel. "Dan, I don't know what to make of you being here."

"Nothing to it, Sheriff. A morning outing before I get back to my banking business. I've got my car up that way a piece."

"Mine's right beside it," Buckner said. He gave a small salute. "You gentlemen have a nice day."

Uncle Daniel asked, "Did Ivan say anything about burying Annie?"

"No. I think he's trying to scrounge some money together. The undertaker won't work for free, and the county's not paying for it."

"I'll speak with my mother," Uncle Daniel said. "We'll work something out. Annie deserves a decent burial."

"I agree," Lon said.

Tony felt a bit perplexed. These men seemed to be more sympathetic to Annie Pyle than he had heard from most people. But inwardly he tended to agree with them.

35

At Lon Shirley's insistence, Tony went home after Uncle Daniel dropped them off outside the bank catty-cornered across from the poolroom. Tony wanted to stay and work, but Lon told him to go home. He said, "You had a very busy couple of days. Go get yourself cleaned up, get some rest, and change clothes. You'll feel better. I'll see you tomorrow if you're up to it."

When Tony got to the house, he was greeted joyfully by Agatha, who then wrinkled her nose and chided him for his dirty clothes.

"You get out of those things quick as you can," she said. "I'll heat water for your bath."

Tony, still not sure how he was feeling, undressed and fell across his bed. He was almost asleep when Agatha came in and told him his bath was ready. She gathered his pile of clothing including his wet shoes and carried them out. Tony wrapped the towel she had tossed him around himself and went to the bathroom. The old brass, four-legged tub was steaming. He had to ease himself into it.

It did make him feel better, and he soaked for a long time. Agatha asked him if he was hungry, but he shook his head. When the water cooled, he climbed from the tub, toweled himself dry, and padded back to his room. He paused outside his mother's door but only briefly. For some reason he wasn't quite ready to face her and tell her of her husband's burial, but he knew he would soon.

On his bed, he pulled up the covers and instantly fell asleep.

Downtown, Grace and Daniel looked at one of the simple posters from the local newspaper office that announced Annie Coaker's burial tomorrow morning at ten o'clock at the cemetery. They were inside the office.

"You've had a busy morning," Daniel said.

"You, too, I would imagine. These notices should be posted up and down Main Street by now. We'll see who shows up."

"Not many will. The men she knew will be too embarrassed."

"You'll show up, and so will I." Grace had decided not yet to mention the letters Ivan Coaker had tried to sell her, and not the two she had burned.

"Well," Daniel said, "if you hadn't paid for her burial, I would have. Thank you, Mother."

"How did Tony take this morning?" Grace asked.

"Like a man. I think it hit Lon a little harder. Happens when you lose a friend."

"The way Annie's death hit you?" Grace hesitated before

adding, "Daniel, that was out of line. I have no business questioning you."

"Feel free," Daniel said. "I haven't lied to you yet."

Grace drew her breath and posed her question. "Did you take the deputy's gun into town last night?"

"Parker's pistol? I never saw it after I tossed it outside when Dave left the house."

Grace drew her breath in slowly. "Okay, we have to assume Dave did take it with him."

Daniel nodded and lit one of his cigars. "I told Louella about Dave. I figured she should know."

"I suppose," said Grace.

"It might get her out of that damned bed and on her feet."

"You're not patient with others, Daniel. About Annie Pyle, I know I asked this before and you told me, but how much contact did you keep with Annie after you and Ruth married?"

"You don't trust me either."

"It's not that," Grace said. "I love you, Daniel. I want to make sure our family's safe."

"Did Ivan Coaker say something to you?"

"He believes you kept in touch with his wife."

"I told you the truth," Daniel said, irritably, "as far as any relationship went. I did see her outside Amanda Hopper's on occasion. We didn't try to hide from anybody. But I rarely spoke to Annie after I met Ruth. When I did, she listened. She was a better listener than my wife. That's all there was to it. I've done some foolish things, Mother, but not what Ruth or Ivan Coaker thinks."

"Thank you, Daniel," Grace said simply.

Daniel sighed as his face reddened slightly. "I told you I was a damn fool. I admit to writing short letters to her. No, not love letters. At least I never thought of them that way. I don't know the exact number of times. Annie was—nice—to me, and I guess I didn't want to lose that. She wrote some letters to me, too, but I destroyed them."

"Since you got married?" asked Grace.

Daniel nodded. "Yeah. And guess what? She thanked me for our friendship. She said she'd never do anything to hurt me. I believed her. Our meetings were strictly business. Do I think Annie loved me? I doubt it. I don't think she loved any one man except for what he might do for her. I swear to you, Mother, I didn't touch her since Ruth and I married. I can't blame you if you don't believe me."

"Hell," Grace said, "I believe you."

"Ruth doesn't," Daniel said glumly.

At the house, Tony's sleep turned into fitfulness. He began dreaming and tossing. Finally he opened his eyes suddenly, remembered where he was and sat up on the side of the bed. He knew it was late afternoon because of the sun having moved past his open window. The breeze seemed cool on his bare skin.

Tony got up and put on fresh clothes. Somebody, Agatha or Carter, had cleaned the mud from his shoes and brought them back inside his room to set them beneath the open window to dry. They still were damp. He took his other pair from the closet and put them on. After brushing his hair back with his hands he went next door to his mother's room.

She was awake, seated up in bed against pillows on the backrest, wearing her nightgown. A book of Elizabeth

Barrett Browning's poetry lay open on her lap. She had been staring out toward the window of the room but looked at Tony when he came in. She smiled and reached out a hand for a touch greeting.

Tony pulled a chair from her dressing table closer and sat beside her bed.

"Daniel told me this morning," his mother said slowly. "I dreamed it last night."

Tony felt relieved. He hadn't known how to broach the subject of his father's death.

"My fault," his mother said.

Now why would she say something like that? Tony shook his head. He still didn't know what to say.

"Did you and Daniel and Lon Shirley bury him?"

Tony nodded.

"But not at the county cemetery?"

Tony nodded.

His mother drew a breath. One hand fluttered up to her breast. "You didn't know him," she said.

Tony shook his head.

"I don't know how Mother feels. She didn't come in this morning. She usually does for a minute or two."

Tony didn't know what to say.

"Did he do what people said he did?"

It was a change of subject that Tony was glad for. He said, "No. Annie Coaker got killed by somebody else. Lon said he would never do anything like that."

The hand at his mother's breast trembled slightly. She lowered it back to place on the book open on her lap. "I hope Lon is right."

They were silent for a long minute.

Tony said, "Did you—?" He wasn't sure how to finish the question, or even if he should. Finally he blurted it out: "Did you ever love my father?"

His mother frowned. "I—It seems like so long ago. I guess it wasn't really that long. I don't know how it happened, but—"

"But what?"

"No one approved. I had to sneak out to meet David. He seemed—so independent, sure of himself. I guess that's something I never felt." She shook her head. "I don't remember all that much now. I don't want to. As far as love, I don't know."

"Lon says you'd be better if you just faced up to things and moved on."

She scoffed. "Lon says."

"He might be right."

"I don't need somebody running a poolroom telling me what to do."

"I'm going to work with Lon at that poolroom," Tony said. "I'm going to stay with the job. It's what I want, Mother. You can help by making sure Grandmother Grace understands that. If I have to, I'll run away."

"Just like him," she muttered, more to herself. "Don't do that, Tony. You need your school and education. You have to think about your future."

"It's a long time off."

"Seems like it now," she said. "But you'll be older fast enough." She was quiet for another long moment. "All right, I'll talk to my mother about it. I promise."

36

By nine forty-five next morning a number of people who had seen the announcements were gathering at the county cemetery just outside the town limits of Vinton.

There were only a couple of automobiles, one of them belonging to the Blaisdell's, a few bicycles, and a couple of horses and buggies, plus the horse-drawn hearse belonging to the undertaker. Volunteers, at the undertaker's request, had carried Annie Pyle's coffin up the slight rise and placed it beside the freshly dug grave. Not far away two grimy caretakers had propped their shovels against headstones and sat down to observe.

Grace and Daniel sat in their car watching the onlookers. Tony and Lon, who had ridden with them from town, were climbing the incline. Earlier, Ruth had bicycled to the church. Unknown to her, Carter had followed on another bike. He now stood across the road from the small gathering. Ruth and her father, Reverend Caleb Jones, had not yet arrived in their buggy.

Daniel, dressed in his dark suit, white shirt and tie, said, “What do you think, Mother?”

“We'll see Annie's killer today,” Grace said, “if we're not already looking at him.” She wore a long, dark dress and a dark scarf.

“You're serious?”

“He'll be here,” Grace said. “He wouldn't miss this final triumph.”

The sheriff's car pulled in behind theirs. Abe Buckner, wearing a reasonably clean uniform and broad-brimmed hat, and the white-haired Judge Parks, dressed in a dark suit, got out and approached to the driver's side of the Blaisdell car. The sheriff peered in at Daniel and Grace and touched the brim of his hat in greeting. Judge Parks nodded to Grace, and she acknowledged him with a nod.

Buckner said, “I suspect you had something to do with this funeral today.”

“Everybody deserves a decent funeral,” Grace smiled.

“I agree,” Buckner said.

Judge Parks chuckled. “Miss Grace asked me to hurry the inquest, which I did. She didn't say why.”

Grace turned her smile onto the judge. “The Coaker brothers need money. Annie had a savings to release to them.”

“They always need money,” Judge Parks said.

Buckner motioned. “Even my deputy got hisself dressed up for this.”

They had already observed Deputy Orville Parker,

wearing an old suit and a string neck-tie and a bowler hat, walk up the hill.

"Did he know Annie before she was murdered?" Grace asked.

Buckner sighed. "That's a personal question you need to ask him. Lots of men in Vinton knew Annie." With the last statement, he looked directly at Daniel. "Just like lots of members of your family were in town the other night."

"Is that a fact?" Grace said, innocently.

"Sure is. Funny how something like a killing brings out witnesses. I was talking to people in shantytown. Seems like Daniel here was seen."

Daniel stiffened momentarily, and then relaxed.

"Then, of course, there was your nigger servant."

"Carter Foote is my friend," Grace said, firmly.

"Your ex-son-in-law, Dave Hunter. Who we still ain't found. And your grandson, Tony, with Lon Shirley."

"My, you got a list of suspects, Abe," Grace said. "How about including Carter's wife, Agatha, or Daniel's wife, Ruth?"

Buckner made a slight snorting noise. "No, Mrs. Blaisdell, nobody seen either of them. But I'm adding to my suspect list all the time. Of course, I figure lots of folks will pick on you and yours, Miz Grace, 'cause of your money. People get like that—jealous, sometimes. So I ain't saying I'm putting a lot of credence in it. Just collecting information."

"That's your job, Sheriff," Grace said. "Oh, I forgot. I heard that you yourself knew Annie quite well."

Buckner swallowed. "Not *really* well."

"Hah!" Grace said and looked off toward the road. "Ah, it looks like the minister's arrived."

Behind the sheriff's car, Reverend Caleb Jones and Ruth Blaisdell halted their buggy. Reverend Jones hobbled the horse while Ruth stood waiting for him. The minister was in somber black clothes. Ruth wore a pale dress that fell to her shoe-tops and a bonnet tied beneath her chin. She didn't look at Daniel or his mother. Both she and her father, with Bible clutched in hand, climbed the little hill toward the group gathered near the open grave.

"It's time, Daniel," Grace said, and they got out to follow Sheriff Buckner and Judge Parks up the incline.

The two of them stood back from the gravesite but within view of it. Closer to the plain wooden coffin stood Lon Shirley and Tony. Lon had his hand on Tony's shoulder as he looked around at the people gathered. Tony looked, too, but wasn't sure for what he was looking.

Tony saw the Baggets, father Harvey and son Henry, from the tavern, probably as well dressed as they had ever been. Both of them bore serious expressions. Not far from them stood Amanda Hopper. There was Deputy Orville Parker as well. And a few of the faces Tony recognized from shantytown, undoubtedly friends of Ivan Coaker. Ivan stood closest to the coffin and stood with his hands folded in front of him. Clifford Coaker was not to be seen, but that was expected if he was recovering from a knife wound. There were also some people Tony couldn't pin names to.

He looked at Lon's stern visage. "What're you mad at?"

"I ain't mad," Lon said, "just thinking."

"About what?"

"That the person who killed Annie is here, and we might be looking right at him."

"What makes you think so?"

"Just figuring," Lon said. "He would want to see if it looks like anybody suspects him."

"Lots of these men look like they're nervous."

"They do, don't they? Probably most of 'em knew Annie pretty well."

"How well?"

"Never mind," Lon said. He tightened his grip on Tony's shoulder. "There's your grandma and uncle. The sheriff and both his deputies are here, and the judge. Makes you wonder what would happen if some crime was committed in town about now."

Then he squeezed Tony's shoulder as the Reverend Caleb Jones was handed the Bible with a page marked by a ribbon from his daughter. The minister opened the Bible, lowered his head, read from the Book of Psalms and then announced that everyone should pray.

Tony observed most of the other people bowing their heads, except for his grandmother and Uncle Dan and Harvey and Henry Bagget. He saw Amanda Hopper give a little smile and wink to Henry Bagget, and Henry quickly averted his eyes. Tony looked sideways and up quickly at Lon and saw his friend's eyes sweeping the gathering.

Reverend Jones began his eulogy. It was brief and very general, emphasizing the hope that God will open the gates of heaven to this young woman they are about to bury. He said nothing about Annie's life, but mentioned that her survivors did include a husband and brother-in-law. He concluded with another prayer and a quotation of "ashes to ashes, and dust to dust," followed by a loud "Amen."

Men returned their hats to their heads. Tony saw that Grandmother Grace's eyes were as sweeping and observant as Lon's at the dispersing group.

37

Now what's on your mind?" Tony asked. He had walked with Lon back into town to stop outside the poolroom.

"Just going to tell Benny Smith to stick around a little longer. I want to talk to a few people again."

Tony made a wry face. "Benny's getting more work in the poolroom then we are."

Lon laughed. "You can stay here with him and run things. What I gotta do will be boring for you."

"No, I'm sticking with you. You can't cut me out now. Want me to saddle Old Bill?"

"We're not leaving town, so we can walk."

Tony waited outside in the bright sunlight until Lon rejoined him. First, they crossed the street to the bank.

Lon asked if he might speak with Daniel Blaisdell, and one of the clerks went into Daniel's office to get him.

Daniel, still in his dark suit but minus his coat right

now, came out and nodded to Lon. "Think the funeral was satisfactory?" he asked.

"Appropriate," Lon said. "Question for you, Daniel, but I don't know if you'll answer me."

"Ask."

"How much money does Annie's account hold?"

Daniel smiled but shook his head. "No, I can't answer that."

"I understand. Enough to make it worthwhile to kill her?"

"You're thinking of Ivan Coaker and his brother Clifford."

Lon nodded.

Daniel leaned in closer. "Just between us, I think ten dollars, or even less, might be enough for Ivan to consider murder."

Lon smiled, too. "Your mom here?"

"In her office," Daniel said. "She won't give out confidential information either."

"No, I wouldn't expect her to. Give her my regards."

Tony and Lon walked Main Street for a block and a half and then turned into *Bagget's Saloon*.

"I thought we was finished here," Tony said.

Lon went to the bar and nodded to Henry Bagget, who still had his white shirt and tie on.

"My ol' man's upstairs," Henry said, "getting out of his Sunday clothes."

"Got one question for you, Henry," Lon said. "Since we last spoke, I found out you were even visiting Annie Coaker in shantytown. She must have had you by the short ones."

"I got nuthin' to say on that subject," Henry said.

"I'll chalk it up to true love on your part. You gotta be smarter than letting yourself get seen by upstanding citizens. And in front of Coaker's house. Either he didn't care, didn't see you, or he figured you were padding Annie's bank account."

"Fuck off, Lon."

"Because if you were padding Annie's bank account, Ivan would figure it was gonna be his money, too," Lon said. "I figured since you were close to Annie you'd want kept up to date. Kind'a makes you wonder if Sheriff Buckner knows anything about it yet, or has even considered you a suspect. It won't be hard for him to get the same information I got."

"What the fuck do you want, Lon? You trying to shake me down?"

"No, I don't want your money, Henry. I want you to tell me who else Annie was blackmailing. One of her victims turned mean on her and shot her."

Henry squinted at Lon. "I said fuck off. Dave Hunter killed Annie. Everybody knows he screwed her every chance he got. She just said no one time, and that done it for him. There ain't no other suspects."

"Does your wife know you were fucking Annie on the side?"

"Lon, I'm gonna come across this counter and beat the shit out of you."

"You might try," Lon said. "Why don't you just tell me how much money you gave her? I know Myrtle, so I can ask your wife."

Henry wet his lips with his tongue. "Stay away from Myrtle. We don't need this kind of trouble."

"You were visiting Annie at Amanda Hopper's place."

For a moment Henry Bagget drew deep breaths. Then his countenance softened. He said, "I knew Annie. But so did most men in this town one time or 'nother. I might'a give her a few dollars. Girl in her line expects it. But I didn't hate her enough to murder her. Now can I have your word, Lon? You won't go saying nothing to Myrtle?"

"For the time being," Lon said. "Unless I find out you did kill Annie."

Lon went upstairs. Tony trailed after him, still not sure what Lon was trying to do this second time around.

Tony asked softly, "How did you know he was visiting Annie at Amanda Hopper's place?"

"I didn't," Lon said. "I just took a shot."

Harvey Bagget opened the door at Lon's knock and let him and Tony inside.

"Seen you at the funeral today," Harvey said. "You, too, kid."

"Same at you." Lon remained standing, hooking his right thumb in his belt at the front. "Harvey, were you fucking Annie too?"

Harvey laughed. "Thanks for the compliment, Lon Shirley. Wish I could say yes."

"Then it's no?"

"That's my story, and I'm sticking to it. 'Tween us men, I might'a tried a time or two, but I hate getting laughed at by these young bitches. She wasn't above accepting money for the effort."

"How much did you pay?"

"Not much." Harvey shrugged. "Pocket money is all I ever give 'er. Like I said, I didn't like her snickering at us older guys. But she sure was a good looker. And she had a way, not a mean way either, of teasing you—kind of flirty if you know what I mean."

"How much did Henry give her?"

"Ask him."

"He's not cooperating," Lon said.

"Hell, Lon, you know why. Myrtle might be a fat little woman but she'd kick his ass around the block and take everything he's got, not that it's all that much. Why are you still after this?"

"To get at what really happened," Lon said. "I kind of think Annie wasn't only accepting money for favors granted. I think she got into somebody who can't afford to be exposed and was milking him."

"Blackmail," Harvey said and stroked his grizzled chin. "Yeah, I can see her doin' that if she thought she'd get away with it. Looks like she didn't get away with it, don't it?"

"Still think Dave Hunter killed her?" Lon asked.

Harvey shook his head. "I can't imagine Annie trying to squeeze money out of Hunter. I never knew him to have much. But the sheriff thinks he's the most logical suspect. Abe says the motive could've been passion, not profit."

"Your son's got his wife to consider. Maybe he couldn't take the squeeze."

"Henry's made a lot'a mistakes," Harvey said. "Maybe that one, too. I don't keep tabs on him, Lon. It is possible Henry got fed up with paying Annie Pyle and killed her."

"Or a devoted daddy could've killed her for him," Lon said.

Harvey scoffed. "I generally let him take care of his own problems."

"Do you know anybody else Annie was seeing?"

"You already asked me that," Harvey said. "No, but if I did I wouldn't tell you just to spread gossip. I don't recall that I owe you a hell of a lot, Lon Shirley."

Lon nudged Tony from the room and shut the door behind him.

38

Lon steered Tony into Amanda Hopper's place once more. It was a little past noon, and the dining room was about a third full, a few couples there but mostly single men who traveled on business for a living. The food smelled good to Tony.

Lon asked for Amanda, and it wasn't long before she came out wiping her hands on a kitchen towel. She stood at the table and smiled down at them.

"Lunch?" she asked. "Got fried chicken today, or maybe some leftover beef stew that can be heated. You get mashed potatoes and corn with it."

"Hungry?" Lon asked Tony, and Tony shook his head. "Cup of coffee for me, Amanda."

"Two coffees coming up," Amanda said and went away.

"She's more cheerful today," Tony said.

"She has to be. Because of the customers."

"Lon, I don't think you're gonna find out anything you didn't already know."

"Very possible," Lon said, looking around at the other customers. "I don't know any of these people."

"Do you think you should?"

Lon smiled and shook his head. "I suppose I could ask every single man in here if he knew Annie Pyle, but Amanda would have me arrested for bothering her people."

Amanda brought two mugs of coffee to the table and set them down. "You just here for my good coffee?" she asked Lon.

"Couple of questions about Annie."

"Lon, I'm busy in the kitchen."

"This won't take long, Amanda. We saw you at the funeral this morning."

"Least I could do for the poor girl."

"Who was Annie's secret boyfriend?"

Amanda half-smiled. "I told you I don't know."

"Would you tell me if you did know?"

Amanda shrugged.

"See? If he's really got some money," Lon said, "you probably wouldn't. You might even want a piece of it for yourself." He held up a defensive hand. "No need to get pissed at me, Amanda. I ain't criticizing you. I mean, if Annie got some, why shouldn't you for keeping his name quiet? I kind'a figure that's one reason you were at the funeral today. You wanted to see her boyfriend, consider if there might be something in it for you if you play it just right. But you got to be careful. You see, if he was the one who shot her, he wouldn't be above killing you, too. I imagine you thought of all that."

Amanda chuckled. "You trying to give me ideas, Lon?"

Lon made an eyebrow shrug. "I said I ain't criticizing. But you got to be careful. He might not be so easy to bargain with. That's all I'm saying. The sheriff and his deputies carry guns all the time. Other men got access to 'em. Since your husband died, you ain't got a man to defend you. What happens if you piss him off?"

Amanda took the kitchen towel from her shoulder and snapped it between her hands. "Coffee's on the house, Lon," she said and left.

"That was smart," Tony said. "You made her mad."

"Maybe I stirred it up too much with her. Amanda's okay people." Lon drank some coffee and stood. "Let's go."

Tony sighed and stood up.

Outside, in the sunlight, Lon said, "Whoever got close enough to Annie to send her running and shoot her in the back had to be welcomed by Annie."

"What?" asked Tony.

"Annie didn't think she was in danger or she would'a raised one hell of a ruckus. It was somebody she considered harmless."

"With a gun in his hand?"

"He probably didn't show her the gun at first," Lon said. "By the time he pulled it, Annie guessed what was on his mind and tried to run."

"Let me guess," Tony said. "You're going to the sheriff's office again."

"Smart kid."

Tony trailed, first beside, then a bit behind him along Main Street. They went into the Sheriff's Office and saw Abe Buckner sitting behind his desk. Tony followed Lon inside.

Buckner looked up at Lon and barely gave Tony a glance. He nodded his hello.

"What'd you think of the funeral service, Abe?" Lon asked.

"Okay," Buckner said. "More people than I expected."

"Her murderer was among 'em. He wanted to know if anybody suspected him."

"That's a big jump in guesswork, Lon." Buckner took a cigarette from his desk drawer and lit it. He drew and exhaled. "What is it you want?"

"I think most, if not all, of the men at the funeral had very close relationships with Annie."

"It's certainly possible," Buckner conceded.

"I heard you were one of them, Abe."

Buckner sat up straighter. "Where did you hear that?"

Tony, with a puzzled expression, looked quickly at Lon.

"Asking questions," Lon said, mildly. "Some people talk."

"Some people are full of shit, too," Buckner said. "Is that all you want? To ask me if I was fucking Annie Pyle?"

"It's a start," Lon said. "Hey, your two deputies were. All you men are single, not that that would matter to Annie. Were you giving her money?"

Buckner's eyes narrowed. He slowly shook his head.

"She was getting it from somebody—and not Dave Hunter. He didn't have any."

Buckner considered and nodded. "You're probably right. And I don't doubt she was squeezing money from her men. Men pay for their pleasure. That won't take Hunter off the hook. Could be that's the reason he snapped and killed her—the fact that he couldn't pay what she wanted. It makes sense to me."

"How about deputies Meyer and Parker?"

"What about 'em? I can't vouch for where they spend every penny, and I can't swear they weren't nailing Annie as often as they could. She would've had something to say about it. What does your anonymous source tell you?"

Lon nodded. "They visited her at Amanda's place. So did you. Real hush-hush, I understand. As the county sheriff, you don't want to get a reputation of using local prostitutes."

"That's why I want to know who told you this shit."

"Can't tell you that," Lon said. "Just wanted to let you know the drift of the wind, Abe. You might want to check on Meyer and Parker for the night Annie was killed."

"That's my business," Buckner said. "Why are you making any of this your business?"

Lon nodded toward Tony. "For this kid. I don't want him growing up with people thinking his daddy was a murderer."

"That kid ain't gonna have any trouble in life," the sheriff said. "He's a Blaisdell."

"His name's Hunter," Lon said.

Lon and Tony left the sheriff's office and stepped outside.

"You lied to him," Tony said. "I never heard the woman say anything about Sheriff Buckner visiting Annie."

"You're right," Lon said. "I wanted to see his reaction."

"What did you see?"

"That he lied, too. He was visiting Annie sometimes."

39

Grace tapped on the door lightly and entered her daughter's darkened bedroom. Though it was late afternoon, the sun was still bright outside but muted by the heavy curtains. Grace stepped over and opened the curtains.

Almost as on a signal, the recently installed cast iron radiator issued a clanging sound as though someone had rapped it with a wrench. She turned and saw Louella sitting up, propped against a pillow, an unopened book in her lap, watching her.

"You need some brightness—some sun," Grace said. She nodded at the radiator. "These damn things make noises, don't they."

Louella didn't respond.

Grace looked at her daughter. "I guess it's worth it to have heat in every room." She approached the bed. "Please come down for dinner tonight. We haven't had a meal as a complete family for some time."

"I'm not hungry, Mother."

"You can sit with us and talk to us."

"I already told Agatha she can bring me some soup later."

Grace sighed and pulled a chair closer to the bed. "I've failed you terribly, haven't I?"

Louella looked away. "Nothing's your fault."

But that's not altogether true, Grace thought. Poor child, you never had much of a chance in life. How much of it was due to my stubborn pride, and how much was out of my control? So many things I might've done differently. Why wasn't I thinking straight when it all started?

In the fall of 1871, son Daniel had been three years old at the time. Grace worked at the bank, learning the business, beside her aging husband, Darwin James Blaisdell. Carter and Agatha Foote were in charge of taking care of the house and of young Daniel. And that fateful afternoon was etched in stone in Grace's memory.

She had left the bank early, told her husband that she was stopping at the general store to pick up two special orders that had been shipped down from Chicago, collected their buggy and horse from the livery stable, and parked them outside the store on a mostly empty Main Street. D. J. Blaisdell had told Grace that he would see her at the house, that he didn't mind walking home.

When Grace came out of the store with the two wrapped boxes, one under each arm, she paid little attention to three men, one huge and two average in size, huddled near the rear of her buggy. Their backs were to her. She put in the packages and climbed onto the buggy seat. What was she thinking about at the time? Probably the contents of the mail-order. Matching fur coats for her and her husband that he had arranged secretly to buy, although he hadn't been able to keep that secret from her.

Before she realized what was happening, one of the three men had vaulted into the seat beside her. She felt the sharp point of a blade against her throat.

"Don't yell," the voice, somewhat familiar, told her. "Don't look around. You do, and you'll be dead before anybody can get here to help you."

Grace felt the buggy sag under the weight of the other two men who climbed in back. "Look at her fancy clothes," a high-pitched voice behind her said, followed by a giggle. "I bet there's something valuable in these packages, too. Who'd 'a thunk it, Jess?"

Now Grace did look over at the man beside her, the one holding the knife. He grinned at her. Jess Simson. She hadn't seen him in many years, not since the day he had fled after killing a man with a pitchfork.

Normally not given to expletives, Grace said, "Shit!"

Jesse laughed. "Go real slow," he told her. "Head on out of town, Gracie. Toward the railroad tracks but not to the station."

Grace urged the horse forward as commanded. Silently, she cursed to herself. They passed the bank, Lon Shirley's poolroom, even the combined sheriff's office and fire department. A dozen times she thought about leaping from the buggy and running for help. But something stopped her. Since then, she had never been able to discern what it was, or if it was anything more than her stubbornness.

At the edge of town she risked craning around to look at the other two men.

One, the small and wiry one, was ugly and scarred across his forehead topped by unruly blond hair. He leered at her through rotten, yellowed teeth. The other man was very big, almost a giant to Grace's way of thinking, with a round face and blank expression, lips slightly parted, and appeared not to be paying much attention to anything. He wore a floppy hat pulled down on his head.

Jess Simson hadn't changed much in appearance except for the gray in his hair. He had the same smirk that she had become familiar with years past, also the same arrogance in his manner. And the same whiskey breath. But he was holding the knife steady against her skin.

All of the men wore frayed work clothes, heavy shirts and trousers, of various colors, and work shoes. The shoes on the giant's feet had the soles pulling apart from the tops and stocking toes sticking out.

"These are my friends," Jess said. "We travel together. The little one there is Nelson. Big guy we call Bubba. Don't even know his real name or if he remembers. He ain't bright, but he is strong."

"How did you know I was in Vinton?" Grace asked, coolly.

"Didn't," Jess said. "We wandered in, spent our last coins in the saloon, and happened to see you stop this buggy and go in the store. We's passing through. I said, 'Hey, fellas, guess what? That's my wife there. Look how she's all cleaned up.'"

Nelson giggled and said, "Yeah."

"So you got money," Jess said. "That's plain to see. You

done all right for yourself, Gracie. Lemme have a look in that purse."

Grace didn't protest when Jess picked up her purse in his free hand and opened it with his teeth. He dumped the contents in back close to Nelson and told him to check it out.

Nelson whistled through his rotten teeth. "Hey, there must be close to forty dollars here. We hit the mother lode."

Jess grinned. "That'll buy a lot of whiskey. Let's see that ring on your finger, Gracie."

Not looking at him, she extended her left hand across to him. He looked at the wide gold band and said, "I don't wanna hafta cut you, so hold real still while I work this off."

It took a couple of minutes but he got it twisted free of her ring finger and put it into his shirt pocket. "That oughta sell for a few bucks."

"Take what you want," Grace snapped. "Then get the hell away from me."

"Nelson, check out those packages."

Grace heard the ripping and tearing of the wrapping paper.

"Shit!" Nelson said and giggled again. "Two of the finest fur coats you ever seen. That'll keep us warm next winter, Jess."

"Warm, my ass," Jesse said. "We sell 'em soon as we can."

"Whatever you say," Nelson said, grumpily.

"Okay, you've got everything," Grace said. "Now get out and let me go home."

"Not so fast, Gracie," Jesse told her. "Take it to the right up here."

They were nearing the railroad tracks and station. Grace

didn't see anyone around. To the right, couple of hundred yards from the station, was a spur on which sat two empty boxcars with their side doors open.

"Hey, we seen these earlier," Nelson said.

Jesse nodded. "Park your buggy over by that front one, Gracie. Take it nice and easy. Don't spook the horse. You guys get out and look inside. Make sure nobody's here."

Nelson and Bubba got down obediently and peered inside the leading boxcar. They looked at Jesse, and Nelson shook his head.

"Hop down, Gracie," Jesse said. "In there you go."

"You son of a bitch," Grace said. "What are you thinking?"

Jesse pricked her skin at the side of her neck with his knife. "Do it, girl, or the next one goes in deeper."

Grace got down. At that point she realized she had made a mistake not trying to flee back inside Vinton. The chance of anybody seeing her plight here was very slim. Shuddering, she allowed herself to be pushed ahead of Jesse to the open boxcar.

The floor was dirty and smelly with filthy straw in small piles. At Jesse's command, Bubba took Grace under her arms and lifted her up and inside. Jesse and Nelson hopped up. Bubba climbed in last.

Grace's breath caught in her throat. "What are you doing?"

"Gonna have a little fun," Jesse grinned. "Guys, who wants to go first?"

Grace tried to run for the opening. Jess hit her high on her right cheekbone with his fist, knocking her down.

Her head spinning, she was barely aware of Jess and Nelson dragging her deeper inside and pinning her to the dirty floor of the boxcar. Jess used his knife to cut away her clothing. He shredded it and discarded it while Nelson and Bubba held Grace down. In just a few minutes she was stark naked.

Jesse laughed. "Go for it, guys."

Nelson looked uncertain. "She's your wife, Jess. You should go first."

"Naw, I had so much of this years ago I don't need no more. It's old stuff to me. You boys take your turns."

"You animal!" Grace screamed at Jesse. "You lying son of a bitch. Tell 'em the truth! You never had me—not once! You're not able. You're not even a man."

That's when Jesse started beating and kicking her, in the face and sides, back and legs. He put his knife away and pinned her shoulders down. "Bitch!" he said. "C'mon, guys! Git on it. Take turns holding her legs apart."

"Okay, I'll go," Nelson said and giggled.

Every time Grace found her reeling senses returning and tried to fight back, Jesse released her with one of his hands and beat her in the face and throat with his fist. She couldn't speak for the bile and blood in her mouth. She passed out.

She came to barely enough to realize that Nelson had finished with her and was backing off to hold her spread legs. Then she felt the weight of Bubba, naked from his waist down to his old shoes, pressing upon her and felt his entry. He still hadn't made a sound. She heard Jesse whoop with delight. Then he hit her again, and she was swept into unconsciousness.

What happened after that had to be related to her by Carter Foote.

40

"Mister Lon!"

Lon Shirley looked up from behind his counter in the poolroom to the tall black man in the open doorway. Lon had only one customer with whom he was swapping lies inside at the time, a slow afternoon,. When he saw the expression on Carter Foote's face, he came around the counter to speak with the man.

"Miss Grace is gone," Carter said. "Something bad might've happened to her."

"What do you mean 'gone?'"

"Mr. Blaisdell came home a little while ago, walked from the bank, and asked about his wife. Agatha and I hadn't seen her. I checked the barn, and her buggy wasn't there. I told Mr. Blaisdell she probably stopped to visit someone because I didn't want him to worry. I came into town fast as I could since he said she was stopping at the general store. They remembered her leaving with a couple of packages but didn't see her after that. Folks don't talk to me. You know that. But the livery guy said she picked up her buggy and left. That was before she stopped at the store. So the horse and buggy are missing, too."

"We'll find her, Carter," Lon said. He looked around at his single customer. "Get out! I'm closing for a while." After he locked his door, he turned again to Carter. "I'll stop everybody I see and ask. She stands out in this town, so somebody's bound to'a seen something. They'll talk to me. We might need transportation."

"I'll take care of that," Carter said. "I'll get us a couple of horses."

By the time Lon had made inquiries, Carter returned from the house and stable with two saddled mares, riding one and leading the other. In a sheath at the side of his saddle he had stuck his double-barreled shotgun. He saw Lon eying it.

"Hope I'm being silly," Carter said. "But I'd rather have it if the need should rise. Did you learn something?"

Lon nodded before he went back inside his poolroom and upstairs to his apartment. He returned with his own shotgun and eyed the horse that Carter had been leading. "I hope he's gentle," Lon said.

"He's a she," Carter told him, taking the gun handed up to him. "Tell me."

Lon pulled himself up onto the saddle and pointed. "Couple of people saw her with three men, one beside her on the buggy seat and the other two in back. They know Grace on sight, but they'd never seen the men before." He took his shotgun back from Carter and held it in the crook of his right arm across his lap. "Said the men looked like hobos or bums. They left town in that direction."

Carter's eyes followed Lon's pointing finger. "Nothing out that way 'cept the railroad station."

"We'll start there. Maybe they passed somebody else."

"I don't like it," Carter said as they urged the horses along at a steady walking pace. "She won't have anything to do with bums."

Lon laughed to ease his inner tension. "You mean like me?"

Carter smiled, too. "You're not a bum, Mr. Shirley."

"Carter, you can cut out the 'mister' crap."

They passed the sheriff's office, and Carter considered if they should inform the sheriff or one of his deputies right away. He saw that Lon wasn't slowing down with the same thought, so he continued keeping his mount a few yards back.

In a few minutes they were at the rail yard. They looked for signs of buggy tracks and found some, then followed them. The trail led around a small bend to a spur from the railroad that had two darkened, but open-sided, boxcars sitting on it. Near the door of the forward boxcar were the horse and buggy.

Carter and Lon dismounted carefully, took their shotguns, and approached slowly from the side. When they were sure there were no men waiting, Carter jumped up into the boxcar, and Lon clambered up behind him.

They found Grace inside. She was huddled on the hard floor, totally naked, covered with blood and dirty straw.

Carter and Lon knelt beside her. Carter gently brushed some of the straw away as Lon felt for a pulse.

Lon expelled his breath. "She's alive, at least for now."

"Sons of bitches," Carter growled. "Look how they beat the poor girl."

Neither man said what he obviously knew to be true. That Grace had been brutally raped. The only movement about her was an occasional twitching of her arms or legs, not much but enough to indicate she might be heading into shock. Once her lips trembled without sound. Her eyes remained tightly pinched shut.

"How bad?" Carter asked softly.

"Hard to tell," Lon said. "She's got some broken bones—ribs, cheek, maybe some other places we can't see. Carter, you need to go for Doc Harris. I'll stay with her."

Carter looked quickly and hard at Lon. "He's more likely to come if you ask him."

"He'll come when you tell him who needs him."

"Please, Mr. Shirley. And hurry."

Lon was the one who rode hard back into town. He tied his horse to the white picket fence outside the doctor's house, bounded onto the porch, and pounded on the door. The woman who opened up for him was Doc Harris's wife, receptionist, and nurse. She listened when Lon told her, and then called the doctor to the front door. He listened.

"I'll get my horse," he said. "Where do I meet you?"

"We'll go together," Lon told him.

Five minutes later both men were headed out toward the railroad yard. They dismounted behind Grace's buggy, and Doc Harris tied his horse to the back. Lon had to help him up inside the dark boxcar. Lon and Carter stood back as the doctor made his preliminary examination. He got up and blew out a long breath.

"I hope she can live," he said. "She'll need looking after. We got to get her into my house. I got an extra bedroom there."

"No," Carter said. "Take her home, Doctor. Blaisdell's house. People there will keep their mouths shut."

"You saying Mrs. Harris or I will gossip?"

"No, but he's right," Lon put in. "If you tend to her at your place, it's bound to get around. She won't want people either looking at her like she done something wrong or feeling sorry for her. She's a fighter, Doctor. Help her. I'm sure Mr. Blaisdell will spare no expense."

Doctor Harris considered and nodded. "Okay, you men will have to assist me with getting her into the back of her buggy. We need to cover her with something."

"I found this," Carter said. He held up a long fur coat that looked like somebody had stuck a knife in it and maliciously ripped it. It had streaks and stains of blood on it. "It's one of the things she picked up at the store. Both empty boxes are out there in the back of the buggy."

"Let's carry her out," the doctor said.

After they carefully deposited the trembling Grace into the back of the buggy and covered her with the stained fur coat, and had the doctor's horse tethered to the rear, Dr. Harris climbed up front and turned the conveyance back toward town. He looked back and called, "You coming?"

"Soon," Carter said. When the doctor was out of sight,

he turned to Lon. "I looked. They didn't leave anything else behind. They can't have got too far."

Lon agreed. "They didn't take the horse and buggy. Mean's they're likely on foot."

"They didn't want to take a chance getting seen with Mrs. Blaisdell's buggy," Carter said. "I thank you for your help, Mr. Shirley. You can go back to your place now, and I'll be along shortly."

"You're not going after them alone," Lon said. "We don't know how they're armed."

"I'll do something about it," Carter said.

"We both will, and we're wasting time arguing."

"They might've already jumped on a train," Carter said, glumly. "I hope not."

Lon shook his head. "East and west freights come through here twice a day, in the early morning and 'bout noon. Eastbound stops two miles up the track at the water tank. That's where guys wait to pile on. They jump off at the edge of the yards in Elston because Elston's got a couple bulls in uniform on the lookout for hobos. So they're either waiting at the water trough or hiking on foot. The descriptions we got of our guys don't make that seem likely."

"Unless they've gone the other way to wait for the westbound freight," Carter said.

Again Lon disagreed. "The west train doesn't slow down until it's in Illinois, and I think they'd wanna grab the first one, which heads to Elston. Anybody wanting to go west from here jumps on when it slows outside our station. The sheriff sometimes has a deputy on hand to watch for freeloaders."

"Then we head east," Carter said.

41

On horseback, even though keeping the animals at a leisurely pace, the two men made better time than anyone could have on foot. Carter and Lon watched the almost invisible trail carefully, looking to both sides to see if there was any evidence of somebody cutting off into the woods. But that would have slowed walkers down even more.

Less than half an hour later they emerged into a clearing alongside the curving track and saw the water supply in the distance. The spout was lifted and tied back against the wooden bowl of the tank, making the object look like a fat teapot.

"Might be police here," Carter said.

Again Lon disagreed. "We just crossed the county line. Unless the railroad hires cops, nobody's gonna come this far from Elston to catch a few hobos. And they won't bother us anyway. We're on horseback. They won't figure we'll leave our horses just to take a little train ride."

Carter saw that Lon was peering intently toward some woods on the other side of the tracks. He asked.

Lon said, "We got eyes on us. More'n one person over there."

They guided their horses to step across the tracks to the other side. Near a wood line an older man sat on a stump in front of a small fire, a blanket across his lap, his right hand out of sight beneath the blanket, his left holding a corncob pipe on which he puffed casually. The man wore the blue uniform pants of an infantry soldier with a simple work shirt and a felt shirt over that with the sleeves cut off, making it more of a vest. He had white hair and a white beard. He watched as Lon and Carter approached and dismounted.

Lon told him whom they were after and what they looked like.

"We're looking for three men," Lon said. "One is a big fella according to the description we got. The other two, I guess, average."

"What'd they do?" the man asked.

"Beat and raped a woman. She might not live."

"They was here," the older man said and made a vague motion with his pipe over his shoulder. "Went that way, back across the tracks in the direction you come from. They wanted to know when the next freight was heading east or west. You know 'em personally?"

"Not a bit," Lon said. "There's a boy over there watching us from behind a tree."

"My grandson," the old gentleman said. "I told him to go hide himself when I seen you coming. We travel around the country, see things, one place or 'nother. I git a little work when I can. We're pretty free. Them guys you want, they're dangerous, right? Must be if they raped a woman. Be careful of 'em."

"You might be lucky they didn't do anything to you," Lon said.

"Well, they might've tried." The old man grinned. "See my pack there? One 'a the little guys, the leader I think, wanted to know what I had in it. I told him nothing of value. He said to his two buddies, the real big one and the other little one, that they'd just have to look for themselves."

He shrugged and flipped his lap blanket aside. In his right hand he gripped a .44 caliber Navy Colt revolver that looked shiny and in excellent condition. It had been the preferred sidearm of many officers during the Civil War, both North and South.

"I showed 'em this, and they backed off in a hurry. Practically ran down toward the water tower. That's why I moved the boy and me out here in the open more, so nobody can sneak up on us."

Lon nodded at the pistol. "I doubt if anybody would want to."

"What're you gonna do when you find 'em?"

"They have to pay for their crimes," Carter said.

42

It was easy to spot the three men. The big one stood out like a giant, and draped over his shoulders was a twin to the fur coat Lon and Carter had wrapped around Grace. The big man's two companions were average height and on the wiry side.

There were other men gathered near the trees, several of them having started fires to ward off the early evening's growing chill, but they appeared to be loners or in their own particular small groups. And it didn't appear that they were exactly welcoming the three newcomers. Suspicion showed on their faces, just as it did when Lon and Carter approached and dismounted. The suspicious eyes rested on the shotguns in their hands. A few of the men stirred and made tentative moves toward the trees.

"Nobody's gonna hurt you," Lon announced. He nodded toward the three newcomers. "Them's the ones we want."

There appeared to be a bit of relaxation among some of the others.

Lon and Carter strode toward the three men. Lon motioned the shotgun toward the clearing near the tracks. "Let's step over here."

"Who the fuck're you?" one of the wiry men demanded. "We don't know you."

"We know you," Carter said. "You beat and raped a woman—maybe killed her."

"That's shit," said the small man, but his eyes suddenly darted side to side. "Leave us be."

Lon was staring straight at the big man. The big one stared straight ahead with vague eyes as though not comprehending any of it. He had a thick nose and broad mouth, huge hands and feet. Lon took this all in as he stepped forward suddenly.

He reversed the shotgun and rammed the butt squarely into the big man's face. The giant crumpled onto his knees, dazed but not unconscious.

The second small man started forward. "You hurt Bubba!"

"Empty your pockets!" Carter stepped forward, leveling his weapon. "Nice and slow."

The two smaller men complied. Carter saw a tiny bulge in the shirt pocket of the first small man and reached out to probe with his fingers. He withdrew Grace's wedding ring and nodded to Lon.

"I found that," the small man said.

"Your names?" Carter demanded.

"Why the fuck you wanna know? A nigger don't give me orders."

Carter shot the other small man's leg out from under him, dumping him in a writhing ball on the earth. The man was screaming loudly. When Carter and Lon looked around, they were alone with these men in the clearing. The other onlookers had faded into the woods.

"His name's Nelson," the first small man said quickly. "The big guy there's Bubba. He ain't bright, but he's strong as a bull."

"And you?"

The man swallowed. "Jess. Jess Simson."

"I've heard of you," Carter said, his eyes squinted.

"Look. Keep all our stuff. You can have the coat Bubba's got on, and that ring. Take the money we got out'a the purse. We just want to go."

Nelson twisted in agony on the ground, alternately moaning and crying out. He kept both hands clutched to his bloody, mangled leg below his knee.

"You were married to Grace a long time ago," Carter said to Jess Simson.

Jess let out a relieved sigh. "Yeah, right. See? We didn't do nothing wrong. The woman and I are still married. What's hers is mine."

Carter cocked the second barrel of his weapon.

Jess took a step backward, lifting both hands palms outward. "Now, look. I don't know who you are, but you got no business doing this. I said you can have this stuff back."

Lon had stepped to the horses and taken a coil of rope

from one of the saddles. He looked around and nodded to Carter before heading to the woods.

"Wait!" Jess Simson called after him. "You can't leave us here with this nigger. He's got a itchy finger. You're a white man. Give us a break."

Lon went into the tree line.

Jess licked his lips. "What's he doin'?"

"He's looking for a tree with a limb thick enough to hang you from," Carter said.

Jess turned and started to run. Carter fired his second barrel, knocking Jess's leg out from under him. Rolling in the dirt, Jess groaned. Close by, Nelson still wept and occasionally screamed. Carter broke the shotgun, plucked out the two empty shells, and reloaded. He snapped the gun together.

Bubba rocked on his knees with his ruined mouth and nose. Blood and teeth particles had dribbled out onto his beard. His eyes were still distant, his arms hung loosely at his sides.

Between groans, Jess Simson cried out, "You ain't the law! We want the law."

"You're getting it," Carter said. "Keep your mouths shut."

A few minutes later Lon Shirley returned from the woods.

"Found a good one," he told Carter. "I don't know how to make a hangman's knot but I got a noose made."

"It'll do," Carter said.

Jess Simson twisted in agony and focused on Lon. "Look,

mister, you're a white man. You can't let that black son of a bitch do this to us. We wanna see a sheriff."

Lon motioned with his shotgun. "Drag your sorry asses over here or I'll shoot you again. You'll just suffer that much more."

Nelson was weeping loudly and rolling in the dirt. One ragged pants leg was a sodden mass of blood. He dug his fingers into the ground and dragged himself forward. Jess Simson bit back his outcries and hitched himself in the direction Lon indicated. The big man, Bubba, got to his feet as though in a trance and plodded along after them. Carter brought up the rear, keeping his gun leveled at Bubba's broad back.

About thirty yards inside the thick woods they came to the tree that Lon had selected. A rope with noose was slung over a thick branch. Jess and Nelson, looking at it in horror, tried to hold back until Carter kicked both of them. Big Bubba stoically moved forward and knelt on the ground beneath the limb. Carter and Lon exchanged a look.

Lon put the loop over the big man's head and pulled back on it. As he had stated, he didn't know how to make a hangman's knot to break a neck. Strangulation would have to do. He and Carter propped their guns against the tree. Jess and Nelson wouldn't be able to get to them, and they wouldn't be running anywhere.

It took almost all of Lon's and Carter's combined strength to draw the rope tight and lift Bubba upward. Even at that, they couldn't get Bubba's feet clear of the ground. He had his knees folded and his toes dragging in the dirt. Lon and Carter heaved. The big man didn't raise his hands or protest.

His eyes bulged, and his mouth opened without a sound. He hung like that, dangling with knees just above the ground, not fighting at all. It took several minutes before his head dropped forward.

Lon stepped forward to check for a pulse. Bubba was dead.

Lon and Carter removed the noose from Bubba's neck and rolled him out of the way. They dragged Nelson, begging for mercy, forward to ensnare his neck. Jess watched in wide-eyed horror.

Carter whipped off Jess's belt in one snapping motion. He used it to bind Nelson's hands behind his back. Nelson stopped begging and started crying.

It didn't take nearly as much energy to hoist Nelson off the ground. Carter and Lon held onto the rope until the small man stopped fighting and twitching, and then held it another couple of minutes. When they lowered the man, he was dead.

Roughly, Lon dragged Jess over beneath the limb.

"Look!" Jess cried. "You're all wrong about me. That woman is my bitch. She's my wife. I got a right to beat her. Ask anybody." Lon looped the rope about Jess's neck.

"If you gotta do it, you do it!" Jess cried out to Lon. "Don't let him do it. Don't let no nigger hang me."

Carter tied the man's hands behind his back with his own belt.

"Please?" Jess said.

Carter and Lon hoisted the writhing man from the ground. They held him aloft several minutes. The wiry man's eyes bugged and his tongue protruded. His face went from red to purple. Finally, his legs ceased to twitch.

Carter and Lon lowered the body and removed the rope.

"Bury them?" Lon asked.

Carter shook his head. "I don't want to touch 'em."

"Seems like we should do something."

Carter relented. "We'll rope 'em behind the horses and drag them to the river. It'll do the rest."

Lon, trying to control his own shivering, nodded.

Carter looked off toward the woods and back in the direction of Vinton. He said, "Then we'll pray for Miss Grace."

43

It had taken a long time for Grace to wheedle the story from Carter. It didn't happen until she was out of danger and recovering, however slowly. The scars would always remain. Nothing the doctor could do about those. But on a daily basis, Dr. Harris came to the house to attend to Grace.

She couldn't remember much of that time, only bits and pieces. But the most pointed memory was the day she told Dr. Harris, and he confirmed it, that she was pregnant again. He asked her what she wanted to do about it, and she said she would talk to her husband.

D. J. Blaisdell, patting her brow and hand, listened to her that evening. He showed no outward emotion except concern for his wife. After moving thoughtfully to the window of her bedroom, he turned and nodded to her.

"This will be our second child," he said. "It's not the child's fault, and it's not yours. You just regain your strength and we'll be all right."

Grace broke down and cried.

She remembered how at first her young son, Danny, wasn't allowed to see her often in her room. He had been told, as was the general story, that his mother had fallen while horseback riding and got stepped on. Danny cried, but Agatha and Carter assured him his mother would be all right. She needed plenty of rest. Later, when she could move without a lot of pain, Danny was allowed in every day.

D. J. Blaisdell insisted on hiring more help at the house, two extra housekeepers to help Agatha, and two men to help Carter with the outside chores. Grace had suspected D. J. had done it for her protection as well. She never told her husband what Carter and Lon Shirley had done to the three men they had found, and she knew Carter never would tell him.

Carter was in to see her several times a day. He looked happier each time she appeared to be recovering. She confided to Carter about the child she was carrying, and Carter merely said, "Mr. Blaisdell is a good man."

He also told her that the first day of her trauma, when she was unconscious, that Lon Shirley had come to the house and asked permission to see her. D. J. agreed, and the doctor said for only a few minutes. Carter said that Lon had sat beside her bed and held her small right hand in both of his. When Carter tapped on the open door, Lon had placed her hand gently at her side and drew up her covers.

Downstairs, Lon and Carter did not talk about anything. Lon trudged away, back to town and his poolroom. Since that time, until the night Annie Pyle was murdered, Lon had not been inside Blaisdell House. Anytime he met Tony, to take the boy anywhere, he had waited outside on the porch.

Lon Shirley was not excluded by the family. A couple of times when he was waiting for Tony to join him in an early morning for squirrel or duck hunting, Daniel had come to the door and invited Lon inside for coffee or breakfast. Lon thanked him but said he had beef jerky and a jug of coffee with him.

Grace remembered all this as she now sat at her daughter's bedside, hoping and praying that Louella could gain the kind of strength the girl had never had. In her mother's presence, Louella drifted in and out of a slight, sometimes fitful, sleep. Grace wondered if Louella cared at all about living or dying.

44

Friday afternoons were generally slow at the *Billiards Emporium*. Most men went to work on Fridays at whatever work they could scrounge for no other reason than to collect a paycheck, however meager. Some dropped into the poolroom late in the afternoon, around five, for a game or two; others hit the bars; and a few conscientious fellows took their paychecks home to their wives.

Tony found Friday afternoon boring. He wanted Lon to keep him on into the evening, but Lon was adamant about Tony's leaving his work at five o'clock. No argument could prevail with the older man.

Shortly after five, while Tony was walking past the livery stable which was the last building at that edge of town before climbing the incline toward Blaisdell House, a figure detached itself from the shadows inside the wooden door and seized Tony's arm. At first Tony started to strike back until, with some shock, he recognized the man. He found himself staring into the pale, waxen face of a staggering Clifford Coaker. Coaker, his eyes bloodshot with tiny pupils, looked like a man wanting to bend forward with a stomachache.

"Where is he, kid? Where's your old man?"

"You shot him," Tony said, bitterly, and then immediately regretted saying it. Lon had told him never to mention that his father had been shot. "He's not around here anymore."

Clifford's features twisted into a look seeking comprehension. "No. I seen 'im—just a little while ago. I got outa bed and followed him into town. Now I don't see him. Is Lon Shirley hiding him?"

"You don't look so good," Tony said, looking at the dirty hand still gripping his arm.

"He ain't the only one messing with Annie behind Ivan's back. I talked to Annie. She said Dan was gonna come see her, that he'd bring her some money. That's what me an' Ivan want—the money. But where'd your old man get to?"

"I don't know. And Lon's not hiding him. You think he is, take it up with Lon."

"No. I got this back and forth hot fever and cold sweats. I don't know what's 'a matter with me. But I won't rest 'til I get Hunter. He stuck a knife in me."

Tony figured the man was crazy. "You that mad about Annie Pyle?"

Clifford had a half-coughing, half-choking fit. He released Tony's arm and straightened himself up with an effort. "Your uncle's gonna give her money. But she can be a real hell-raiser. Ivan an' me want the money. You see how it's gotta be ours."

"Uncle Dan ain't giving her money," Tony said.

"Sure he is. He wants them letters he writ to her. But, see, Ivan an' me got 'em hid. He was there, right near our house last night," Clifford said with an effort. "I come back from the river to get another jug an' I seen 'im. Kinda sneaking around, keeping in the shadows. It was him all right. Ain't the first time he's been lookin' in at Annie. I thought about askin' him if he was bringing money to us. But then I knew Ivan would wanna be the one to deal with him. So I went back and told Ivan."

"Last night?" Tony queried, certain the man was out of his senses now.

Clifford groaned, but drew himself upright again. "Listen. I'm gonna find your ol' man, that's for sure. He can hide, but I'll find 'im. So don't lie to me, kid."

"I'm not."

Clifford sucked in his breath as he blinked. "I better git back home 'fore Ivan gits there. He won't like that I gone out. He tol' me not to move around too much. I'll tell Annie not to tell him."

Clifford moved back into the shadows. Tony caught a glimpse of him a few seconds later as he stumbled out the back door of the stable. Then he was gone around the corner.

Letters? Uncle Dan wrote letters to Annie? Tony ran back to the poolroom and told Lon.

Lon nodded thoughtfully. "You're right, Clifford's gone nuts with his sickness. You steer clear of him and his brother. Don't believe anything they tell you. Main thing is, don't let 'em get near you or think they can use you some way. As for your Uncle Daniel, he's not dumb, Tony."

Tony shrugged. "He might be if he thought nobody'd ever find out. Clifford claims Uncle Dan's been there in shantytown lots 'a times looking in on Annie."

"Don't you worry 'bout it," Lon said, "Clifford's hallucinating." He gently shook Tony's shoulder. "Listen to me. You keep your distance from either of the Coakers if you see one. Always look around you. Ivan might be more predictable than his brother. Clifford might do anything. Promise me now, and keep your eyes open when you go home."

"Should I tell Grandma or Uncle Dan?"

Lon considered. "It's up to you. I can't tell you what you should do."

"What about those letters?"

Lon shrugged it off. "We don't know that there are any."

On second thought, once he got home, Tony decided he would keep the information to himself. He wondered how insane Clifford really was with his injury. He certainly was wrong on his dates about seeing Uncle Dan spying on Annie Pyle, so that meant he could be wrong about everything—which was what Lon surmised. But, to be honest, Tony wasn't sure how much Uncle Dan could be trusted. And the idea of letters out there somewhere intrigued him.

"Why don't they find out who really killed Annie?" he asked.

"Tony, I'm sure Sheriff Buckner is trying to do just that. Least I hope so."

"And if he's not? If he's already decided?"

Lon could only shrug at that.

Okay. If Lon Shirley's inquiries had hit a wall, then Tony would have to take it upon himself to do some investigating. So why not start at home where he might be able to gain more information without letting on to Uncle Dan that he was suspicious? The idea of letters was locked into his mind.

His Grandmother Grace got home earlier, as usual, and Tony caught her in the foyer to pose a question to her. "Does Uncle Dan always tell you the truth?"

Slightly bemused, Grace looked at him. "Well, as much as I can expect, I suppose. Where did you come up with a question like that?"

"I want to know what you really think," Tony said.

"Do I think your uncle is honest? I certainly do. Do I believe he tells me everything? I do not. Anymore than I believe you tell me everything that goes on at that poolroom and what you and Lon Shirley talk about. Did Lon say something to make you ask?"

"No," Tony said, grudgingly. "But it seems like everybody's willing to believe my father killed Annie Coaker, and nobody's doing anything about it."

"That's out of our hands, Tony. It's the sheriff's business."

"And he's not doing a thing."

Grace considered it. "We don't know what Abe Buckner is doing or what he thinks. And I don't like to see you unhappy. You got a birthday coming next week. You won't be a little boy anymore. We'll celebrate."

"Uncle Dan's not home yet. How about Aunt Ruth? Is she upstairs?"

"No. She said she was going for a walk." Grace tilted

her head at him. "Your mom's in her room. You should visit her."

"I will," Tony said. "I'll go up now. I want to change my shirt anyway."

His grandmother smiled in surprise. "Well, now," she said, "that's a first. I usually have to nag you to bathe and change clothes."

"Are you coming upstairs?" Tony asked.

"No, I'll stay here awhile. I might sit for a spell on the porch."

Tony went up. Stopping in to see his mother took only a moment. She was listless as usual, smiled at him from her bed, wanted to stroke his hand for a moment, and then allowed her eyes to drift closed.

Tony asked, "Do you think Uncle Dan's honest?"

His mother opened her eyes. For a second it looked as though she didn't understand the question. Then she smiled.

"Well, sure," she said.

"Did you know about him and the murdered woman, Annie Pyle?"

His mother was more careful in her response this time. "I heard that he was seeing her, but that was a long time ago."

"What if he killed her?"

"Your Uncle Dan? No."

What should Tony have expected? Of course his grandmother and mother would stick up for his uncle. Tony excused himself by telling her he was going to his room to clean up for dinner.

Instead he drew in his breath and entered Uncle Dan's

and Aunt Ruth's bedroom, his first time in there in longer than he could remember. He sensed a severe hopelessness to his mission, but he had to see for himself. Uncle Dan just might have kept some incriminating letters.

What would he do if he found them? Tony had no idea. Possibly he might want to turn them over to the sheriff. Lon Shirley seemed to have confidence in the sheriff. Tony wasn't even sure what letters exchanged between a man and woman might mean, if anything.

The closet was where he looked first, moving Uncle Dan's .22 rifle aside, and pulling a chair over to stand on it to peer at the upper shelf. Then it occurred to him that there probably would be no hiding place in the closet if Uncle Dan wanted to keep those letters out of Aunt Ruth's sight.

He went through the pockets of his uncle's suits, pants, and coats hung in the closet without success. He didn't bother with Aunt Ruth's garments.

Next, Tony searched beneath the mattress on the bed to no avail. Then his gaze settled on the small writing desk in the room. He tried the single middle drawer but it was locked. He did notice that the lock had been scratched as though someone had pried at it. Maybe Uncle Dan had forgotten his key, or lost it, and had to force his way into the drawer. Tony looked about the area but couldn't find a key. He stepped back and considered.

The gun that had killed Annie Coaker mystified him almost as much as the supposed letters. It was the same thing Lon Shirley had said.

Fact: the deputy's gun had been at the house that night. Fact: Uncle Dan had tossed it outside to his father. Fact: it had been the murder weapon in shantytown, so—how did it get there? Someone had to take it from the vicinity of this house. On the surface it would appear to have been his father. But suppose it wasn't? It might have been Uncle Dan later. Or even Carter. Did one of them leave it with Annie? And did someone else—somebody like one of the Baggets, one of the deputies, perhaps the sheriff himself, maybe even Amanda Hopper—pick it up and use it on Annie? It could even have been her husband, Ivan Coaker, or his nearly demented brother, Clifford.

Whatever—Tony gave up hope of discovering anything inside Uncle Dan's and Aunt Ruth's room to provide answers. He slipped out and shut the door quietly, just in time, too, because Ruth was ascending the stairway as he went to his own room. He was aware that she was watching him from behind.

45

Dinner that evening was a tense situation for Tony. Whether actual or not, he imagined that his Aunt Ruth knew about his misadventure that afternoon in hers and Uncle Dan's bedroom. If she spoke of it in front of his grandmother, he would have to think of some way to cover it up. Concentrating on a possible excuse, he ate little of the meal.

To his relief, Aunt Ruth never said a word. However, she did cast him a sort of knowing look, or else he imagined it that way. His Uncle Dan, other than being unusually quiet while eating, didn't appear to know anything. Neither did his grandmother.

As they were finishing their after dinner coffee, Aunt Ruth stood up and announced that she was going into town to see her father. Uncle Dan sighed but said nothing. His grandmother barely nodded.

Tony made his announcement: "Grandma, I got to

go back to Lon's. I left a book there I'm reading. It's really important."

"It can keep until tomorrow," his grandmother said.

"What's it about?" asked Uncle Dan.

"Oh," Tony said, thinking fast, "all about ships and pirates out at sea. It's real exciting."

"What's the name of it?" asked his grandmother.

"I—I forgot."

Uncle Dan chuckled. "I know how that is. Sometimes I get two-thirds through a book and can't tell you the title. Let alone the author," he added.

"Tony—I" Grace stopped abruptly and sighed. "You're growing up fast. Do what you think is right. I'm glad you informed us because I would be worried if you simply left without a word."

Tony nodded. "Thank you, Grandma."

"Yes, I want you to be honest with me." Her statement made Tony wonder if it was some retaliation for his asking her earlier that afternoon if Uncle Dan was honest with her.

"He'll be all right," Uncle Dan said.

Grace nodded. "But don't be staying out all night. Tell Lon Shirley I'll skin him if he keeps you out late. You can go in with Ruth. That way I won't worry about either of you so much."

Aunt Ruth reappeared from upstairs. She had taken a shawl instead of a coat from her bedroom to put around her shoulders since it was a warm night. Tony followed her outside. When he looked back, he saw that Grandmother Grace and Uncle Dan were still at the dining table with their coffees.

On the porch, Aunt Ruth said, "I'll take one of the bicycles. You don't have to go with me."

"Grandma expects me to."

"What she don't know won't hurt her," Aunt Ruth said. "What were you doing in our room this afternoon?"

Tony experienced a sinking feeling. His first impulse was to bluster it off, that he hadn't been there, but not only would that have added another wrong to his list, but it would make his word useless. Feebly, he said, "I thought I heard a strange noise in there. So I looked."

"A strange noise?" Aunt Ruth said, mildly.

"Like maybe a window was open and a bird got in. It happened in my Mom's room last week."

Aunt Ruth was silent a moment before she said, "I see. Very well. Don't be investigating strange noises in my bedroom in the future."

"I won't. I promise." Feeling conflicted, Tony breathed out heavily. "I'll follow you into town. I'll bike in, too."

"Don't try to keep up with me," she said.

Tony let her get ahead of him on the bicycle she selected but kept her in sight. It was still daylight since the days were long now. Aunt Ruth breezed along Main Street, which was generally vacant during the supper hours, and headed in the direction of her father's church. Tony stopped at the poolroom.

Young Bennie was behind the counter. Two customers chatted with each other at one side. Lon Shirley was nowhere in sight.

"Where's Lon?" Tony asked.

Bennie's reply was an elaborate shrug and big grin.

Tony stepped outside and went around back to climb the stairs to the bedroom above. The door was unlocked. Lon was not there either.

Tony, frowning, looked both ways along Main Street. There were few people outside, but considerable noise was coming from the two taverns. He went into the nearest one, the smallest, and looked. No Lon. Across the street the bank was closed at this hour and would stay closed until Monday. He crossed over and down a block to *Bagget's Saloon.*

The smoke and noise assailed him when he went in. Both Harvey and Henry were behind the counter. He finally got Harvey's attention and asked. No, Lon hadn't been in that the Baggets could tell.

Tony's next stop was *Amanda's Rooming House.* He didn't see or speak with Amanda Hopper, but one woman in a foyer told him that she hadn't seen Lon Shirley. Tony went outside and thought about it.

He was a bit angry. It occurred to him that Lon might be on the trail of Annie Pyle's killer and hadn't told him. Tony felt a bit betrayed. He tried to tell himself he was being silly, but it didn't alleviate the betrayal feeling.

Tony got on his bike and rode Main Street. He stopped at the Sheriff's Department and looked in. There was no one there, not even the generally tired looking receptionist.

Hunting? Fishing? Lon probably would have told him if he had been planning something like that.

Tony pedaled toward shantytown and soon was on the worn, rutted, dirt pathway. People, mostly women, were in chairs and rockers in front of their shacks to gossip. Most of the men probably were in town at the bars. The sky was darkening rapidly now with the sunset, and the mingled odors of chicken shit, the outhouses, and manure hung heavy.

Tony rode to the end of the street, stopped and looked at the Coaker residence. There were no candle lights or lamplights showing from inside. Tony straddled his bike for a few moments considering. Two doors down was a dilapidated fence in front of another shanty. He walked his bike to the fence and propped it there. He knew it was a risk leaving something that valuable out here in plain view, but his curiosity about the Coaker shanty overcame.

This is really dumb, he thought. He stepped upon the rickety porch of the Coaker house and close to the front door. No sounds came from inside, and no light was on, at least as far as he could tell through the burlap coverings on the window. Should he knock on the door? If somebody answered, what would he say?

He tried the outside latch. It turned and the door opened inward.

The first thing that hit him was the smell. Tony almost gagged on it, worse than anything he could recall. How could somebody live in such an odor? He had smelled farm animals before—horse stalls—cow barns, even the row of outhouses behind the shanties, but nothing as bad as this. How in God's name did somebody like Annie Pyle manage to live here? She had to have had a very good reason.

Holding his breath, Tony stuck his head inside. God, it was dark. His eyes had not adjusted enough for him to see anything. Then from somewhere came a groan. Tony backed out quickly and shut the door.

He retreated to his bicycle and stood thoughtfully. It

probably was Clifford Coaker inside, not Ivan. Either way he didn't want to be recognized. But the question was still there: what to do now?

A voice behind him asked harshly, "Why are you here?"

Tony whirled around so suddenly that he knocked his bicycle over. His heart stopped pounding when he saw the speaker. It was Lon Shirley with one eyebrow arched inquisitively.

His emotions settling, Tony asked, "How about you?"

"I asked you first," Lon said.

Tony shrugged. "I was looking for you." His tone became accusatory. "You're trying to find things out without my help."

"I told you to stay clear of the Coakers. Now look at you," Lon said. He didn't sound angry. "Let's have it. Why?"

"Letters," Tony said. "I was trying to find out if there's letters from Uncle Dan to Annie Pyle. I think Uncle Dan might've killed her because of some letters."

Lon appeared to consider Tony's theory. He said, "Your bike?"

"One of 'em."

"Come on."

Lon had Tony walk the bicycle around behind the shanty. Here the outhouse odors overcame any others. Lon had Tony lean his bicycle up against the wall of one of the toilets.

"It stinks here," Tony said for lack of anything better he could think of.

"Yeah, well, you're spoiled," Lon said. "So you're looking for letters?"

Tony exhaled and nodded.

"What'd you expect to find? A stack of letters on a table with a sign that says 'Here, Tony, are the letters you're looking for. Annie's letters.' Did you think that?"

"I—don't know." Tony felt his face flush with embarrassment. He had to strike back. "What about you?"

"Me, too," said Lon, his face warming in a smile. "You got me thinking, kid. I don't know we can put much faith in what Clifford Coaker said, but there could be some truth in it. I also don't think Clifford just imagined it. He ain't real bright, and now that he's hurt, well—" Lon left it unfinished but clear.

"Well, what, Lon? Do you believe it about the letters or not?"

"It's possible, and even makes sense. I was going at it from the wrong direction. Annie wasn't killed because of some romance. It was about letters and money, and especially the money. Why else would she even stay in this pigsty? I do know your Uncle Daniel was smitten with Annie, but so was lots of men. So let's say he did write letters to Annie and she kept 'em. Annie was pretty clever. If she encouraged Daniel to write to her, I bet she encouraged other men to do it. It was blackmail she was using."

Tony's voice sounded hopeful when he said, "Then maybe it wasn't Uncle Dan that killed her."

"You're getting smart," Lon said.

"Carter could'a done it to protect the family. So what do we do?"

"First thing is wait 'til it's full dark," Lon said. "Just a few minutes. No need to let other people see us breaking into Ivan's house. So we be patient."

"It stinks back here. Can't we be patient somewhere else?" Tony's brow suddenly furrowed. "Hey, you said break into Ivan's house. We're really gonna do it?"

"Right now Ivan is at Bagget's Saloon. Some kind soul left money at the bar for Ivan to have a few drinks. He won't be back right away."

"You're that kind soul."

"Well, I hope it's worth it," Lon said. From his jacket pocket he produced a half-candle. "Even brought us a light. Listen. When we go in, you let me go first."

"I heard a groan inside," Tony told him. "I think it's Clifford."

"Who else? Stay behind me. He's unpredictable and might be armed."

"Ready for a big stink?" said Tony.

46

They slipped back to the front of the house and onto the small, rickety porch. Lon slowly pushed open the door. Once more Tony recoiled from the horrendous odor. He didn't hear any groaning this time. After shutting the door, Lon struck a match and lighted his candle. The little light illumined the one-room cabin. A lump on the bed rolled in a blanket told them where Clifford was.

There was little furniture, and none in very good condition, inside the place. A cluttered table, a wood burning stove, threadbare burlap over the windows, a baseball bat with a taped handle propped in a corner, Tony could see all this in the candlelight. There was a beaten-up old chest of drawers against one wall. Tony went to it while Lon stepped closer to the bed.

There weren't any letters that Tony could find in the drawers. Wherever Ivan had put them, he had found a good hiding place.

"We better go," Lon said softly. "Quick and quiet."

"We ain't looked everywhere."

"Clifford's dead."

Tony froze. "You sure?"

"I ain't a doctor, but I can't find a pulse. He seems dead to me."

"Did Ivan kill him?"

"No. We'll chalk Clifford up to your daddy. But I think Ivan probably killed Annie."

"Why, if she was getting money?" asked Tony in a whisper.

"Maybe she wouldn't share with her husband. Let's get out of here."

The shack's door opened suddenly, letting in the outside light which was somewhat brighter than total darkness and silhouetting Ivan Coaker in the doorway.

Ivan's voice boomed: "What the hell!"

Lon blew out the candle and reached for Tony. His hand brushed off Tony's jacket before he got a good grip and pulled. With his impaired arm he pushed Ivan aside and hauled Tony out into the night.

Stumbling and running, they went around the shanty toward the row of outhouses.

"Get home!" Lon shouted to Tony.

Tony's voice caught in despair. "How?"

His bicycle was missing from behind the shanties.

They ran along the uneven pathway.

A rifle shot cracked out. Lon grabbed Tony once more and hauled him behind one of the outhouses. There were two more quick shots.

At Lon's urging, they ducked and weaved in and out among the outhouses until a bigger opening between two of the shacks appeared. Lon pulled Tony with him. They made it to the street. Ivan's voice was still screaming at them.

47

Sheriff Abe Buckner was back in his office. He raised his brows. "Ivan shot at you?"

"Yeah," Lon Shirley said. "But he was so drunk I doubt he could hit anything point blank."

"Somehow I ain't surprised," Buckner said. "What you want me to do about it now?"

"That was added information," Lon said. "The bigger thing is Clifford's dead. Ivan might be dumb enough to think I killed him."

"That don't surprise me either," said Buckner. "Clifford's been dying since he fell on his knife. I'll have the doc go out there. And you let me handle Ivan."

"Also," Lon said, drawing it out, "this boy's bicycle was stolen."

Buckner tilted back his chair so he could swing his booted feet onto the corner of his desk. "And just how did that happen?"

"It was out of our sight briefly."

"Why?"

Tony kept looking from one man to the other.

"Well," Lon said, "we felt there might be something in Ivan's shack to point to Annie's killer."

"So you trespassed?"

"Yep."

"What were you looking for?" Buckner asked.

Lon didn't say anything, so Tony answered, "Letters."

Lon shot him a look.

"Letters?" Buckner asked.

Lon sighed and nodded. "We have reason to believe Annie was blackmailing people she knew. Men. She was collecting money from somewhere to put into a bank account."

Buckner half-smiled. "That somewhere was between her legs."

"Abe, were you one of the men paying her?"

"No, and I don't appreciate that."

"People say you did go for those spread legs."

"That's nobody's business, and they better not say it to my face." Buckner sat up straight. "I got no quarrel with you, Lon, and I don't want us to get started with one. The information I'll take and see where it goes. Quit trying to do my job."

"Just want to make sure you're doing it, Abe."

"Urban!" Buckner barked loudly.

Deputy Urban Meyer entered the office.

"Take the automobile," Buckner ordered. "Find Doc Sanders and take him to shantytown, to Ivan Coaker's house. We think Clifford died."

"That's a big loss," Deputy Meyer said, sarcastically. "You wanna crank it up for me, Sheriff."

"I do not. Now get to it."

Deputy Meyer shrugged and departed.

Buckner leaned back and put his feet once again on the desk corner. "Anything else you'd like to share?"

"The bicycle?" Lon said.

"Do you have any identifying markings on it?" Buckner asked Tony. "Your name? Anything somebody can't scratch off?"

"I don't really know," Tony said.

"Will you recognize it if you see it on the street?"

Tony looked sheepish. "Maybe," he said and shrugged.

"Lot 'a help there," Buckner grumbled. "You be the one to tell your grandma you lost a bike. Them things can be valuable if the wrong person gets a hold of it."

Lon said, "It's probably sitting inside one of those shanties now."

"Uh huh."

"Can't you find out?" asked Tony.

"Not without trespassing, like you fellows did," Buckner said. "Why don't you go on about your business while I attend to the Coakers."

"Abe, I'd like to find out if I'm right and Clifford is really dead," said Lon.

"You're welcome to wait out in the hall 'til Deputy Meyer gets back," Buckner told him.

Lon nudged Tony. "We've been dismissed."

Buckner grinned.

They did wait outside the sheriff's office, sitting on one

of the hard, wooden benches. Tony didn't say anything. He felt foolish and stupid for losing the bicycle. He kept playing in his mind how he was going to tell his family about his carelessness. Lon Shirley simply sat with his head leaning back and his eyes shut.

It was almost an hour before Deputy Meyer stomped back into the station. Tony and Lon watched him go inside the sheriff's office and lean forward with his hands spread on the desk. Buckner and Meyer spoke together, and Buckner nodded. He came out into the corridor.

Lon lifted his eyebrows at the sheriff.

"Clifford's dead," Buckner told him. "Doc Sanders confirmed it. Him and the undertaker's going about moving the body now. Doc says Clifford prob'ly got an infection from his wound."

"Ivan?" Lon asked.

"No sign of him. One of the neighbors reported to Urban that Ivan was running around like a mad man, waving his rifle and shooting it off."

"Ah," Lon said.

Buckner had strapped on his pistol belt and now adjusted it. He looked at Deputy Meyer. "Go get Orville and tell him he's on emergency duty for tonight."

"Take the car?" asked Meyer, hopefully.

"No, I'll take the car," Buckner said. "You guys get your bicycles out and pump like hell. Problems?"

"You're the boss, Sheriff," Meyer said. "How 'bout the extra deputies? Do we notify them?"

"No, we'll keep it contained. Ivan won't be goin' far. We arrest him for his own protection."

"And drunkenness," Meyer added.

"Main thing is to disarm him." Buckner looked at Lon. "Think he'll be coming after you?"

Lon shrugged. "He's not a good shot unless he gets close enough, but he recognized us. If he tries, I'll crack his skull."

"Gotta keep the boy safe." Buckner nodded at Tony. "What're you sticking around for? The boy should go home before I get his grandma on my back." He looked at his deputy again. "Check out Ivan's favorite places. He won't go far. He's got no transportation."

"Unless he's the one that stole my bike," Tony said.

Lon nudged him. "Let's go, kid. Let the sheriff get on with his job."

To be on the safe side, Lon walked Tony back to Blaisdell House.

Carter Foote sat in a wicker chair on the porch with his shotgun propped beside him.

"Trouble?" Lon asked.

Carter glanced at Tony and nodded. "Ivan Coaker is drunk. He shot a hole in our front door. I figure I'd see if he tries coming back."

"Anybody hurt?"

"No. He went back toward town, cussing like a fool." He looked at Tony again, longer this time. "Your grandma was worried 'bout you, boy. You better get in and tell her you're okay."

"Why did Ivan come here?" Lon asked.

Tony paused on the porch to listen.

Carter said, "He claimed Missus Blaisdell cheated him

out of money. He said he won't let anybody get away with that. I stopped Mr. Daniel from going out the door after him. I could see Ivan was armed."

Lon scratched his chin. "He's crazy 'cause his brother died. Should I explain to Tony's grandma what happened?"

"I can do it," Tony said. "I gotta fess up anyway to losing the bike."

He went inside the house and shut the door, leaving Lon and Carter talking outside. His grandmother met him at the door of the study and ushered him inside. She hugged him and ruffled his hair. Tony saw that Uncle Dan was also in the study and saw the two brandy glasses on the table near his grandmother's armchair. Uncle Dan looked relieved to see him as well.

Grandmother Grace said, "Your Uncle Dan was about to go looking for you. We were worried with that idiot running around shooting at us."

They listened as Tony explained everything. He left nothing out and looked crestfallen when he admitted he had lost the bicycle.

"We can replace it if we have to," Daniel said. "Anyway, we have more."

"You're not mad at me?" asked Tony.

Uncle Dan and Grandmother Grace shook their heads.

48

At his grandmother's request, Tony departed the study and went upstairs to visit his mother. She, too, had been concerned about his safety.

Daniel put on a denim jacket and came back to see Grace in the study. She asked him where he was going.

"Now I've got one more member of the family to worry about. Ruth went in late this afternoon to see her daddy and have dinner with him," Daniel said. "I trust they're safe in the church, but I'll feel better knowing."

"Take Carter with you."

Daniel shook his head. "I want Carter to stay here and keep his eyes open. I'll be all right."

Grace nodded, but the concern showed on her face. "Just be really careful."

"I will, Mother. Don't worry about me."

"You taking a gun?"

"Hell, no," Daniel said. "I'm afraid I'll use it."

Daniel, keeping a lookout for any indication of Ivan Coaker, walked from the house to Main Street. He saw men outside the taverns gabbing together. They would have heard by now. For all Daniel knew, Sheriff Buckner might already have Ivan in his jail. It was on his way to the church, so he decided to check there first.

He saw a knot of men outside one of the taverns talking.

"You guys look pissed," he said.

One man broke away from the group. Daniel could smell the whiskey breath. The man scowled.

"That fuckin' Ivan Coaker shot a dog in the street. The dog wasn't hurtin' nobody. In fact, it was real friendly. Ivan let it get close, then just up and shot it. Bastard."

"He's crazy," another man added and belched loudly.

"That ain't all," said yet another man, just joining the group. He thumbed over his shoulder. "You know that old horse Lon Shirley keeps in the stable in the alley? Ivan shot the horse."

"No shit?" said the first man.

"Right in the head. Lon's headed out to look for him. I'd say Mr. Shirley is pissed."

"I'll bet."

Daniel left them and hurried across to the poolroom. Bennie was inside behind the counter. He gave Daniel a lopsided grin.

"Is Lon in his apartment?"

Bennie shook his head.

A customer said, "I think he's going after Ivan Coaker. I wouldn't get in his way."

Daniel went outside and continued down Main Street toward the church. When he got there, he saw one of his family's bicycles propped up near the front door. Daniel went in and called out, "Ruth! Reverend Jones!"

Ruth answered him and came out of the shadows of one of the pews. She looked surprised and a bit perplexed to see her husband.

"Ivan Coaker's gone crazy," Daniel explained. "He's shooting up the town. Somebody bound to get hurt."

"I'm safe here, Daniel," Ruth said.

"Where's your father?"

She lit a candle near the simple alter. "Some of Daddy's parishioners live in shantytown. There's a woman very ill. She can't come to church. Daddy's gone to minister to her and comfort her. We heard about Ivan before Daddy left."

"I hope he doesn't run across Ivan," Daniel said. The candlelight brightened the interior of the church proper. "What are you doing?"

"Meditating," Ruth said with a soft smile. "It's the next best thing to praying. I was thinking things through, asking for God's guidance."

"About?"

"Personal things, Daniel."

"Have you eaten?"

"Daddy fixed something for both of us. Cooking is one of his many skills, *and* blessings. Are you hungry? There may be some soup left."

"Had mine," Daniel said. "I'd like to take you home now. You ride the bike, and I'll walk alongside."

"Aren't you afraid of Ivan Coaker?"

Daniel grunted softly. "I'm wary of him. I hope he's not crazy enough to shoot at you."

"You care for me."

"Well, yes."

"But you won't seek forgiveness," she said.

"From you, yes, if it's necessary," Daniel said. "I don't need forgiveness from anybody else. Look, Ruth, if we've got any chance at all?"

"What's that?" she asked suddenly.

Daniel heard it too. It was the fire bell summoning volunteers. He frowned.

Both of them went to the front door, opened it, and peered outside.

There was a reddish-orange haze in the sky, wavering slightly, not too far off.

"Somebody's house is burning," Ruth said. "Come with me."

She led him back into the church and to the winding wooden staircase that led up to the steeple and the church bell. They stepped out into the cool night air and stood in the steeple box, a sort of widow's walk around the structure. The entire town could be viewed from here.

"It's in shantytown," Daniel said. "If the wind's right, that whole area might go up."

Ruth pointed down toward Main Street. People were scurrying toward the fire. Fire department members had led the water-laden wagon, now hitched to two horses, into the street. Some of the regular volunteers were throwing on their firemen's helmets and slickers, running toward the wagon. Others, on foot or riding bicycles, hastened in the direction of the blaze. Ruth and Daniel saw tongues of flame now reaching upward.

"You stay here," Daniel told her and ran down.

49

The crowd gathered. The sky filled with hot ash and flecks of burning wood.

The primary burning shack was at the end of the street. It was Ivan Coaker's house. The two houses nearest it were being doused with water, hand-pumped from the horse-drawn tank. Some folks scurried to rescue chickens from the nearest coops.

Faces of the spectators gleamed in the firelight.

"That one's a goner," a man standing next to Daniel said with a headshake. "Lucky there's not much wind."

Daniel nodded as he scanned the onlookers. He could not see Ivan Coaker among them. He did see Lon Shirley, standing stone-faced, and nodded to him.

Daniel stood for several minutes, watching the firefighters extinguishing small subsidiary blazes and moving onlookers back to a safe distance. The Coaker shack was gone in seconds, leaving charred rubble at the spot; but, at least, the nearest houses were spared. Daniel realized that was very fortunate. The fire that had lighted the evening sky had subsided.

A touch on his shoulder startled Daniel. He turned to see Carter Foote peering past him.

"No way to save that," Carter said.

Daniel frowned. "I asked you to stay home and protect my mother and Tony."

"Would have," Carter said, "but Miss Grace asked me to come in and see about *you*. Ivan won't be coming around the house." He backed the bicycle up and mounted it. "I'll go home now."

What did he mean by that? Ivan won't be coming around the house? How could Carter know?

Daniel turned back to stare at the smoldering ruins.

Dr. Sanders, himself a fire volunteer, was in close with his peers. Even retired Doc Harris was present, as watchful as was everyone else. Sheriff Abe Buckner and Deputy Orville Parker, stepping gingerly over and around obstacles, tentatively approached the remains of the building. When Daniel glanced around again, he noticed that Lon Shirley was no longer with the gathering, not that he could see anyway.

That still left the problem of Ivan himself. Had Lon gone in search of him again? Or, a thought he didn't like occurred to Daniel, had Lon set the blaze that destroyed Ivan's home in retaliation for the shooting of his horse? That didn't quite sound like Lon Shirley, but the thought couldn't be dismissed.

Daniel stood and watched for a few more minutes. Now that the danger was almost over, many of the onlookers dispersed and moved toward their own homes. Kids still clustered about in hopes of seeing more fire, most of them running and chattering among themselves.

Daniel looked around for the reverend Caleb Jones but couldn't spot him. He decided to return to the church and try to persuade Ruth to come home with him.

Reverend Jones had beaten Daniel back to the church. Jones and his daughter were sitting outside in the coolness of the evening on the front steps. The minister stood up and extended his hand to Daniel.

Daniel sat beside his wife. For several seconds nobody said anything.

"It was Ivan Coaker's house," he said finally. "I still have no idea where Ivan is."

Reverend Jones nodded. "He might've torched it himself. He's an unstable man as well as an alcoholic."

"You don't think we're in danger here?" Ruth asked.

"Shouldn't be. He's not altogether stupid." Jones patted her hand. "You have nothing to worry about. God protects the innocent."

Daniel winced. He didn't believe that for a second, but he didn't want an argument. He always had the feeling whenever he was around his wife and her father that they were baiting him into some kind of theological discussion.

"Don't you believe that, Daniel?"

Trapped, he thought. Daniel drew a breath. "I think bad things happen to good people, and sometimes good things happen to bad."

"Where do you fit?" asked Reverend Jones.

Daniel fell silent.

"Answer him, Daniel," Ruth urged.

Finally Daniel said, "I don't have an answer."

"Come now," chided Jones. "We know whether we're saved or not. It's a simple prayer of faith."

How did we get onto this, Daniel wondered. He was afraid of it. "Sometimes I don't know what's simple," he said. He rose from the step. "Let's go home, Ruth. I'll walk alongside."

"We'll pray first," Ruth said. "For your immortal soul."

"My daughter is a wise woman," Reverend Jones said, smiling.

Daniel stalked away several feet before turning. "You pray *for* me, both of you."

"What's bothering you, Daniel?" asked the minister, still with the little smile on his lips.

"His conscience," Ruth said. "You go ahead, Daniel. I'll be along soon."

"I'm still worried about Coaker."

"I'm convinced our girl is protected," the minister said.

"Nevertheless," Daniel said, "I'll wait 'til Ruth's ready to go."

50

The town of Vinton retreated almost gently into its normal slumber by the following morning, which was Saturday, putting Ivan Coaker's shooting rampage and the burning of his house in the background. At breakfast Tony listened to his Uncle Dan's account of the fire and saw very little, if any, reaction from his grandmother. Ruth had finally agreed to come home with Uncle Dan but, so far, had not shown herself for breakfast.

"You going in to the poolroom today?" Grandmother Grace asked Tony.

Tony looked up from his breakfast fruit and nodded, waiting for something else. She didn't oblige him with further comment.

Finally she said, "You be alert and careful. I don't trust the Coakers one bit."

Uncle Dan said, "There's only one Coaker now."

"The crazy one."

"They both were crazy."

"You just be careful," Grandmother Grace admonished Tony.

"I'll drive him in the car," Daniel said.

"I can get there faster on my feet," Tony said.

"You're an impetuous young man," his grandmother said, "like Lon Shirley was."

"What's that mean?" Tony asked. "And how do you know so much about Lon?"

"Lon should've left Vinton a long time ago," Grandmother Grace said. "Struck out on his own somewhere else. He could've made something of himself."

Daniel laughed. "He has made something of himself. He runs the best poolroom in town."

"The only poolroom in town," Tony said.

They both laughed. Even Grandmother Grace smiled.

Carter came into the kitchen to get a cup of coffee. He nodded to everyone in the dining alcove, and then carried his coffee away.

Uncle Dan said, "Mother, you sent Carter to look after me last night. I wanted him to look after you."

Tony's grandmother shrugged. "I had a brandy in the study. Carter left his shotgun with me. I know how to use a gun. Really, Daniel, I wasn't all that worried about Ivan coming back here. But I didn't want you to catch a stray bullet."

"Do you think he burned his own house?" Tony asked.

"Could be," Uncle Dan said. "But more likely it was an accident. People that saw him said he was drunk."

"I wonder what Lon thinks about it," Tony said.

His grandmother half-smiled. "Ask him."

Tony got up.

"Sure you won't take your uncle's offer of a ride?" she asked.

"No, I'm going now."

The day was mild, so less than fifteen minutes later Tony arrived at the poolroom. Bennie stood outside beckoning frantically to him. Tony ran the final half block and saw the sheriff's car parked crookedly on the street. Bennie was so excited, flustered about something that all he could was wave his arms and gasp for breath.

Tony went inside and saw Sheriff Buckner and Deputy Orville Parker facing Lon Shirley in front of the counter. He stopped and looked from one man to the other.

Lon saw him, gave him a little half-smile, and said, "Looks like I'm being arrested, Tony."

Tony's jaw dropped.

Lon spoke to the sheriff with a nod toward Parker. "Your boy can take his hand off his gun. I won't take it away from him, Abe."

"Arrested?" Tony asked.

"It's bullshit, you know," Lon said to the sheriff. "You won't need the handcuffs."

"What for?" Tony asked in astonishment.

Lon looked at him. "They think I mighta' murdered Ivan Coaker."

"Ivan's dead?" Tony drew a breath. "How?"

"Apparently he was in his house that burned last night."

"That ain't what killed him," Sheriff Buckner said. "Doc Sanders found out, and Doc Harris confirmed it. He got his head beaten in with a baseball bat." He nodded toward Tony. "This kid is a witness, Lon. Right in front of him you said if Ivan ever came at you you'd break his head. Well?" He shrugged. "Sorry, son," he said to Tony. "You did hear him say that to me."

Confused, Tony blinked. "But—but Ivan shot Lon's horse."

"That's the reason," Buckner nodded. "Can't say I might not have done the same thing. But I gotta do my job."

"It's okay," Lon said to Tony. "Don't you worry. Just take care of our business. Bennie can help you."

The sheriff and deputy took Lon outside and put him in the car. Onlookers stopped on the street to stare. Tony ran back toward the house since the bank wasn't open for business on Saturday and his grandmother or Uncle Dan wouldn't be there. He found his grandmother looking over some flowers she had planted at one side of the house.

She looked up, a bit surprised to see him in such a state. He blurted out the news.

"Arrest? Lon?" Grandmother Grace said and frowned. "Why on earth?"

"The sheriff says he murdered Ivan Coaker last night. But I know Lon didn't do it."

Uncle Daniel had heard some of Tony's outburst and came out through the screened door. Tony repeated it to him.

"I'll go see what I can find out," Uncle Dan said and left.

Grandmother Grace had Tony go into the kitchen and take a glass of water.

"You just take it easy," she told him. "We'll figure out what's going on."

"He didn't do it, Grandma!"

"I believe you," she said.

Tony waited nervously. He paced the downstairs, then went upstairs, looked in on his mother briefly, and paced the hallway there. When he came down and went outside, his grandmother looked as unruffled as ever as she patted the ground around her flowers with her gloved hands and sprinkled water. She smiled at him but said nothing. Tony stomped about the porch and finally sat in one of the wicker chairs.

Uncle Dan returned on the bicycle and said, "No charge will be filed against Lon. Our county prosecutor, Suggs, says there's nothing substantial to hold him on. Tony, he'll be back to work in a little while."

"Why did Abe arrest him?" asked Grandmother Grace.

"Apparently Lon was upset with Ivan Coaker and threatened to break his head if he came after him or Tony."

Tony nodded vigorously.

"And," continued Uncle Dan, "Ivan got his head busted last night with a baseball bat Ivan kept in his house. His body was terribly burned in the fire but it couldn't conceal the cause of death. Doc Sanders called it, and old Doc Harris confirmed it. So Ivan had to be dead before the fire started."

"Then somebody else burned the house to hide the murder," Grandmother Grace said.

Tony listened intently.

"It appears that way. Abe felt he was just doing his job by arresting Lon because of the threat. But if everybody who threatened somebody got arrested, we wouldn't have many people around. That's how Suggs looks at it. He needs more evidence than a verbal threat."

Grandmother Grace peered at Uncle Dan. "Now why do you suppose anyone wanted to burn down Ivan's house?" The tone of her question indicated that she already had an answer.

But Tony answered it quickly for her. "The love letters Ivan and Clifford were supposed to have. They got burned up." "So you know about that," said Grandmother Grace. "We know Lon had no reason to destroy the letters—if there were any."

Uncle Dan nodded.

Tony said, "He wanted to find out who killed Annie Coaker, so he wouldn't burn the letters." For several seconds he stood in thought. "I'm going to the poolroom and wait for Lon."

It was several minutes after Tony got there before Lon Shirley arrived. Tony had pitched in to help Bennie in the poolroom. He ran to Lon when he saw the big man.

"It's okay," Lon assured him. "You fellas got everything under control?"

Bennie nodded quickly.

"I'm gonna see about talking to some people. I shouldn't be too long."

"I'll go with you," Tony said.

"You don't have to," Lon told him. "Probably nothing to it."

Tony was in the doorway. "Where we going?"

"Shantytown," Lon said.

51

The man Lon wanted to see in shantytown was Phipps. When Tony asked him why, Lon said, "He's a nosy busybody. If anybody keeps up on his neighbors' activities, it would be Phipps. Besides, he likes attention and likes to talk."

"He might not have anything to talk about," Tony said.

"That's possible, too."

They found Phipps sitting in a rocking chair in the shade beneath the battered porch roof of his shack. The old man watched them approach. He had on old pants, unlaced boots with the tongues hanging out, and a shirt that showed grime around the collar. As with the previous time Tony had seen him, the man needed a shave.

"What'cha need this time?" he asked Lon Shirley. "Wanna see where they found Ivan's body?"

Lon grunted half-humorously. "Naw. Were you here before the fire started last night?"

"Right here, sittin' on my porch."

Lon took a seat on the front stoop, allowing Phipps' position in the rocking chair to be above him. Tony remained standing near one of the porch uprights.

"Bet you saw most everything that happened," Lon said.

Phipps grinned.

"I'm interested in what you saw."

"When?" asked Phipps. "Before or during the fire?"

Lon gave him a big, friendly grin. "How about both? But start with before."

Phipps spat a stream of tobacco juice out near Tony's feet. Tony jumped out of the way.

"The woman," he said, "that come running out of old Ivan's house little while before the fire started. She looked scared."

"A woman," Lon said. He and Tony exchanged a look. "Was this woman a frequent visitor at Ivan's house?"

"First time I seen 'er in this neighborhood was when she run out. I seen 'er in town a couple times."

"Was Ivan home at the time?"

"Well, here's what happened, see? I seen her go up to Ivan's door and knock. Nobody answered, Clifford bein' dead an' all, Ivan out shootin' up things. She opened the door and went inside. She was there a few minutes 'fore Ivan come down the street swearing and waving his rifle. He was prob'ly out of ammunition and goin' home for more, or another bottle if he had one. They never lasted long with Ivan or his brother. Anyway, he went in, and it wasn't a couple minutes later that the woman come tearin' out and down the street."

"Do you know the woman's name?"

"Yeah, I know her name," Phipps said, "and so do you. I ain't never done business with her. You might'a. She lives in town—runs the rooming house there."

"Ah," Lon said. "Amanda Hopper."

"That's her."

"And you never saw Amanda visit Ivan before?"

Phipps thought. "Naw, I'm sure that's the first time."

"She was scared, huh?"

Phipps nodded. "What I figure is Ivan walked in on her in his house. Mood Ivan was in would scare anybody."

"Did Ivan come out after her?"

"Naw. He didn't come out."

"And the fire started right away?"

"No, that was a bit later," Phipps said. He thumbed over his shoulder at his own house. "I went in 'cause my sis fixed a little supper. After I et, I came back out to sit here. Then I seen the smoke and the first flames. All hell done broke loose. Ever'body run over to see if we could help, but, boy, that fire really shot up. We didn't know if Ivan was still in there or not. Found out later he was. He probably passed out drunk and couldn't wake up even when it got hot."

"Amanda Hopper was the only person you saw go in or out of Ivan's?" Lon asked.

"I jus' told you."

"Nobody else that wasn't normally around here?" Lon asked.

Phipps grunted. "Well, the fire brung lots 'a people running. Ever'body wants to see somethin' burn, I guess. Yeah, there was lots 'a folks from other parts of town rushing here. Hell, it lit up the whole sky."

Lon sat quietly for a moment. Tony looked from one man to the other.

"Got what'cha want?" Phipps asked.

Lon pushed himself to his feet. "Yes, thanks. Good to talk to you again, Mr. Phipps."

Phipps shrugged and spat more tobacco juice.

When Tony and Lon were walking back to the center of town, Tony asked, "So what does that mean?"

"It means Amanda knows a lot more than she's been telling us," Lon said.

"I guess that means we go back for some more of her coffee," said Tony.

At Amanda Hopper's rooming house, Lon managed to get her to sit with him and Tony in the vacant dining room where a young girl was setting up things for the upcoming evening meal. Amanda poured out three cups of coffee and sat at the table with them.

Lon got right to it. "You were seen leaving Ivan's house last night just before the fire started."

Amanda blinked. "Couldn't. Nobody could'a seen me just before the fire started. I was here." She emphasized it with her finger pointed down at the table between them. "I got girls who can confirm that. We went out front when the sky lit up."

"More than one person saw you," Lon said.

Tony glanced at him quickly. He figured Lon was testing Amanda.

"Great," Amanda said, sarcastically. "But not when you said."

"You knew Ivan wasn't there, so what were you looking for?"

Tony waited. For a moment he thought Amanda wasn't going to reply.

Then she shrugged. "My friend Annie had been his wife. I hoped to calm him down," Amanda said, eying Lon over the rim of her coffee cup.

Lon snorted. "Come on, Amanda. This is me you're talking to. I'd think you'd like to find out who killed your good friend. Did you think it was Ivan?"

"Do you?"

"That's very possible," Lon said, "but he would have to have had a very good reason. And the reason with Ivan was always profit. How did you figure he might profit from his wife's death?" He waited, both of them studying each other. He asked, "Is that why you waited for Ivan to come home and then beat him to death with his own baseball bat?"

Amanda scoffed a short laugh.

Lon continued, "Then you started the fire to conceal the crime."

"Lon, do you really think I would take on Ivan Coaker—the mood he was in—and plan to kill him? I might be tough sometimes, but I ain't stupid. You are reaching, my friend."

"But you knew he was dead."

"Not when I left," said Amanda. "He scared the hell out of me when he walked in on me." She sipped more coffee. "I was afraid for my life. I had no idea what Ivan knew, or thought he knew, or what Annie might've told him. He always did scare me."

"So that's it," Lon said. "It was about Annie. You're

beginning to make a little sense. Annie's letters, am I right?"

Amanda shrugged. "I wanted them. Ivan was running 'round like a crazy man, so I figured I might slip in his house and find the letters. Annie told me about them. She was gonna bring 'em to me for safe keeping. Said I'd get a piece of her action as long as I didn't tell nobody. But she got murdered before I got the letters."

"Did you actually see any of the letters?"

"No. I said Annie kept 'em."

"Did she tell you who she was writing to, or about?"

"No, Annie could keep secrets with the best of 'em. But I don't think she lied to me. She had something on somebody, or more than one somebody. There was a smugness about her. She was getting money from someone."

"And then she got pregnant," Lon said.

Amanda wrinkled her nose and thought for a couple of seconds before responding. "No, that was a lie. She never got knocked up at all. But it was okay with her if the rumor said otherwise. It gave her a stronger hold on the man she wanted. She said he won't have a choice about taking care of her. They would be going away soon."

"Leaving Ivan with nothing."

"Ivan started and finished with nothing," Amanda said. "Nobody will feel sorry for him or his lousy brother."

Lon thought and said, "You believe Annie's real lover found out she was using him?"

"And killed her? Could be," Amanda said. "Now, let me ask you, Lon. What are you gonna do about what I just told you? 'Cause I'll deny everything if Abe Buckner starts sniffing around."

Lon shrugged. "First of all, I ain't sure it's the total truth. But I'll take it for now. If anybody comes forward and says you were in Ivan's house last night, you'll have to come up with an excuse. Abe Buckner wants answers now that two doctors confirmed that Ivan was murdered."

"As if I could do that," she said.

"Wouldn't take much strength after you hit him the first time," Lon said. "Just keep pounding 'til he's finished. Then start a fire to try and cover it."

"I didn't do it," Amanda said.

"I'm just telling you how Buckner might look at it. So you better get a good smart story lined up. I won't be telling him you was there."

"Thank you," she said, simply. She took several long breaths as she studied Lon's expression. She sipped her coffee and said, "I knew what Annie was doing, of course. I was pretty sure Annie'd keep our little secret, but, in his frame of mind, I was scared Ivan might hurt me. I wanted to assure him I didn't have any copies of Annie's letters."

"Do you?"

"No."

"You'd like to have them, wouldn't you?"

"You mean would I like to milk some of these fat cats who think they're so much better'n women like me and Annie, bet your ass I would. But I don't have her letters, Lon. I think everything she had went up in that fire." She finished her coffee and pushed the cup aside. "When Ivan showed up, I got the hell out. I told him to leave me alone, that people knew I was in his house. They didn't really, but I wanted him to believe it. Will I lose sleep over the fact that Ivan's dead, I will not. But I heard he passed out drunk and died in the fire."

"A fire deliberately started to destroy any evidence Annie might've left behind." Lon finished his coffee and rose. "Amanda, if I was you, I'd be very watchful. If you got a gun, keep it handy—in your purse, or your pocket."

"I told you," she said, "I have no letters."

Lon nudged Tony, and he stood also. Lon said, "The person who killed Ivan don't know that."

52

Monday was Tony's birthday, but the family celebrated it on Sunday since everyone was free of work. Agatha made a special meal and baked a cake for him. Grandmother Grace's present included a new suit and new shoes. She told him he should look like a banker. Tony put on a brave smile that he hoped showed some appreciation. Uncle Dan's present was a couple comfortable work shirts. Inserted in this present was a card in which Uncle Dan said the shirts would be fine for working in the poolroom, too. Tony saw Uncle Dan smiling at him and gave him a nod. Carter, along with Agatha, bought him a new pair of work shoes. A birthday card with two dollars in it was Aunt Ruth's gift.

All in all, Tony was satisfied except for the time he had to model the suit his grandmother had ordered for him. He felt totally out of place looking like a little rich boy. More insulting was that he had to have his picture taken in it.

Everything had been arranged. His mother even left her room for the showing and gave him a kiss.

Monday morning as Grandmother Grace and Uncle Dan were getting ready to leave for the bank, Sheriff Abe Buckner's car pulled up out front. Tony's grandmother and uncle went out to speak with the sheriff, and Tony, after getting himself appropriately dressed for the poolroom, stepped onto the porch. Carter was there, watching, listening, arms folded.

"I'm just investigating, Miz Blaisdell, like I'm supposed to," Buckner was saying. From his stance in front of the porch he pointed at Carter. "I'm just telling you what people are saying there in shantytown. Your boy's been seen more'n once hanging about. He was there the night Ivan got killed."

"He's not my *boy*," Grace said sharply. "He's my friend and a member of this family. I'll thank you to remember that, Abe. And if Carter wanted to fight with Ivan Coaker, or kill him, he wouldn't have to hit him from behind."

Buckner shuffled his feet before looking up again. "I just know what I'm bein' told."

"For that matter," Uncle Dan said, "I was in shantytown that night, too. Most of the town was. The fire was an attraction."

Buckner nodded stiffly. "I know, Daniel. I heard about you. Just like I heard about Lon Shirley. I didn't come here to accuse nobody. I guess I came here to ask questions and hope you folks can cooperate."

"Apparently, the only person not seen that night close to this family," said Grandmother Grace, "was Dave Hunter."

"You're right," Buckner said. "Nobody's heard from or about Dave Hunter. So it don't look like he killed both Annie

Pyle and Ivan Coaker. I just don't like the idea of somebody thinking they can git away with murder in my county."

"Is that all you wanted to tell us, Abe?" asked Grandmother Grace.

Buckner nodded and finally said, "That's it." He climbed back into his car and drove off.

"Well," said Uncle Dan, "it's getting to him."

"Or he's acting like it is," said Grandmother Grace. She turned to Carter. "You worried about anything?"

"Not a thing," Carter said.

"Then neither am I," she said and stopped before brushing past Tony to re-enter the house. "How about you, young man?"

Tony gave her a lopsided grin. "Lon will be opening the poolroom 'bout now. I'm going to work."

"Happy birthday," she said.

"You said that yesterday."

Tony jogged all the way downtown to the poolroom. Inside, Lon had a single customer, and they both were drinking coffee. Tony helped himself to another mug and poured coffee. He peered around Lon to see what he was doing.

Lon had spread a sheet of paper on the counter and was drawing with a pencil. Tony saw a square shape with the word "house" inside it, then a crude drawing of a pistol out in front of the house with an arrow from the house to the gun. The rest of the page was filled with doodles. As Tony watched, Lon drew another arrow from the gun off to the side of the paper and printed above the line "to town."

"When you gonna give up on that?" Tony asked.

Lon pulled a crudely wrapped something, wrapped in old newspaper, and put it on the counter in front of Tony. "Happy birthday," he said.

"Kid's getting big," the customer observed.

The compliment pleased Tony. He ripped away the paper and beamed. His present from Lon was a new baseball mitt, a small, individually fingered fielder's glove, and a new baseball. Tony's eyes shined as he thanked Lon.

Lon nodded as he returned to look at his drawing.

Tony carefully placed his presents on a shelf and again peered around Lon. "I asked if you figured anything out."

Lon shook his head. "Nope. Got me puzzled. I talked to Daniel and to Carter. They both left the house the night Annie was murdered and came into town. They both claim they never seen the deputy's gun again after Daniel threw it outside. I just can't figure some guy passing by, picking the gun up, deciding it would be a good thing to kill Annie Coaker with, and taking it to shantytown and doing it."

"I know," Tony said. He lowered his voice. "Uncle Dan or Carter is lying. Has to be." Then he beamed. "I got a present for you, too."

"It ain't my birthday," Lon said.

"So what? I don't even know when your birthday is."

"And you ain't gonna know," Lon said. He studied the drawing. "Well, I know Agatha didn't grab the gun and come into town. Neither did your grandma. So?"

"Don't you want to know what your present is?" Tony asked. "It's from Grandma and Uncle Dan."

Lon peered at him.

"They're gonna get you another horse. They talked about it yesterday. You get to pick it out."

Lon grunted and shook his head.

"It's a gift they said. Don't you want it?"

"Nope."

"Why not?"

"I'm gittin' too old to mess around with another horse. They're a lot of trouble to keep clean, not to mention the expense for grain, hay, and grooming. I appreciate the offer but won't accept."

The customer spoke up. "Hell, Lon, you could always sell it and make some money."

"That's not the reason I'm doing it, or they're doing it," he said.

Tony frowned at his friend. "What if we wanna go hunting or fishing? We gonna walk all the way to the river with our supplies?"

"No, I'm modernizing," Lon said.

Tony's eyes popped wide. "You're getting an automobile?"

"No, I'm getting a bicycle," Lon said. "A two-seater, for you and me. It'll have one 'a those little sidecars for our shotgun or fishing poles or anything else we wanna take with us."

"Lon, I seen you on a bicycle," Tony said. "Ain't nobody with worse balance than you."

"That's why you have to sit up front and guide."

"Why don't that make me real happy?" Tony said. "You want me up front so you'll figure I got to pull harder."

"Well, you're a lot younger. I'll be along for balance. What is they call it in the navy? Ballast."

Tony peered around Lon at the drawing. "Like I was telling you—"

"Nobody else came in that night."

Tony tilted his head. "Aunt Ruth did. She came in to see her father, the minister. That's why Carter came in. Grandma told him to follow Ruth and make sure she was okay. I think she stayed the whole night at the church. Her daddy's got a back room."

Lon stared at him. "I thought your Aunt Ruth came to see her pa before that gun ever showed up at the house."

Tony frowned. "No, I'm pretty sure she didn't leave until after my daddy."

"Pretty sure?"

Tony shrugged. "Well, I don't really remember too good, but I think so. Aunt Ruth comes in often to see her daddy. If it's late, she spends lots of nights in the spare room."

"Your family all in the bank today?"

"They will be," Tony said, "in a few minutes. Carter and Agatha will stay at the house unless they got shopping. They look after my mother, too."

"How about your Aunt Ruth?"

"I guess she's there."

"Tony, I think we should have a talk with Ruth. We'll check with your uncle first."

53

Benny assumed duties in the poolroom and Lon and Tony angled across Main Street to enter the bank. Lon asked a male teller if he would tell Daniel that they wanted to see him privately.

Uncle Dan came from his office and motioned them inside. He invited Lon to sit, but Lon declined.

"Daniel, what I'm going to propose might seem out of line to you. I don't want any hard feelings between us. I believe we need to discuss something with your wife."

Uncle Dan was silent for several seconds, apparently in thought, before he finally nodded. He said, "The gun the night Annie was murdered."

"You've considered this," Lon said.

Uncle Dan's second nod was barely perceptive. He said nothing.

Lon said, "It's so damned unlikely that somebody just

came along, picked it up, and took it to shantytown to kill Annie."

"I know," Uncle Dan said softly. "Ruth hated her for imagined wrongs and evils, but I can't believe she'd kill someone. She'd fear for her immortal soul."

"I believe you," Lon said. "I think we should ask."

"Now?"

"Is she still up at the house?"

"She was," Uncle Dan said, "when Mother and I left for work." He took his suit coat from the coat tree. "I'll go with you. I insist on it."

"Wouldn't have it any other way," Lon said.

Uncle Dan went into Grace's office and shut the door. The subject of their discussion could not be heard by Tony or Lon. Uncle Dan came out and said, "Let's go."

The three of them walked Main Street to the end and climbed the hill to the house.

Carter answered the door and nodded with a smile to Lon Shirley. He noticed that Daniel was standing a bit back, near the bottom of the steps to the porch. Lon told Carter they would appreciate it if they could speak with Daniel's wife.

Carter stood silent for a moment. Looking at Daniel, he said, "It's about the gun."

"You didn't pick it up," Lon said.

Carter shook his head. "When I followed Miss Ruth, I looked and couldn't find it. She carries a large tote bag sometimes. 'Course, I was busy getting a bicycle for myself so I could keep her in sight." He hesitated. "I thought about the possibility. Even thought about talking it over with Mr. Dan." Now he shrugged. "I couldn't bring myself to do it."

"Yeah, that would be hard," Lon said. "Can you ask her to speak with us, Carter?"

"I guess it had to come to this finally," Carter said. "I know she hated the woman, but it's difficult for me to believe she'd actually shoot someone." He heaved a long breath. "I'll see if she'll speak to you. I can't make her."

"Wouldn't want you to," Lon said.

Tony still stood open-mouthed. Uncle Dan shuffled his feet, head down as they waited. When Carter was back inside the house, and Lon had turned to stare off from the porch, Tony asked, "What if she claims she didn't?"

"Would she lie?" asked Lon.

Uncle Dan shook his head slowly. "Lying would be a grave sin. I should've lied a long time ago about some things but didn't. Ruth has a much more solid foundation in her faith."

"That she does," Lon nodded.

"Seems to me if you lied about anything, you'd lie about killing somebody," Tony said.

"Or where we bury bodies," Lon said.

Carter came back and said, "She's not here. Agatha saw her leave just after Miz Grace and Daniel drove off."

"Going to the church?" Lon asked.

"Probably," said Carter. "She thinks we're spying on her, and, in a way, I guess we are."

"And that's my fault," Uncle Dan said.

With a glance at Tony, Lon asked, "How's Louella this morning?"

"She has good days and bad days," Carter said. "More bad days than good. Agatha couldn't get her to eat breakfast."

"You wanna say anything to your mom, Tony?" asked Lon.

Tony shrugged one shoulder. "What would I say? She might be asleep now."

"What do you think, Daniel?" asked Lon.

"It's up to Tony," Uncle Dan said.

Tony smiled his appreciation. He felt it was terrible that he didn't want to visit with his mother more often than he did. He made it twice a day, at least, but they were difficult times. Often he wondered if she cared one way or the other.

"Thank you, Carter," Lon said to the other man.

"Need for me to go with you?"

Lon said no and thanked him again. He and Tony and Uncle Dan headed back toward Main Street.

Tony was totally puzzled as to what his Uncle Dan and Lon Shirley were going to do. Somehow the thought of confronting Aunt Ruth in any kind of aggressive manner was disturbing. He felt like telling the two adult men to "let it go, that it wasn't worth it." Why hurt somebody else? If people wanted to believe his father had committed the murder, then so be it. He didn't care what they thought of him, or his father.

The white church steeple came into view at the far end of Main Street. It seemed to Tony that they slowed their pace. Uncle Dan looked seriously troubled. One of the family bicycles was propped outside the wooden steps leading up to the church entrance.

Uncle Dan let out a long sigh. This was not to his liking.

Aunt Ruth appeared at the open doorway, tilting her head at them. She wore a simple gray frock this morning with black shoes. She showed a little smile.

"Well," she said, possibly with a touch of humor, "the sinners of Vinton have finally come to repent."

Uncle Dan, shaking his head slightly, looked away.

Lon Shirley said, "It's about the gun."

Aunt Ruth showed little if any surprise. "Ah," she said, and left it at that.

"Ruth?" Uncle Dan started.

She interrupted him. "Sooner or later, I expected you'd want to know."

Okay, thought Tony. She did pick up the deputy's gun. But would she go to shantytown and kill the woman she thought was trying to steal her husband?

"You took the gun the night Dave Hunter was at the house—the night Annie Coaker was killed," Lon said quietly.

"I did," she said.

"Why did you take it?"

"I'm not sure I have an answer for that," she said, still hinting a smile.

Lon was kneeling, inspecting the tires of the bicycle. He looked up. "These tread marks resemble the ones behind Coaker's house in shantytown."

"It's most likely the same bicycle," Aunt Ruth said. "I only use one or two."

Uncle Dan looked distraught. "Ruth? Did you kill Annie?"

"I did not," she said.

"She didn't," Lon said.

Tony looked from one man to the other.

"Where's your father?" Lon asked.

"Inside," Aunt Ruth said. "Praying. Praying for salvation for all of us."

"Bully for him," Lon said. "Tell him we have to talk."

"I heard you," Reverend Caleb Jones said from behind his daughter. He stepped from the shadows behind her onto the stop step. "I hope it's not too late for any of us. Even me."

Tony looked at the minister. He was dressed in his black suit with black shirt with white clerical collar. He looked sad.

"Too late for what, Reverend?" said Lon.

"Saving grace."

Uncle Dan started to speak, but Lon restrained him with a quick grasp of his arm.

"You want to tell us about it, Reverend? You're hurting now."

"Oh, I believe you know," Jones said, quietly. "You're clever." If there were anything in the set of his eyes or his mouth, Tony couldn't read it. But he understood.

Lon said, "Nobody can blame a man for falling under Annie's spell. It's too hard to be immune with something like that. What attracted her to go after you, Reverend? Was it your money? Your inheritance? Everybody knows that for a preacher you're quite well off. Or was it true love—maybe starting that way? You must be a lonely man living a lonely life. It would be simple for Annie to threaten you with exposure as your lover. I bet you had to promise her many things."

"Many," Jones nodded. "Things I couldn't deliver on."

Lon nodded. "She got more and more demanding. But why did she marry Ivan Coaker of all people? You must know why."

"Ivan forced it," Jones said. "He found us together one night near the river. Can you believe it? Like two love-struck kids we frolicked by the river, and Ivan saw us. He threatened to let everybody know if I didn't pay him off. I did, but he wasn't satisfied. He said he'd marry the tart and just charge me a small amount every month. In my stupidity, my confusion, I went along with it, even talked Annie into it. I figured what with the money I've got, and the collections, I could afford to keep Ivan in whiskey. It worked for awhile."

When he stopped talking, Lon nodded. Lon said, "Then Annie got very greedy. She wanted more than the presents and love you gave her so far."

Ruth made a sobbing sound and turned her face away.

Jones said, "Annie said we had to leave here, go to some big city where we could live the life she wanted, that we could marry once I leave the church. She wanted to be respectable. How could I tell her you don't get respect that way, even if I did marry her? But, of course, I couldn't. My congregation didn't care for her. I owed something to my congregation."

Aunt Ruth sobbed again. "For God's sakes, Papa, you've paid them over and over again."

"Shush, daughter," Jones said. "When Annie found out I couldn't make an honest woman out of her, she became bitter. Her demands became greater. So did her threats. She said she could drop hints about what kind of fallen minister I am. Did I love her? Yes, I loved her. I'm sorry, Ruth, but I did. No dishonor to you or your dead mother. I put myself in a terrible hole."

"You're a good man, Papa," Aunt Ruth said, tearfully.

"A good man going to hell."

"Don't say that!" she cried.

Lon Shirley said, "So Ruth gave you the deputy's gun that night. Was it her idea, or yours?"

"Mine alone," Jones said.

"No! Mine, too," Ruth cried. "It was in the back of my mind. I knew something had to be done."

Jones shrugged. "I couldn't let her go to shantytown to commit murder. I took the bicycle and tried to stay away from any main street or path. I had seen Annie earlier. She was delivering the cash I'd promised Ivan. I planned on waiting for her to leave. I knew she would because she preferred staying at Amanda's. Ivan and Clifford came out first. They were heading off to buy whiskey and take it with them. I slipped into the house while Annie was putting her shawl around her shoulders. It occurred to me that the Coakers might be blamed for her death. I guess she figured what I had in mind."

Lon said, "She tried to run, and you shot her. Then you slipped back to where you'd parked the bicycle and took the path behind the houses. Everybody else was running out into the street. Only the barking dogs bothered you."

"Scared me," Jones said. "I didn't know until the next day that Dave Hunter was getting blamed for the killing. For a few brief minutes I felt relieved, that I was free of a huge weight. It didn't last."

"Your conscience," Uncle Dan said, looking from the father to the daughter.

"I guess you can call it that," said Jones with a shrug. "Now it doesn't matter. Where do we go from here?"

"You might as well tell it all," Lon Shirley said. "You killed Ivan Coaker, too, and torched his house."

The minister's eyes narrowed. "Ivan wasn't as dumb as I thought. He figured it out and increased his demands. I had my excuse to be in shantytown that evening and I heard about Ivan's rampage. I waited in his dirty, stinking house until he came home. He didn't even see me. I struck him with his own baseball bat. Then, yes, I set fire to the house. Now, again, I ask you—what do you want to do?"

"What do you think *you* have to do?" Lon asked.

"Of course," Jones nodded, somberly. He said to Uncle Dan, "Will you please take Ruth home now? No, I mean it. Go with him, daughter." To everyone, he said, "Will you give me time to put some things together? I'll turn myself in to Sheriff Buckner. Will you trust me on that?"

Lon looked at Tony and Uncle Dan, then nodded slightly.

He said, "That's a good idea."

54

The fire that consumed Vinton's new church must have started in early afternoon. Tony, at the poolroom, heard the shouts and commotion outside. He and Lon stepped into the street to see businessmen and the fire department volunteers running in the direction of the black smoke boiling up from the white steeple a few blocks away. It brought all commerce to a halt as people crowded into the street and kids, excited by the prospect of witnessing another conflagration, shouted and ran toward the church.

Lon didn't bother trying to find Bennie to take charge of the poolroom. He and Tony jogged toward the scene. Tony saw his grandmother standing out in the street in front of the bank staring in that direction. He didn't see Uncle Dan. The last he had seen of Uncle Dan was taking his wife back to the house.

The fire was all the way out of control before the first volunteers arrived to try and fight it. It obviously was of no avail. Whatever had caused it to start continued to make it burn rapidly. The stain-glass windows blew outward to shower on-lookers with tiny sharp particles. Black smoke boiled upward from the openings followed by shooting flames.

Tony felt Lon's strong hands on his shoulders, keeping him back a distance from the fire.

Lon turned him. "Let's go, boy."

"Lon, it ain't burned out yet," Tony said.

"Will be in a few minutes. There's no saving it. We're in the way here."

Reluctantly, looking back over his shoulder, Tony accompanied Lon along Main Street toward the poolroom. Tony's grandmother was still standing in front of the bank looking toward the church. The other clerks had come outside to stare and comment. When they had about reached the poolroom, Tony saw his Aunt Ruth running, sobbing between screams, toward the fire. Uncle Dan was trying to pull her back, but she refused to be restrained.

"Don't you want to see the end of it?" Tony asked.

"I know the end of it," Lon said. "You can wait for me at the poolroom."

"Where you goin'?"

"See the sheriff."

"I'm going with you," Tony said.

They went to the sheriff's office, and Lon saw the deep gouge in the outside door. It hadn't been there earlier.

Inside, Deputy Orville Parker was kicked back in the sheriff's chair. He swung his feet to the floor when Lon and Tony came in.

"Abe ain't here," Parker said. "He ran down to the church fire. Me, I gotta sit here and look after things."

"Who nicked up your door?" Lon asked.

"Don't know," Parker said. "It upset Abe some. He was frowning when I come in. What's the fire look like?"

"A big fire," Lon said. "Luckily, the church is set away from other buildings. It's almost over."

Parker nodded as he bit at a thumbnail. "Feel sorry for Reverend Jones. He put all that money and work into building that church."

"We'll wait out here in the hall," Lon said, "so you can nap peacefully."

He and Tony sat on one of the wooden benches. "What are we doing here?" Tony asked.

"Waiting for the sheriff."

"I mean, why?"

"I want to talk with him. You don't have to stay."

"No, no, I'll stay," Tony said, but his voice was not enthusiastic. "You gonna tell him about—?"

"Don't say anything," Lon cautioned quickly.

It was another half hour before Abe Buckner came in, puffing out his breath and looking disgusted. He stopped and peered at Lon and Tony.

"We're waiting for you," Tony broke the silence.

"Go talk to Orville," Buckner said.

"Can't," Lon said. "We want to talk about the confession you got."

That stopped Buckner fast. "What?"

Lon nodded. "The one that was pinned to your front

door by a dagger. I bet that dagger is in the shape of a crucifix with a little silver Christ on it."

"Come in my office," Buckner said.

Tony and Lon followed him inside. Buckner said to Orville Parker, "Orville, you go out now and see if there's any help you can give those people down at the scene."

"Sure, boss," Parker said, looking relieved to be getting out of the office.

Lon watched him leave. "I take it he don't know about the dagger and the confession."

Buckner nodded with a sigh, removed his gun belt to hang it up, and sat behind the desk. He motioned Lon and Tony to a couple of straight-backed chairs. Slowly, from a desk drawer, Buckner took out the crucifix-dagger and placed it on his desk. From the same drawer he took out a paper that had been punctured by the dagger point. He handed the paper over to Lon.

Lon read it quietly.

"Well?" Tony asked.

Buckner gave Lon an inquisitive look, and Lon nodded to indicate it was all right for Tony to hear. Lon read it aloud:

I'm a weak man. I succumbed to the charms of Annie Pyle. I paid Annie for her affections. She wanted more, much more. I tried to buy time by paying her to marry Ivan Coaker. That did not satisfy her as her demands increased. She wanted nothing less than marriage to me and moving to someplace else. I was desperate. I took your deputy's gun and shot her. Ivan guessed the truth and demanded more money to keep quiet. The trap I was in was built by myself. I found Ivan drunk because of Clifford's death and struck him with a baseball bat. Then I set fire to his house and left him to die. I am a fallen minister.

Signed: Caleb Jones

"I don't know when he stuck it on the door," Buckner said. "Once this fire got started, I tried to find Caleb outside the church. I didn't see him."

"You won't," Lon said. "After everything's calmed down, you'll find him inside."

"Damn!" Buckner said.

The three of them sat in silence for a couple of minutes.

Buckner nodded toward the confession. "There's a postscript."

Lon read aloud:

P.S. Abe, I hope you can find some way to soften my disgrace and my scandal for my congregation. I don't want the people to lose faith because of one man's (my) evil ways.

Lon handed the confession back to Buckner. This time the sheriff folded it and put it inside his uniform shirt pocket.

"Well?" said Lon.

"I've been thinking," Buckner said. "How 'bout you?"

"I want a statement from you to this town, and to this boy's folks, that Dave Hunter is cleared of any charges. You received new information."

"Okay," Buckner said. "Let's get back to the minister. Who else knows about his involvement?"

"The Blaisdells do, or will," Lon said. "His daughter knows. Nobody's likely to say anything. I know Tony won't. Nobody in the family will have reason to. It's in your hands, Abe."

It took Buckner another full minute before he finally nodded. "Okay. Evidence has come up to show that in a fit of rage Ivan Coaker murdered his own wife and tried to have it blamed on Dave Hunter. After Clifford's death, in another rage Ivan attacked whoever was close. In self-defense one of his neighbors struck him and left the house. It appears that Ivan, groggy and staggering, collapsed again, this time knocking over his lamp and causing the fire. I'm sure Dr. Harris and Dr. Sanders will agree to that. In keeping with my duty as an elected county official, I had to bring a number of people in for questioning. A lot of people have threatened Ivan Coaker in the past. This is what brought the information out. Because Ivan's death was not intentional, the prosecutor and judge will not pursue charges against any single individual." He paused to rock back. "Does it make sense to you?"

"Sounds like you got it all figured out," Lon said. "I'm sure that's exactly what happened."

55

Four days later a procession made its way along Main Street to the railway depot at the edge of Vinton. The hearse led the way; several people followed on foot. Interestingly, to Tony, many people, men and women, had dressed up for the send-off. Tony knew he would be glad when this was all over. The past three or so days had been difficult for him to pretend any deep sorrow despite Aunt Ruth's crying jags that lasted most of the time.

Reverend Caleb Jones's body had been discovered and removed from the shambles of the destroyed church. Nobody would ever know what caused the blaze, but, apparently, the minister had tried to fight it single-handedly until overcome by smoke and flames. It was a terrible tragedy for the small town.

Before he left the house this morning to go to the poolroom, Tony broached the subject with Uncle Daniel.

"She's leaving?" he asked.

Uncle Dan nodded. "Yes. She's going home to Pennsylvania where she and her father have folks."

"Is that okay with you?" Tony asked.

"Has to be. It's what she wants."

"She's your wife."

Uncle Dan tilted his head at Tony. "Not long. Ruth spoke with Judge Parks, and he agreed to an annulment order. It seems we didn't do some things that normal married couples do."

"Like having sex," Tony said.

Uncle Dan laughed. "Well, I guess that's something I won't have to explain to you as you get older. I want you to understand that there's no ill will between your Aunt Ruth and me."

"We certainly don't want ill will," Grandmother Grace's voice carried from the open doorway. She wore a white and gray dress that contrasted with the black in which Aunt Ruth had wrapped herself.

"Looks like you're going to a party," Tony said. "You must think it's gonna be a real occasion."

"In a way, it is," Grandmother Grace smiled. "No point in walking around with long faces if you don't have to. You going to ride in with us?"

"No, I'm staying at the poolroom," Tony said. "I said goodbye to Aunt Ruth after breakfast. She said she preferred it like that. I think she's afraid I'll say something out of turn."

"That's true," nodded Uncle Dan. "She doesn't want anyone to know what really happened with her father."

"See, this way I don't have to dress up like the rest of you," said Tony.

"Wise beyond your years," said Uncle Dan.

Tony left the house first and walked into town. He went straight to the poolroom.

Lon was behind the counter, serving coffee to his first customer of the day.

"Wow," said Tony to his old friend, "you really got yourself dolled up. New shirt and everything."

"Ain't new," Lon said. "It's clean. How come your grandma lets you come in your work clothes?"

"I won't go to the depot. Aunt Ruth don't want me to. It's seems phony to me anyway. I'll stay here." Tony paused a moment. "I'm surprised you're going."

"For your Uncle Dan," Lon said. "He came to your daddy's send-off."

"I read the paper," Tony said. "Sheriff Buckner cleared my father of everything."

"He kept his word. Now we'll keep his secret."

Thirty minutes later they heard a distant train whistle on the still morning.

"Lots of people," said Tony.

He was peering out from the open doorway to Main Street. The procession was moving slowly, somberly, led by the hearse. Right behind were Grandmother Grace and Uncle Dan in their automobile. Tony was surprised to see that his mother, tucked inside a blanket in the back seat, was attending, too. Behind the family car came Carter Foote on a bicycle pulling a wagon. The wagon was heaped with a trunk and three suitcases. The sheriff's car with Buckner behind the wheel was following close. Most people, well-dressed surprisingly enough to Tony, were walking; some rode their own bicycles.

Tony lost sight of them as they moved on down Main Street.

The train to Elston was in, taking water, mail, other shipped goods, and the few passengers waiting to get aboard. Daniel stopped the car back from the planked walkway and waited while Sheriff Buckner parked beside him. The sheriff got out and headed toward the tracks. Daniel and Grace got out.

Ruth was waiting outside one of the boxcars until two men hoisted her upward and inside. She stepped back as the coffin was loaded; then she reappeared in the open doorway.

Lon Shirley edged in closer.

"Bless him!" someone shouted. "Your father was a saint."

Ruth lifted one dainty hand to silence the crowd. "Indeed he was," she said, loudly. "Will you join me in a silent prayer for his immortal soul?"

"Ayes" and "yes's" were shouted out.

The moment of silence lasted three minutes. Lon thought it was an awfully damned long time. Someone nudged against him, and he looked over to see Grace standing next to him, her shoulder touching his muscular upper arm.

"Bless you!" someone shouted from the crowd.

"No, bless you," Ruth said. "You were my father's flock, our congregation. Despite this tragedy you must carry on in your faith. He would wish that for you. Believe me when I tell you my father loved you, everyone of you."

Lon leaned closer to Grace and whispered from the side of his mouth, "Some more than others."

"Be kind, Lon," Grace whispered back.

"I'm always kind," Lon whispered.

Standing close beside him, unseen by anyone else, Grace moved the little finger of her free hand, the hand closest to Lon, and hooked it around Lon's index finger. Lon smiled.

One of the porters had come back to speak with Ruth in the boxcar doorway. She conversed with him out of earshot and then said something to Carter Foote, who had unloaded the luggage and trunks and was tossing them up into the back of the car where another handler was stacking them. Finished, Carter backed away and retreated to his bicycle. He passed Lon and Grace and gave Lon a little nod.

The boxcar door slid shut. Ruth had insisted on staying inside with the remains of her father. They had arranged as comfortable seating as possible for her.

Lon had had enough. After a final pressure on Grace's finger, he moved out of the crowd and stopped at the Blaisdell automobile. Louella, still huddled in the back seat, gave him a wan smile. She stopped him to speak.

She said, "Lon, I want to express how much I appreciate what you're doing for Tony."

"Glad to, Lou," Lon nodded. "Tony's a great kid. He'll do you proud."

If anything, her smile faded a bit more. She said, "Mother's grateful, too. She says Tony is her heritage, her legacy, now. We don't know what Dan's going to do about getting married again and having a family."

"He'll work it out," Lon said. "You have to take care of yourself."

"I'm afraid it's a little late," Louella said. "I had a moment there. I'm just—not—I mean—" She stopped, sounding a bit embarrassed. "You'll keep looking out for Tony, won't you?"

"Of course," Lon said.

Louella reached out a trembling hand, and Lon took it gently. He was amazed at how weak, flaccid, and shaky it was.

When Grace and Daniel returned to the car, the train was moving away from the station. Grace took her place in the passenger seat, and Daniel got behind the wheel. Carter came around to do the cranking, but Lon beat him to it and winked at him. Carter nodded with a smile and stepped back.

With his good hand Lon cranked the engine for the Blaisdells and gave a little salute. The crowd was dispersing quickly. Those with bicycles departed first. The walkers knotted in small groups, or singly, and moved back toward Main Street. Daniel and Grace backed away and drove off.

Lon helped the sheriff, also, by cranking his engine. Soon he and Carter were practically alone by the depot.

Carter sighed and climbed on his bike.

Lon grinned at him. "We've come a long way, Carter."

"Long way, Lon," Carter agreed and waved. "And we got a long way to go."

Lon trudged back up Main Street to his poolroom. Tony stood in the doorway.

"Got her sent off okay?" Tony asked.

"She's on her way," Lon said. "I hope you didn't let anybody cheat us while I was gone."